Readers' praise for Jodi Compton

'The writing is superb, the action sequences are
... ngly gritty and real ... Hailey is such a
... ully complex character that I lost my heart to
... with n the first few pages of this book ... *Hailey's*
... about friendship and family and honour and
... that bind them all together. And how far you
... o to keep your word and to make things right'
... favouritebooks.blogspot.com

'... thriller that had me guessing until the final
pa... . Jodi Compton certainly has a hit on her
... with this one and I'm keen to see how she
... s the main character in books to come'
... milorambles.com

'... elling ... Jodi Compton is skilled at keeping the
... ast whilst also keeping readers on board.'
... emmalee1.wordpress.com

'If you want a fresh look at the L.A. crime scene from
a totally different perspective then this could be the
book for you – it doesn't disappoint'
http://imeanttoreadthat.blogspot.com

ALSO BY JODI COMPTON

SYMPATHY BETWEEN HUMANS

THE 37TH HOUR

HAILEY'S WAR

DON'T
LOOK BACK

JODI COMPTON

SIMON &
SCHUSTER

London · New York · Sydney · Toronto · New Delhi

A CBS COMPANY

First published in Great Britain by Simon & Schuster UK Ltd, 2011
A CBS COMPANY

This paperback edition first published 2011

1 3 5 7 9 10 8 6 4 2

Simon & Schuster UK Ltd
1st Floor
222 Gray's Inn Road
London WC1X 8HB

www.simonandschuster.co.uk

Simon & Schuster Australia, Sydney
Simon & Schuster India, New Delhi

A CIP catalogue record for this book is available from the British Library

ISBN: 978-1-84739-375-3
eISBN: 978-1-84720-675-6

Printed in the UK by CPI Cox & Wyman, Reading RG1 8EX

For Anastacia

Author's note

Hailey's Latin and Spanish are taken from my own studies of those languages. Thanks, though, to copy editor Maureen Sugden for catching an error in my Latin late in the editing process.

DON'T
LOOK BACK

"*I*t's me. Hailey."

"*I know.*"

"*I thought maybe something was wrong with your voice mail. I left you a message, and you never called back. . . . Well, listen, I'm coming home to L.A.*"

"*Is that right.*"

"*I . . . CJ, what's wrong? Are you pissed because I left town without saying good-bye? I wanted to, it's just—*"

"*Why would that piss me off, Hailey? Feel free to come and go as you please. Go down to Mexico and*" *nearly get yourself killed, then come back and tell me nothing."*

"Where did you hear about that?"

"You showed your mother the scars from where you got shot. She told my mother about it, who told me. It's great hearing this stuff thirdhand, by the way. It's not like you and me mean anything to each other."

"You mean everything to me, dammit. It's just that . . . it's complicated."

"Your life is complicated because you make it complicated. If it ever gets simple, you'll go out and recomplicate it by any means necessary."

"That's not fair. You don't know what happened."

"Whose fault is that?"

"I kept you out of it because I was trying to protect you."

"Yeah? Let me make that easy on you, then. I don't want to see you when you get back into town. Don't call me, don't come around my place. Understand?"

"CJ . . ."

"Do you understand?"

I've been slow to realize it, but a lot of what's happened in the past four months has to do with my cousin CJ and the conversation I had with him on New Year's Eve, just days after losing one of my fingers—and nearly my life—to a mobster's hired thugs. Since then my behavior has not been unimpeachable. *Impeachable* would be a very fair word to describe my actions. Or maybe *acting out,* as the psychologists say.

But the Good Friday killings, as the media is calling them, I had nothing to do with those. Because at the time I was over four hundred miles away, committing an entirely different crime.

PART ONE

a day in the life

1

good friday/early april

You never realize how few stars pierce through the light-leached night sky over Los Angeles until you get out of the city. Way out. That's where I was tonight, at a little past eleven, in the desert on the edge of a lonely secondary highway near a railroad crossing, straddling my motorcycle and looking up at the sky. About the only thing I recognized in the dazzling treasure chest above me was the arched three-star handle of the partially visible Big Dipper.

Experts say that my generation can recognize, on average, two to three constellations and six to seven species of trees but over a thousand corporate logos. Supposedly a lot of us also can't find America on a world map, either.

I say, does it really matter whether Americans can find America on a map? What are we afraid of, that people will go to Canada and not be able to find their way back?

In my prior life as a sincere person, I would have gotten really bent out of shape about young Americans' geographic illiteracy. Not anymore. A lot of those teenagers who can't find the USA on a map can tell you, block by block, which gangs control which territory in their part of town, where it's safe to walk and where it's not. That's what keeps them from getting killed. Nobody they know has ever been shot for not finding the United States on a map. People know what they need to know.

I know, for example, that there isn't much out here in the desert except, about four miles east, the laboratories of a major pharmaceutical company. And I know that the company's delivery drivers are instructed to stop, like school buses do, at the railroad crossing. My reconnaissance on a previous night suggests that nearly all of them do. By the time they cross the point where I am now, they're lumbering back up to twenty or twenty-five miles per hour, a manageable speed at which to have a blowout. And one of them is definitely going to have one.

That was why I'd come out here: to hijack a truck with my old friend Serena "Warchild" Delgadillo. I had a mask and a baseball cap in my backpack and a Browning Hi-Power in a holster concealed at the small of my back, and coiled at my feet was a homemade spike strip, like the kind that police toss across the road to end long-distance pursuits.

The spike strip had been the most time-consuming part of our prep work. Neither Serena nor I was particularly good with tools, and we'd spent hours in the chop shop of a *vato* affiliated with El Trece, Serena's gang, trial-and-erroring our way to a workable spike strip. Then we'd painted it a non-reflective black so it wouldn't glint in the headlights of an oncoming vehicle.

My cell phone, set to its two-way-radio function, crack-led to life. "*Órale,* check it out." Serena was on the opposite side of the road, in an SUV with a V6 engine and its back-seats removed for greater cargo capacity.

I saw now what Serena had seen, a pair of headlights shimmering silver-white in the distance. "Is that it?" she asked. "Is it showtime?"

"Give me a minute," I said, still looking into the distance.

Waiting, I ran a hand under the hair on my neck, lifting it up and letting it back down. I could feel sweat on the nape of my neck. Most of California had been in the grip of an early-spring heat wave. It would have been more comfortable to pull my hair back, but my motorcycle helmet wouldn't fit over a ponytail. Neither would the ski mask.

The truck drew closer, and I was sure of the shape of the headlights and the size and mass of the vehicle. I raised the phone again. "Yeah," I said, "that's our guy."

I swung my leg off the bike, scooped up the chain, ran to the edge of the road, and threw it across, watching it skitter and land mostly straight.

The drug-company truck slowed at the tracks, then

accelerated again. But only for a moment. There was no dramatic sound, no pop or hiss of air as the tires were punctured, but I saw the brake lights and the truck slow, and then it lumbered to a stop at the edge of the road.

I pulled in the spike strip so we wouldn't accidentally trap an unwanted second vehicle, then pulled on my mask. I was wearing gloves already, not because I expected to leave prints anywhere but because I'd stuffed the smallest finger of the left glove with newspaper so the driver wouldn't be able to tell police that one of the robbers was missing a finger on that hand.

The driver's door of the delivery truck opened, and a man climbed out from behind the wheel. He wanted to know what had gone wrong. *It's a little early to be using the past tense, "gone wrong," buddy. Things are about to go wronger.*

Serena, masked like me, walked out of the shadows behind the man and clicked off the safety on her Glock.

"Put your hands up and keep them up where I can see 'em," she said.

He stiffened, his gaze going from her masked face to the gun and back to her face.

"Don't be afraid," Serena said. "It's just a little robbery. Happens several thousand times a day in America. Take a walk over to my associate"—she raised her chin at me, standing across the highway—"and please note that she, like me, is armed, so don't make any sudden moves, like you're reaching for something."

When he got to my side of the road and I'd gotten behind him with the gun, he said, "I have kids."

"Then be smart," I told him. "You're just going to lie down in a ditch for few minutes, that's all."

"That's okay, I guess," he said, his voice stiff and uncertain.

I walked him about thirty yards off, to the dry bed of a drainage ditch. "Go on," I said. "Lie down on your stomach and lace your hands on the back of your neck."

He navigated the downslope carefully, like a guy unused to being outdoors, then got to his hands and knees, then lowered himself to his belly. He placed his hands on his neck, like I'd said.

I raised the cell with my free hand and radioed Serena. *"Paratus,"* I said. *Ready.*

"Venio," she said.

Serena's first comment on the Latin language, when she'd seen me reviewing flashcards in study hall when we were both fourteen years old, had been, *Weird.* Now she was studying it herself. It was baffling to both the English and Spanish speakers who surrounded us. More than that, it was highly economical, ideal for text messaging. You could say in three words of Latin things that would take six or seven in English.

Once Latin had been the language of my early-adolescent ambitions, of a cleaner, purer self. Now it had become a code between outlaws.

I heard the engine of an SUV start up, and Serena backed down the shoulder of the road to the truck, her headlights off, only the reverse lights visible. Normally Serena drove a Chevy Caprice, but the SUV was borrowed for tonight's mission.

Well, it was borrowed in that Serena had gotten it from one of the *vatos* in Trece, but I had no illusions that he hadn't stolen it. We'd ditch it somewhere right after unloading our cargo.

I could easily have ridden with Serena in it, but my motorcycle was part of our escape plan. If things went wrong, she could jump on the back of my bike and we'd be gone. The SUV wasn't much of a getaway car, V6 or not, but my bike was a different story. It was an Aprilia, built for speed. There wasn't much on the road that could outrun it, including the average police-issue Crown Vic.

Once Serena and I had made the spike strip and I'd done reconnaissance on the truck routes and found a safe place to do this, the plan had fallen together with wonderful simplicity. Done right, it would take about five minutes. Serena would know exactly what she needed from the truck, what was resellable and what wasn't. She had been robbing pharmacies back when I was still . . . well, back when I was still sincere.

After we'd pulled back the spike strip, it didn't matter if a car came along before Serena was finished unloading. The delivery truck was safely off the road and the SUV parked well to the side of that, lights off, in the shadows. People drive past stalled vehicles all the time. Samaritans are rare.

The driver, lying in the ditch with his head turned to the side, said, "My older daughter's in an Easter pageant on Sunday."

"Be quiet," I said.

What I wanted to say was, *For God's sake, I'm not a serial killer. You don't have to flood me with biographical information so I'll see you as a person*. But I didn't, because that was a little too lighthearted and reassuring. When vics get reassured, they get overconfident, and then they do stupid things. I didn't want this guy fantasizing about getting some kind of special commendation from the company after thwarting a robbery, up in front of a whole auditorium full of applauding executives. That would be bad, because if this guy acted up, I knew I couldn't shoot a union-card-carrying hourly employee whose daughter was going to be in an Easter pageant. But Serena, across the road, might.

Then my cell phone crackled again. *"Ecce,"* Serena's voice said. Loosely translated, *Heads up*.

There was a second pair of headlights coming down the road. The same size, the same shape.

I'd done some scouting on this location, but my observations hadn't indicated that the trucks ran on any sort of schedule. The plan tonight had been to simply wait until one came. I certainly hadn't been expecting a second truck so soon.

I raised the radio: *"Voles?"* I asked Serena. *You want to?* *"Faciamus,"* she said. *Let's do it.*

I couldn't leave the first driver unwatched to go get the second from Serena, so I added, switching to Spanish, *"Cuando traigas el conductor aquí, seas tierna."* *When you bring the driver over here, be gentle.* I'd switched to Spanish because Serena's Latin wasn't very advanced yet, and I didn't want there to be any confusion, not when people could get hurt.

"Claro," she said, and her dark silhouette moved quickly and lightly across the highway to get the spike strip. She bent

and sent it skating across the asphalt, and we were ready for the second truck's approach.

Ten minutes later I heard Serena slam the cargo door of the SUV, finished with the loading. I waited for her to pull onto the highway before I spoke to the two drivers lying on the ground. "Count to a thousand before you get up," I said. Serena had taken their keys. They'd be out here awhile. "I don't want to see either of your heads prairie-dogging up into my line of sight before I'm out of here, okay?"

As I turned to go, the second driver, a woman, spoke. "I don't know how you live with yourself."

"Deb, shhh," the man said.

I stopped and looked back. "The company you work for has made record profits off its erectile-dysfunction drug, which was only a minor variation on impotence drugs already on the market," I said. "How much of that money did they put into research on malaria or the rarer cancers? They did find money in the budget, though, for research on a new weight-loss drug."

The woman said, "That's not a justification."

"I'm not in the justification business," I said.

I scrambled up the steep side of the ditch, then turned back, adding something I knew they wouldn't understand. "That duty-and-honor thing? I'm over it."

2

I've never had strong feelings about the God-versus-Darwin debate, but if I ever doubt that humans evolve, I have only to look back at my life. I'm only twenty-four, and already I've left a series of selves behind me: Army brat, West Point cadet, aimless L.A. twenty-something, San Francisco bike messenger, and now, second-in-command to a rising Latina gangster.

I know where you probably got hung up: *Go back to the part about West Point—what was that?* Yeah, it's true. I don't recommend it, but here's how, in five easy steps, you get from being in the top fifteenth percentile of your class at the United States Military Academy to jacking trucks in the desert.

Step One: Get diagnosed with a tiny but inoperable brain tumor that severely blunts your fear and compromises your judgment, thus disqualifying you from Army service and wiping out all your plans for the future. Step Two: While sober and obeying all traffic laws, accidentally hit and kill a child who darts from between parked cars on Wilshire Boulevard. Step Three: In an attempt to make symbolic amends for that death, get involved in protecting a pregnant runaway from a mobster. Nearly get killed, twice. Step Four: Survive that and come home only to get slapped down by the one person you've loved and counted on since childhood.

That was my cousin, known to the world as Cletus Mooney, the Grammy-winning music producer. To me he was simply CJ. We'd been born ten days and nearly a thousand miles apart, and met for the first time at the age of eleven, when my mother and I, shortly after my father's death, had moved in with his family in their farmhouse outside Lompoc, California. CJ and I had taught each other to kiss in the shade of the willow tree outside his parents' home. It wasn't right to say we were "inseparable," because I'd gone to West Point and he'd gone to L.A., to find a way into the music business without a single contact. But our emotional bond had been unbreakable. Until New Year's Eve and that disastrous phone call.

Here's the difference between rich people and the rest of us: When most of us have arguments with the people we love, we slam out of the house, let the screen door bang shut behind us, and walk around the block a couple of times until we cool off. But when you've got the kind of money CJ now had, you don't have to stop at a block or two. You can let the screen door bang shut behind you and be halfway across the world. Which is basically what he did. At first CJ had been back east, recording at a friend's studio in New York City, but now he was in Africa, traveling and looking for talent in the music clubs of Dakar, Nairobi, and Accra. No one knew when he planned to come back. God knew he hadn't left any contact information for me. I'd sent him a postcard with my new address on it but hadn't gotten any response.

Which brings me to Step Five: Go lick your wounds with an old friend, a career criminal whose antisocial ways increasingly make sense to you.

That was Serena. When it came to personal evolution, she made me look like a piker. If you knew me at twelve, you'd recognize me at twenty-four, and not just because I still have the same port-wine birthmark high on my right cheekbone. That couldn't be said of Serena.

When I'd first met her, back in the seventh grade near Lompoc, she resembled the *telenovela* character Betty La Fea, with harsh black bangs cut straight across her forehead and braces her immigrant family went into debt to afford. She'd also had an unbecoming layer of baby fat on her face, though she wasn't at all overweight; she'd been a speedy and accurate striker on the soccer team where I was a midfielder.

By ninth grade, in the halls of our high school, Serena appeared as a proto-gangbanger, outlining her lips in pencil three shades darker than her lip gloss and shaving off her eyebrows to redraw them. Then, after moving to Los Angeles with her family, she'd reinvented herself as a virtual boy, with a shaved head, Pendletons, and khakis, and run with the Thirteenth Street clique, or Trece. After a stint in jail, she emerged visibly feminine again but no less committed to *la vida,* and she'd formed a clique of girls she called her sucias, supposedly a "girls' auxiliary" to Trece, but who banged just as hard. Serena had dreamed since childhood of a past life in Vietnam—choppers hovering over the jungle, chaos and fighting—and believed herself to have been an American GI who'd died over there. That was the source of her gang moniker, Warchild, and her conviction that life is war, this time around no less than the last.

The coach who knew the twelve-year-old soccer player, the teachers who shook their heads over the fourteen-year-old underachiever, the gang-suppression officers who ran down alleys after the sixteen-year-old gender-bending *chola*—none of them would recognize the woman she'd become now. And in fact, conventional wisdom said it was virtually impossible for Serena to be what she was at age twenty-five: the leader of El Trece.

The things we'd done last winter had only raised her profile in the neighborhood. There was more than one version of events in circulation, but basically it was said that Warchild had punked this Italian mobster up north, stolen his grandbaby (or baby, in some inaccurate accounts) right out from under his nose, and gotten away clean.

Of course, Tony Skouras had been Greek. And Serena

had taken the baby out from under the noses of hospital staff, not Skouras and his people. And it was me who'd found the kidnapped Nidia Hernandez, arranged a safe home for her baby after her death, and paid the price in the brutal torture session in which I'd lost my finger. But I was philosophical about how much credit Serena got for things I'd done. It wasn't like I really needed that shit to stick to me. And it made a great addition to the Warchild *leyenda*.

When she came back to town after the Skouras business, she'd begun paring her sucias down to a core group of dedicated older girls. Hoodrats who only wanted *familia* to drink and party with no longer needed apply.

This was the state of affairs when the leader of Trece, Payaso, had been arrested and sentenced to a year in Chino, leaving behind a very unexpected edict: "Warchild's in charge."

Granted, it was temporary. Serena had understood that he probably had an ulterior motive: Another male might not so easily relinquish his role once Payaso returned from prison. Serena might have seemed the safest choice. That was a viewpoint she didn't acknowledge publicly. Respect from males was hard enough to come by and to keep.

So she'd installed me as her new lieutenant and protection, dismissing her old second-in-command, Luisa "Trippy" Ramos, as a dangerous loose cannon. Trippy, furious and resentful, had defected to Tenth Street, Trece's nearest rivals. This wasn't as rare as you might think. Once ganged up, bangers loved to say that their affiliation was *por vida,* but the truth was that gang sets or cliques lived so close together that after a slight or betrayal it wasn't unheard of for a gang member to switch loyalties, or "flip," to another clique.

I'd been happy to see the last of Trippy. On the surface she'd seemed a lot like Serena: strong, coolheaded, not easily scared. It took time to see that she was, underneath, psychologically unstable, with an almost nihilistic need to fight. She was a bully, too: I'd heard her brag about beating up a pregnant girl and knew she had no qualms about jumping rival girls three or four on one. She'd hated me as well, to the point that she'd sometimes spoken about me in the third person when I was in the room, as though I were absent, or not fully real. She'd never believed that Serena would advance me ahead of her, hence her outraged defection to Tenth Street.

But after she'd gone, I'd learned that there were other people in Serena's neighborhood who couldn't understand why she would give pride of place to an Anglo girl. Serena had met the criticism coolly, saying, "Insula was my homegirl before all these other homegirls, back in the 805, when teachers thought she was gonna be a soldier girl and I was gonna go to secretarial school someday."

In time it became part of the Warchild mystique that she had a white, blond, ex-military chick as her second. It was as if Serena had an exotic weapon; I was her ivory-handled switchblade. And Serena knew that having me around made her safer. I had training that her other girls didn't. I was a good fighter and shooter. When Serena and I were out on the street, I always had my Browning at my side and, often, a baby Glock on my ankle. But the other part of that was this: I wouldn't shoot unnecessarily. I respected guns and what they could do, and I was careful in a way Serena knew her girls wouldn't be.

Funny to look back on it now, but I hadn't wanted to become a sucia. It was a commitment she'd extracted from me last year, when I'd asked her for Trece's backup in taking on Tony Skouras. When I took my beating and joined, Serena had given me the street name "Insula," Latin for *island*. She'd meant it as "someone alone or separate," and that had reflected the understanding that we'd both had, that I was joining her clique mostly in name. Neither of us had foreseen that after the Skouras business was over, I'd become her lieutenant. I hadn't foreseen coming home to L.A. so restless and angry.

Some of that anger was because of the brain tumor, which had stolen away my Army career and much of my future. I had been in my third year at West Point when things went wrong, except it didn't feel wrong. I was simply never afraid. That wasn't normal for someone at a military academy. The curriculum was designed to push you out of your comfort zone. *Jump out of this airplane. Walk into this room and get gassed without a mask so you'll always remember what it feels like. Compete at the levels we've set for you or you'll go home in civilian clothes and everything you've done here will be for nothing.* It was supposed to be frightening. Except then it wasn't. In my third and fourth years, "What the hell" had practically been my mantra: *What the hell, I'll go first. What the hell, I'll try it. I don't care. I'll do it. I'm not scared.*

Then my tumor, so small and unknown, outed itself. My fearlessness brought me too close to the edge of a high bluff in a training exercise, and I fell. A precautionary MRI showed the tiny white glowing spot in my amygdala. Inoperable, the doctor said, and no matter that it was slow-growing and I was in perfect health otherwise, the "emotional anomalies" the tumor was causing made me unfit to serve as an officer in the United States Army. And it wouldn't stay asymptomatic. I would not celebrate my thirtieth birthday.

But the truth was, I'd been dealing with the collapse of my life's plan for a long time before I became Serena's lieutenant. The simmering resentment that I felt when I came back from San Francisco couldn't fairly be blamed on that. Nor was it even how badly Skouras's men had punked me up north, their mutilation of my left hand. No, to be honest, a lot of my anger was about CJ.

So my career as Insula, Warchild's second-in-command, began in earnest. I needed to be needed, and I found that in the sucia life. It was me who had seen that if the pharmacy robberies Serena pulled two or three times a year were profitable, truck hijackings would give us a bigger haul at a fraction of the risk. And on the streets I was Serena's protection. In private I was the confidante she needed more and more.

Serena was under an appalling amount of pressure. I think I was the only one who saw what her new status cost her. Because in the gang life, even when things are good, they're never really good. Gangbangers call it *la vida loca,* but privately I thought of it as *cura nigra,* or "black care," the Roman phrase for trouble and worry. I'd seen the graffiti at the edges of her neighborhood, left by rivals, that said SUCIA KILLER and WARCHILD 187. The first time, I'd smiled bitterly, thinking, *This is how the glass ceiling breaks in the ghetto, with death threats on a wall.*

The pressure didn't come just from rivals on the street. There were rumors that Magnus Ford, the feared LAPD gang-intelligence officer, had taken an interest in Warchild.

Gang suppression is one thing. It's a war of attrition, hassling the street-corner guys, making petty arrests that often don't stick, doing intervention with the youngest gangbangers who might still be saved. Gang intelligence, or organized-crime intelligence, is something else. Magnus Ford was the quiet force behind the arrests of several high-level Mexican Mafia shot callers. There were rumors that he was a fed planted within the LAPD. Nobody knew what he looked like. He was apparently so valuable that he was never photographed, not for the newspapers, not even on law-enforcement websites.

Thinking ahead, Serena had taken steps to protect herself from threats on both sides of the law. For example, the rented house that I used to call "Casa Serena," with the orange tree out front and the couch or floor space for any of her homegirls who needed it, was no more. Serena was now living NKA, or "no known address." Sometimes she crashed with her homegirls, other times with her brothers, occasionally, when money permitted, at a Vietnamese café-bar where they rented rooms upstairs for assignations. The main thing, for Serena, was that no one know where she slept.

She didn't ever acknowledge the stress she was under, but for several months she'd been having stomach pains; intermittent, but sometimes bad enough that she'd retreat to one of her sleeping places and lie down, handing off her pager to me and telling me to TCB—take care of business—for a while.

I'd told her more than once that she should see a doctor. She said the pains always went away. I said they always came back. But she still hadn't been through a clinic door.

I guess that all this is a long explanation of why I stayed at Serena's side: My most subtle and unspoken role in our relationship was not just to protect her from danger but to keep her from *being* a danger. The odds had been against her getting even as far as she had. Age twenty-five was past time for a hardcore gangster to be in the grave. I knew that Serena knew this, that she thought about the endgame and the money that would fund a transition to a better life. And I knew she was willing to take risks to get it.

What I'm saying is, increasingly I saw Serena as a loaded gun. I was the safety on that gun.

Or maybe this is all a lot of justification, of the type I told the drug-company truck driver I didn't do anymore. Pare it down to its simplest, and it's this: Some people like to say the greater the sinner, the greater the saint. What they don't tell you, I guess, is that the reverse is also true.

3

"Hey, Hailey, did I tell you about my new girl?"

It was a little more than an hour after the Great Truck Robbery. We were at a storage facility off Olympic, where Serena rented a small walk-in locker. It was there that she stored her boxes of stolen pharmaceuticals, a few unregistered weapons, and some emergency cash. There was an overhead light of two long fluorescent tubes, but we hadn't turned it on, working instead in the glow of a flashlight set on its end and pointed at the ceiling. Serena never drew attention to her presence when she visited her unit.

"I don't think so," I said. "New like newly jumped in?"

"Uh-uh. That's what I wanted to talk to you about,"

she said, pushing a box backward on the shelf until it was flush with its neighbors. "Diana wants to fight you. For her initiation."

There aren't a lot of choices in the gang life. One of them, though, is the initiation ritual. In too many places, for girls, it's sexual: They roll the dice and have sex with that number of their gang-brothers-to-be. The hardest part to understand was that many girls were offered the choice of taking a group beating—the conventional jumping-in ritual for guys—or the sexual option, and they willingly chose the latter. It was less an act of cowardice than an acknowledgment that a life of emotionless sexual use was inevitable.

Serena had never tolerated anything like that. For a girl who wanted to be a sucia, the only way had been to take a group beating, just like a guy. But lately, since I'd come back to L.A., there was a second option: a three-minute, one-on-one fight with Warchild's lieutenant, Insula.

The only two girls Serena had initiated lately had chosen the group beating. Certainly that wasn't less painful, but it was impersonal at least. A one-on-one fight was different: It was the gladiator thing, everyone watching to see if you proved yourself. It was intimidating in ways that went beyond *I might get hurt.*

"You sound pleased," I said.

"Yeah, I've got hopes for this girl," Serena said. "She's got a lot of *corazón.*"

She sat on her heels and snapped open the latch to a fire-safe cash box, looked inside, and took out a sheaf of bills.

She rolled them into a cylinder and wrapped a rubber band around them. I knew what she was doing: taking away some of her savings for storage elsewhere, at one of her sleeping places. Serena split up her money like a tourist separates traveler's checks in case of a purse snatching. This was despite the fact that almost no one—including none of the guys in Trece—knew about her storage unit.

This was why Magnus Ford, the LAPD's "Shadow Man," was right to be interested in Warchild Delgadillo. She was a planner.

Serena stood up. "Okay," she said, moving to the door. "Why don't you come over to Diana's place for a while?" she suggested. "I'd like you to meet her."

"Sure," I said. I was already giving her a ride to wherever she was spending the night, since we'd ditched the SUV and were down to only my bike as transportation.

Serena closed the door behind us and pushed the shackle into the body of the padlock.

Her directions took us to a four-story building in her neighborhood, a blocky gray building with a secure entry and bars on the first-floor windows. Serena had a key to the outer door, and I followed her into the entry landing. The heavy door clanged shut behind us, locking out the perils of the outside world. Serena called an upstairs apartment on the intercom.

"*Bueno,*" a girl's voice said.

"It's me," Serena said. "Insula's with me."

A loud buzzing filled the entryway, and Serena pulled

open the inner door, revealing a stairwell that smelled strongly of old cigarettes.

Upstairs, she knocked on the apartment door: three raps, pause, a fourth. To an outsider it would have seemed silly; the secret girls'-club knock. Or at least paranoid, since she'd called up seconds earlier, identifying herself to the girl within. But such caution was the key to Serena's survival to age twenty-five, ripe middle age in gang years.

The door opened, and a tall girl stood in the breach. She didn't resemble the sucias I knew. Where they invariably had long hair, Diana's cocoa-brown hair was cut short in defiance of girl-gangbanger fashion dictates, and her eyes, almond-shaped like Serena's, were free of harsh eyeliner and shadow.

She nodded to Serena first, but immediately after, her eyes flicked to me, with the undercurrent of curiosity I was used to by now. In her case I imagined it was also a sizing up: I was her opponent-to-be, soon.

We exchanged *what's ups* and Serena and I came in. The place wasn't very big. The kitchen grew into a living room, the division marked by the end of the kitchen's tired linoleum. A door set into the far living-room wall indicated a bedroom. It was all dim, only the lamp on the living-room floor lighted, and the hood light over the stove. The windows were closed, and I knew why: Even on the third floor, Diana didn't want the unmistakable scent of marijuana to get out. It was rising as steam from the big, ten-quart pot on the stove. Diana was making oil of chronic.

The first time Serena and I had done it, it had been just for fun: simmering marijuana and cooking oil together in a big pot of water to infuse, then freezing the water in a bowl so that the green sludge congealed on the surface, all the easier to scrape off and melt back into marijuana-infused oil, or "oil of chronic" as Serena named it, that could be mixed into foods or swallowed like a spoonful of medicine. With hip-hop music playing on the radio in the sunny kitchen at old Casa Serena, it had seemed little different from homegirl cooking, making pan dulce on a Saturday.

I don't know when Serena got the idea to turn oil of chronic into a business sideline—a boutique drug trade—but there was no question she'd found a niche. Her clientele was small and select, most of them entertainment-industry people. Though marijuana was nearly as available as Wrigley's gum in Los Angeles, these were people who ate at Spago. They weren't going to pass around a slimy joint like it was 1973. Serena understood this, and she gave them the same quality control they expected in their cabernet sauvignon or sparkling water. Serena dealt with only one supplier of high-quality marijuana, a grower hidden deep in a national forest in Northern California. She bottled her product tastefully in small shaker bottles that she bought at a kitchen-supply outlet. And she didn't actively seek new customers, just let word of mouth do its work.

A lot of people would say, *With a product like that, why stay small? Why not go big and watch the money roll in?*

Serena knew better. A larger operation would draw the

attention of the big fish in La Eme, who'd take over, and then Serena would be an employee in her own operation, making only a small cut, and that couldn't be allowed. She'd paid her dues for years on her prescription-drug heists, just as the guys of Trece did on the cocaine and grass they moved in the neighborhood. But the oil-of-chronic sideline, that was Serena's endgame, her retirement plan.

Serena went over to peer into the vat, as if she were inspecting the work of a sous-chef. Then she went to the refrigerator and pulled out a bottle of Corona, looking questioningly at me.

"Just one," I said. "I gotta drive."

"You can sleep here," she said.

The bedroom was lived in and messy, with mismatched furniture and a thirteen-inch TV perched on the dresser.

"Where does Diana sleep?" I asked.

"She sleeps on the couch when I spend the night."

"But there's got to be other people living here."

"No, just her."

That was odd. In the barrio—not just in gang life— crowded homes were the rule. A whole apartment for one teenage girl, no matter how small—that was almost unheard of.

Serena said, "I've been helping her pay the rent here."

"What about her family?"

"Dad's in prison, Mom's a flake with a meth habit. Good times."

That wasn't an uncommon story; many of the sucias

came from broken homes. Serena had often made room for them in her old house, but I'd never known her to pay rent for any of them. "You must like her."

"Like I said, she has a lot of potential." Serena set her bottle down and reached into her jacket, taking out the roll of bills she'd brought from the storage unit. She peeled several off the top. "Here," she said, handing them to me.

"Thanks." I didn't count them. We didn't negotiate my pay for riding with her; we didn't even talk about it. It was understood that when times were good for her, financially, they were good for me. She opened the top drawer of the dresser and put the rest of the money inside. Then she flipped on the TV set atop the dresser. The audio began right away, hip-hop music, but the picture tube was slow to warm up.

"Look," I said, "if Diana's so different, if she's got a lot of brains and potential, why not steer her in a different direction, like toward college?"

This was sensitive territory. It didn't matter that I was now as morally compromised as anyone in Serena's OC underworld; I was still white and college-educated, and she was quick to get hot about anything like preaching on my part.

But she calmly said, "Let me put it in terms you'll understand: *Virtus laudatur et alget*."

" 'Virtue is praised and made to freeze'?"

" 'Virtue is praised and left to freeze,' " she corrected. "That's what happens to good girls around here. The nice boys, some of them get a football scholarship or something, but the girls? There's nothing for them. Diana could study and work and study some more, and then she'd get killed in a drive-by anyway, or shot by accident by the cops, and the neighborhood do-gooders would light a few candles, and then they'd forget her. It woulda happened to me, if I hadn't gotten ganged up and learned to look out for myself." She repeated herself: "Virtue is praised and left to freeze—you're living proof of that."

"Me?"

"Look what happened to you at West Point. You worked your ass off to become what they wanted, and then they hosed you off the back steps because of something that's gonna make you sick someday in the future?"

"It wasn't like that. The tumor raised a question of whether my judgment would be sound enough for me to serve as an officer."

"Yeah, but what did they do to help you, after your whole life went down the drain? They gave you, what, a ride to New York City to catch the Greyhound home? Great."

I shrugged, not wanting to argue the point anymore. Serena didn't, either, changing the subject. "Hey, who'd have thought I'd be schooling you in Latin?"

"Yeah," I agreed. "Pretty good."

She walked into the bathroom, and I heard the shower start running. She'd left the TV on, and now it was playing a hip-hop video, standard scenes of ghetto fabulousness, booties shaking in a packed nightclub. The logo at the bottom corner of the screen was that of a late-Friday-night video program, one that came on after the network talk shows were over.

I sat down on the bed and began unlacing my boots.

"Hey, y'all," the host of the program said, "did you see, at the beginning, the guy coming out of the club as Nia and her girls are going in? A long drink of water with reddish hair? That's none other than Nia's producer, Cletus Mooney, making a cameo. I wouldn't kick that boy outta bed, 'cept maybe to do him on the floor, know what I'm saying? Up next—"

I got up and snapped off the TV set. Then, barefoot, I opened the sliding glass door and walked out onto the little balcony. *Balcony* was too romantic a word; this was a boxy platform seven feet long by four feet deep, mostly for smokers to be herded onto so they could indulge their vice. Concrete dividing walls came all the way out to the railing on both sides, a security measure, so that no one could infiltrate from a neighboring deck who wasn't ready to take a serious risk climbing over with his ass hanging out above the street.

I put one leg over the railing and straddled it, then shifted around to sit with both legs over the railing, on the outside, heels resting gently against the bars. The sidewalk, three stories below, would be hard as iron if I fell, but the breeze was cool on my face, so I leaned out a little, looking up at the night sky.

For God's sake, I hadn't even seen CJ's image on-screen, I thought, exhaling. I'd only had to hear the host talking about him, and the picture had sprung immediately to my mind's eye: my beautiful cousin, holding the door for a flirtatious pack of clubgoing girls. CJ loved women, and they loved him back. He went in for variety rather than long-term relationships, dating a steady stream of cocktail waitresses, Laker girls, and backup dancers, but his ex-girlfriends never seemed to have hard feelings after things were over. Back when I was spending more time in his circle of friends, one of them had tried to engage me in some us-girls talk, saying, "Man, Cletus just *gives* himself to you in bed," before I'd managed to cut her off, feeling heat in my port-wine birthmark, the part of my face that still blushed.

The thing was, when I'd first met him, CJ had had almost none of the things women saw in him now. Or rather, everything was there, but in a raw, early form that the other kids in the halls of junior high school couldn't recognize. His musical gifts had been pretty well hidden. He'd picked up the piano almost faster than his mother could teach him, but he'd never played in public. His hair, worn shorter than now, was almost kinky, and he couldn't put on weight and muscle fast enough to keep up with his height. His accent, to Californian kids, was comical, the sound of backwoods unsophistication.

Those were the days when CJ and I had been each other's closest companion. It was also in those bad days that, underneath his parents' willow tree, we'd learned French kissing from each other, because we'd had no one else to practice with. Then we'd kept doing it long after we could no longer justify it as a learning process. We had to love each other, because we were unlovely to everyone else.

All this is a long way of explaining the resentment I felt when I saw his picture in entertainment magazines, CJ in a nightclub banquette with glittery club girls or carrying his girlfriend-of-the-month on his back on Leo Carrillo Beach. I understood what they saw in him, but dammit, I'd seen it first. I hadn't needed the big career or the eight-figure bank balance or the A-list friends to love Cletus Mooney. I just had, and now I was the only one who wasn't allowed.

Serena's voice floated out from the bedroom. "So I was thinking— Jesus, do you have to sit like that?" she said sharply, looking up at the no-hands way I was sitting on the railing, leaning forward with my elbows resting on my thighs, like someone following a ball game on TV. "If you fall from up there, you'll break your neck."

"Why would I fall?" I said, not turning around. "If I was sitting on the kitchen counter like this, you wouldn't say that."

"If you fell off the counter, you'd get up again. Can you please come in, so I don't have a heart attack?"

I shifted my weight and swung a leg over, then backed up until I could rest my spine against the concrete wall, sitting sideways. "Is this better? Because this is about all the concession to safety I'm willing to make."

She leaned against the slider's framework. "Sometimes I really wish I knew how it felt to be you."

"Blond?"

"Fearless."

"I didn't say I'm never afraid," I told her. "I'm just . . .

blunted. Haven't you ever been drunk and you did something you'd never do sober? Your feeling was just, 'What the hell, I'll do it'?"

"That's not the same thing," she said.

"Isn't it? Why do you think they call alcohol 'liquid courage'?" I said. "It's an extreme example, but think of people on PCP. They'll do anything. Nothing scares them."

"That's different," Serena said. "Those people are out of their minds. Nobody jumps off a roof just because it's not scary to them."

"Exactly," I said. "I wouldn't, either. I'm rational. But when things happen where I should feel afraid, there's just an absence."

"So it's better," she said. "Because you're not uncoordinated, like a drunk person would be, or half asleep, like someone in a hospital on downers would be. That's all it is, like a drug with no side effects?"

Other than eventual death from brain cancer?

"I guess," I said. "There aren't that many things you can compare to my situation. There are kids that seem to be born with a really high fear threshold, maybe from brain damage sustained during difficult births. They do a lot of heart-stopping things on their bicycles or jump off rooftops. Afterward they don't understand why people are yelling at them. When people say, 'You could have broken your neck,' they say, 'But I didn't. What's the big deal?' "

"And you feel the same way," Serena said.

"Not exactly," I said. "I haven't had this problem all my

life. I remember what used to frighten me, and I know what scares other people. That guides me."

"Hmm," she said, inspecting one of her thumbnails. "I guess it's good you say that."

"Why?"

"There's something we gotta talk about. It's Trippy." Her face was serious in the ambient city light.

"She hates us, yeah. This is not news."

"She hates *you*," Serena corrected quietly. "I hear things, Insula. She's been telling anyone who'll listen that she's going to kill you. She's saying this is still her neighborhood and she's not afraid to come onto my territory to put a bullet in you."

"Let her try," I said, shrugging. "She loves to wave a gun around, but she's a lousy shot."

"You're so full of shit," Serena said. "You just said that what scares other people guides you, but I'm telling you this is something to be scared of, and you're, what, blowing me off?"

"I'm not blowing you off. It's just, I've had more dangerous enemies than Trippy Ramos, and I'm still standing. Grudges like Trippy's, it's kid shit. She's just blowing off steam."

"Whatever. I had something to say to you—now I've said it. I'm going to bed." She turned and left.

The truth was, she probably had a point about Trippy. Grudges could be deadly in the ghetto and the barrio. This wasn't "kid shit" to Luisa Ramos. I'd taken her place and dealt a terrible blow to her ego. In antiquity, in the present, in organized crime, in corporate boardrooms, these kinds of clashes played out everywhere. Loss of position, loss of face: one of humanity's most primal wounds. Why was I still here, making myself a party to it? Because of Serena. My loaded gun.

I looked inside to see her standing in front of the dresser where she'd stashed her money. Now she pulled from the top drawer a bottle of pills, not one of the little orange ones that patients get but a larger wholesale one that she'd kept after a pharmacy heist. I didn't have to watch her spill the little white oval pill into her palm to know what it would be: Ambien.

She washed it down with Corona and, still standing in front of the open drawer, crossed her arms and pulled her T-shirt over her head. The dog tags she wore as a necklace caught briefly in the collar, then fell back to bounce against her hard breastbone. Usually the tags were out of sight under her clothes, but Serena never took them off, in honor of the past life she believed she'd lost in Vietnam. I'd once encouraged her to travel over there, to see the country that occupied her dreams, but it didn't seem that she ever would.

In the dim electric light of the bedroom, she was thin enough to count ribs. Weight loss, stomach pains, Ambien sleep—the glamorous gangster life.

The bottle of Corona I held was still half full, but I didn't want any more. Briefly I considered letting it drop from my hand, three stories down to the sidewalk, just for the nihilistic pleasure of seeing shards of glass and white foam explode against the pavement. No. Reckless was one thing, but pointlessly antisocial was another.

I got off the railing and went inside. Stripped down to her panties, Serena had climbed onto the bed, wrapping the spread, but not the sheets underneath, around her; it'd been ninety-nine degrees at midday and would likely stay warm all night.

"You want me to look for a movie or something?" I asked, but then saw that Serena's eyes were already closed. Ambien is quick.

I began getting undressed as well.

Home, right now, was an apartment in the Crenshaw district. Like Serena, I understood the virtues of being NKA; the apartment was my compromise. My name wasn't on the rental contract nor any of the utilities. Instead I paid cash to a young woman as white as me, who was a schoolteacher with the Los Angeles Unified School District. She was gaming a federal program that gave teachers in "underserved communities" a sizable tax break to live where they worked. So she'd taken the modest second-story apartment, then immediately rented it off the books to me and moved to Hollywood.

It took me a little while to get used to living in the land of *ay yo* instead of *órale,* but I was accustomed to outsiderhood. And Crenshaw was the last place that Serena's enemies—by extension my enemies, the ones who spray-painted SUCIA KILLER on walls—would look for me.

It wasn't home, but I hadn't had a real home for some time now.

4

The next day dawned bright, promising to be as hot as yesterday, and I was out of the apartment at ten, before Serena or Diana had risen. I was thinking of two things: one, that maybe the Blind Guy was at his bench in the park, and two, how good a chocolate-filled roll from a favorite *panadería* would taste.

I'd first seen the Blind Guy several weeks ago and still thought of him that way, even after learning his name, Joe Keller. He'd drawn my attention the first day I'd seen him, for two reasons. First, he'd looked enough like CJ—young and tall and loose-limbed, with curling red hair—that my heart had briefly skipped, until I'd realized it was highly unlikely

that CJ would be sitting around an East L.A. park by himself. Second, I'd seen the white cane that immediately marked
him as blind.

The cane was the reason I went over to talk to him that
first afternoon.

"Hi," I'd said. "My name's Hailey."

"Joe," he'd said.

"Look, I could lead up to this by making small talk first,
but I won't. The thing is, this neighborhood is one where
maybe you want to bring a friend if you're going to hang out.
I know it probably seems like a lot of nice people, kids and
mamis with strollers, but there's a lot of gang activity here,
too. In fact, the bench you're sitting on is pretty marked up
with gang graffiti."

I'd gone on, "And while I'd like to say that gangbangers
have scruples about jacking the elderly or the disabled, mostly
they don't. They see someone like that, by themselves, and
it's like the rest of us feel when seeing something we need in
a store marked half off. It's like, 'Hey, I can't pass that up.' "

His face had been inscrutable, with the dark glasses adding to that impression. When he didn't respond right away,
I'd said, "I've offended you, right?"

"No," he'd said. "You might have, but then the analogy,
the half-off discount, really redeemed it." A small, sardonic
smile had lightened his expression, and then he'd said, "What
about you?"

"What about me?"

"You're young, female, apparently alone, and, from the

sound of your voice, white. How much are you discounted for those guys?"

I'd smiled privately, wanting to say, *A piece of me is gonna cost them,* but I hadn't. Instead I'd said, "You have a good ear. I am white. Blond, even."

"Oh, good. I like blondes."

"But you're blind!"

"Just on principle."

I'd laughed, even though my act of Good Samaritan-hood was going very differently from how I'd expected it to. "Well, great," I'd said. "The world can always use another man of principles. By the way, you personally? Very much red-haired."

"I'm a redhead? Jesus, nobody tells me anything."

I'd taken a seat and stayed awhile, long enough for him to tell me that he had an elderly, chronically ill uncle in the area whom he came around to care for, and that he liked to walk out and get a little sun while the old guy was napping.

He'd asked me how much I knew about the gangs in the area—did I have friends in the life?—and so on. I'd evaded his questions, just telling him that I came around to visit an old friend from junior high, not elaborating. I'd had a suspicion that he was leading up to asking me for a source to buy marijuana from, but then he never did.

The second time I'd seen him, I'd asked him if he was a student—he dressed very casually—but he'd said, "I'm done with school," somewhat flatly, so I hadn't pursued it. Nor did I ask him what he did for a living. He was clearly able-bodied, and I heard both intelligence and a certain amount of education in the way he talked. Yet he seemed to have a lot of free time, and I wondered if he was on disability. But again I didn't ask, afraid again of offending him.

When I arrived at the park today, I saw the Blind Guy from a distance, red hair like a flag, eyes hidden as always behind the shades, his face tipped up toward the sun. His skin was pale; he didn't freckle, like a lot of redheads would have.

When I was close enough that I knew he could hear my footsteps, I said, "Hey, it's Hailey."

"Morning," he said. "Have a seat."

I maneuvered around his outstretched legs to get to the open space on the bench. He had long legs; I figured him for about six-three, standing. "Have you eaten?"

"Yeah, but I can always eat. What've you got?"

"Something from the bakery," I said, opening the bag. "You like cinnamon rolls?"

"Because you want the chocolate for yourself?" he said. "You thought I wasn't going to smell that, did you?"

"You want the chocolate one instead?"

"No, it's fine, whichever." He held his hand out in my general direction.

I reached into the bag and drew out the cinnamon roll but then stopped, distracted. On the back of the bench, just between us, someone had scratched the message INSULA 187. The exposed wood looked pale and splintery, therefore fresh. It was new.

I had seen threats against the sucias in general and Serena in particular, but never against me personally. This was Trippy's handiwork, made all the more striking because the park was dead center in the middle of Trece territory, where a member of Tenth Street shouldn't have dared to go. Serena was right. This was a sign of true dedication to a grudge.

"Hailey?" Joe prompted me.

"Sorry," I said. "Distracted."

I took the cinnamon roll out of its wrapper and gave it to him.

"Thanks," he said, tearing off a small piece. "I thought maybe I hurt your feelings, teasing you like that."

"No, it was funny," I said. "How's your uncle?"

"About the same," he said.

He'd never been talkative about his uncle's illness, and I'd never pressed him on it. So we sat for a moment, eating in silence. The breeze played with his hair, and he brushed it back. His hair was redder than CJ's; my cousin could almost be called a strawberry blond.

"Joe," I said, curious, "what color are your eyes?"

Immediately, he put up a hand, palm outward and fingers spread in front of his face. "Hey, you're not reaching for my shades, are you?" He sounded alarmed.

I pulled back. "No," I said, surprised by his reaction.

He relaxed a little and put his hand down. "Sorry," he said. "It's a thing with blind people. Some of us are sensitive about our eyes, like deaf people are about their voices. I usually know someone awhile before I go without sunglasses around them."

"Oh," I said. "I'm sorry."

"No, I am," he said. "I shouldn't have assumed you were going to try to take off my shades. The other thing is, blind people get used to folks touching us without warning. People think it's okay if it's well intended, like when someone just takes your arm and pulls to show you which way to go. I don't like it."

"I wouldn't, either," I said.

"I don't think you're like that," he said.

"Thanks," I said.

Then, for a minute, I wanted to tell him about my tumor. Because then I could say I understood what it was like to not want people to think of you as an "asterisk" person. If I told people about my cancer, I'd never just be Hailey again. I'd be the girl with the deadly little poison pill deep in her brain. Or maybe it'd come off like one-upmanship. So instead I said, "If we keep running into each other, eventually I'm going to say something stupid about you being blind. It's inevitable. I mean, you're probably giving me too much credit."

"Don't worry about it." He shifted position slightly, touched his white cane. "Listen, do you have a phone number? I'm not hitting on you," he added quickly, "but it'd be nice to know someone in the neighborhood, just in case I get stranded after the buses stop running, something like that."

I had a brief idea of his hands on my stomach, the way

riders hold on to you when they're riding pillion. "Sure," I said. I dug into my backpack, found a pen. "Hold out your hand," I said. "I'll say it out loud, but I'm also going to write it on your palm."

"You do know how being blind works, right?" he said quizzically.

"I know, but this'll help you remember. It's tactile rein- forcement. We learned about it in school." I ran the pen point back and forth across my own skin, along the base of my thumb, to get the ink to flow. "Hold out your hand."

He did, and I recited the numbers slowly as I wrote them. "There," I said.

"Thanks."

"I should get going."

"Are you going to work?"

"Not right away."

"You've never said what you do for a living."

"Oh," I said, "the usual dead-end wage-slave stuff."

5

twelve hours later

"**C**ome on, girl! Harder! You can hit harder than that, babe!"

I wasn't sure who the guy with the clear, sonorous voice, intelligible over all the rest of the chaotic crowd noise, was yelling to, me or my opponent. I liked to think that I'd been fighting here long enough to have supporters in the crowd, but there was a good chance he was encouraging my opponent. Generally the men who came to illegal fights favored the prettiest girls, and "Kat" qualified. She had gold-brown braids and light olive skin; the men had whistled their approval at first sight.

Every week, beyond the mesh of the cage in which I

fought, I saw many of the same faces in the crowd, and it was always heavily male. Some were motivated by the prospect of illegal gambling gains, others simply loved to watch fights. I don't know what drew them here when there was boxing and mixed martial arts on TV about every night of the week, as well as club fights at gyms around L.A. But some people need that thrill that comes from knowing it's illegal.

This was the Slaughterhouse.

It was Serena who'd gotten me into this line of work, in the early days after my return to L.A. One Saturday afternoon, when neither of us had plans for the evening, she'd asked me, "Do you still like to watch fighting?"

"Sure," I'd said.

"Do you want to see some fights?"

"You mean, like on HBO?" I didn't think either of us knew anybody who had premium cable.

She said, "Not at all like HBO."

The venue she took me to was just west of the river, in a mixed-industrial neighborhood near the Fashion District. The building had once been a meatpacking plant, hence the name. Now the main floor was empty and refitted with an octagonal cage and bleacher seating on all sides.

Though most of the fights were between guys, Serena told me that a girl could get a hundred dollars just to fight and five hundred dollars to win. The steep difference between winner pay and loser pay was designed to weed out the dreamers and wannabes.

"Really? Five hundred?" I'd said. The next week I'd gone

back alone. I wondered if Serena had known all along that I would.

I learned pretty quickly that there was more to the Slaughterhouse than just fighting. I'd had good boxing instruction at West Point, where I'd also learned some submission moves, and I'd carelessly assumed that those things alone would make me a crowd favorite. I'd been wrong.

Jack, one of the two brothers who ran things, called me into his office early on to ask two things of me. First, he wanted me to improve my kicks.

"You box great for a chick," he'd said, "but if the guys out there just wanted to see boxing, they'd turn on the TV. They come here to see a mix of styles, street moves and Asian stuff, and kicks are especially a crowd pleaser. You're making enough money—go find a dojo you like and learn to mix up your moves a little."

"All right," I'd said.

"The other thing is," he'd said, "do a little something with your looks. Hey, don't get hot. This place isn't all about good fighting. It's a spectacle. The guys out there aren't gonna get behind you if you're dressed like a college girl on her way to lift weights. They'd rather watch a hot girl with sloppy moves. It doesn't matter how good your chops are—if you can't get the crowd behind you, I can't keep giving you fights."

Jack and I probably never quite saw eye to eye on how I should look when I came down to the ring, but I made some changes. About once a month, I went to a small salon off

Melrose, redolent with the scent of chemicals and pulsating with Eurodisco music, and I let the girls brighten and streak my hair. I got temporary tattoos, flames up my arms from wrist to elbow, a sunburst rising over my tailbone. Sometimes I thumbed black kohl thickly under my eyes to create an angry, deadened gaze.

As Jack predicted, the guys liked it. But everything I changed about my hair and body was short-term; I never did anything permanent. I suppose a shrink would say it was my way of declaring that none of this touched the essential me.

I didn't always win. In particular I remember one girl, white like me, from somewhere out in the Central Valley. Five-foot-eleven, hard fat, staring at me with the impassive gaze of a bear looking at a wildlife photographer. That was one of my hundred-dollar nights.

It wasn't uncommon for me to hurt the next day, win or lose, but Serena always had Vicodin.

"Come on, baby! Head kick! Kick to the head!"

Being a good fighter, it's not any one thing. Technique is a lot, of course. But size is, too, because reach lets you hit opponents while staying out of range, and weight lets you put more force into the blows. It's just physics: Force equals mass times velocity.

Kat threw her first hook, and I dropped low over my heels, letting her fist graze above my head. The men whistled and jeered.

Experience matters. That's a close cousin to technique, but not the same thing, because experience also means a fighter who knows that bleeding stops, bruises heal, pain goes away. That lets you keep your head when things aren't going your way.

Kat dug a low left hook into my ribs. I couldn't get out of the way in time and had to absorb it. It wasn't a very hard blow. Good. If that was all she had, it wasn't enough.

A lot of people think anger helps. I tend to think that's a myth. An angry fighter with no skills may throw more punches, but flailing blindly will get you knocked out fast.

Confident now from landing a blow, Kat stayed in close, trying again to hammer my ribs. Mistake. I threw both my arms around her neck, taking advantage of her proximity.

The other thing that doesn't help as much as people think? Brains. You hear about "thinking fighters," but those individuals are rare and very, very good. Maybe, for them, time seems to slow and they can anticipate, plan on the fly. I can't; most of the guys I know can't. The firstie who'd coached me and the rest of my company's boxing team used to say, *Learn as much as you can outside the ring, but when you're in the ring, stop thinking. Let your muscles think for you, because your brain won't do it fast enough.*

Still clinching Kat's neck, I threw my right knee into her midsection and both heard and felt the way it punished her. She would have doubled over, except that I put my hands on her shoulders, then shoved lightly to get her out at the end of my range, and threw my hardest straight right into her face.

I've heard men, experienced fighters, say they'll sometimes block body blows with their heads. I believe them, but

I've never done it. Next time you see a picture of a human skull, notice the gap, the absence of bone, at the nose. It's a fantastically vulnerable place to get hit. Something about it goes straight to your brain and rattles you to the core. It's hard to recover from.

Kat didn't. She backed up, raised her arms against another blow, and then waved me off. She'd decided to have a hundred-dollar night.

After she was out of the cage, Jack's brother, Mav, beckoned me to talk to him through the mesh of the cage. I went over.

"Short fight," he said.

"Sorry." But I wasn't.

"You want to go again?" he said. "I've got another girl who's ready."

I wiped at a bit of hair that had come loose from my braids and fallen into my face. "Sure," I said.

I'd like to say that was how I had a thousand-dollar night, but it wasn't. It was how I had a six-hundred-dollar night.

The Slaughterhouse had real locker rooms, left over from its days as a working factory, but there was no water service anymore, so no showers. Cooling off, I checked out my reflection in the tarnished mirror.

"You look fine," a voice behind me said.

She was younger than me, Alice, a white girl of twenty. We hadn't yet fought each other. I'd seen her once outside the fights and barely recognized her. She was a clerk at Home

Depot during the day, and her pale blond shoulder-length hair was curly in a way that could have been natural or could have been an unfortunate perm. Her face and eyes were both round, giving her a vacuous look, and under street clothes her body looked a little plump. Her middle-class customers at Home Depot, the ones pricing Corian countertops and hardwood flooring for their home-improvement projects, probably looked at her and thought *white trash*, then double-checked their receipts for mistakes.

At the fights she was someone different. She laced her hair back into multiple narrow braids against her skull. The blankness of her face became cool hardness. And in sports bra, board shorts, and bare feet, the roundness of her body was clearly the roundness of muscle, like that of the dray ponies that had once worked in coal mines.

"Go kick some ass," I told her. *Good luck* wasn't something we said. It wasn't about luck.

Alice went out to the ring, and I got my backpack from a locker and took out my street clothes. It was after ten, probably just cool enough outside to justify changing from my shorts into the jeans I'd brought, and my simple white T-shirt and crimson hoodie. I was sitting on a bench lacing up my boots when I heard my cell phone buzzing. The number on the screen was Serena's.

"Hey, *ésa*, where are you?" she asked. Then, without waiting for an answer, "You shouldn't be on the street, wherever you are. The cops are looking for you."

That was fast, I thought, remembering last night and

the truck robbery. Then, "Wait a minute, just me? Why not you?"

"It's not about last night," Serena said. "A couple of people got killed, up in San Francisco."

"And?"

"You're the suspect."

"What? You're kidding me, right?"

"No, it's on the news," Serena said.

"You mean, like, last year, when I lived up there?"

"No, it was yesterday, they're saying."

"Well, then it's a mix-up," I said. "It's just somebody with the same name. My last name's not uncommon, and my first was only the most popular—"

"I know that, but it's not just a name thing," she insisted. "This is who they're describing: Hailey Cain, twenty-four years old, blond hair, brown eyes, birthmark on the right cheekbone. And—" She paused here. "Hailey, they're saying that your thumbprint was on one of the used, what do you call 'em, casings."

That's not possible.

I was silent so long that Serena said, "I know, Insula, I didn't believe it, either. It was Diana who saw it on the news first and called me, and I said, 'No way, that can't be right.' "

Then she said, "The other thing, the big thing, is that one of the two vics was a policeman. *Prima,* they think you're a cop killer."

PART TWO

to the limits of fate

6

Cop killer. I didn't need Serena to explain the implications of that for my safety.

"What the hell is going on?" she said.

"You're asking me?"

"What're you gonna do?"

"I don't know," I said.

"Where are you?"

"At the Slaughterhouse," I said. "I was about to go home, but now I'm not so sure I should."

It was true that my Crenshaw apartment wasn't trace-able to me through any kind of bill or rental contract, but my neighbors had seen me coming and going, and I'd introduced myself to several of them by name. More than that, I stood out in Crenshaw. I'd known that before, but it hadn't bothered me. Now I had to worry about it.

"I'll come get you," Serena said.

"No," I said. "Hold that thought. There's someone else I want to call."

After we'd hung up, I scrolled through my list of old calls, finding a number I didn't use enough to know by heart. Tess answered on the third ring, her voice, as always, slightly British-inflected.

"It's Hailey," I said. "Have you seen the news?"

"Yes," she said.

"Do you believe it?"

"No," she said, "I don't."

"Then I need your help."

Tess D'Agostino, the biological daughter of San Francisco organized-crime figure Tony Skouras, had already saved my life once. Last winter she'd called off her father's henchmen and brought to an end the torture session that otherwise probably would have ended with me floating facedown in the bay; more than that, she'd brought me back to her hotel and overseen my recuperation herself. At first I hadn't known how far to trust her—she was a Skouras, after all—and I'd been brusque to the point of rudeness, but Tess had been serenely polite in response.

A few days later, she'd called me to suggest that if I stayed in San Francisco and if she in fact took the reins of the

Skouras syndicate—which officially was a shipping line and several related import businesses and unofficially brought Asian heroin, stolen artworks, and illegal Eastern European and Central Asian immigrants into the ports of San Francisco and Oakland—she would have use for me. In other words, she wanted what I'd gone on to provide for Serena: a right hand, protector and sounding board.

When she'd called me, I'd been walking on the Golden Gate Bridge. It had been a bright and promising morning, I still wasn't quite used to being alive when I was supposed to be dead, and despite the rough treatment I'd just suffered, my life at that moment had an anything-goes character, and I'd agreed to meet with Tess that evening to discuss her offer further.

That night she'd bought me dinner on Fisherman's Wharf. In the intervening hours, my mood had shifted a bit. The bright hour on the bridge was over, and the ghost of my newly severed finger had ached increasingly throughout the day. Over dinner, made more frank than I might have been by a martini and pain meds I'd taken for my hand, I not only turned down any potential job, I discouraged Tess from taking over the Skouras empire altogether.

"You seem to look at me as some kind of hero because I took it on myself to protect a baby whose parents I hardly knew," I'd told her, "but I didn't volunteer for that—it chose me. I'm not a hero. Me, my closest friend, most of the people I know—we're like an evolutionary chart of morally compromised people. I might be a little farther to the right on that chart than most of them, but you, you're not one of us at all, and I can't think why you'd want to be. And you will be if you take over your father's businesses. You won't change them. They'll change you. It's inevitable."

I don't kid myself that my advice could have had any effect on someone as self-assured as Tess D'Agostino, but she'd apparently come to the same conclusion. She sold nearly everything, keeping only her father's minority share in a film and television studio here in Los Angeles. Then she'd used the proceeds of the sale of the other Skouras businesses to buy a majority share. In short, Tess had become a studio head, and she lived locally.

I was reaching out to her now because she had no discernible link to me. No one knew that we knew each other, and thus no one would expect me to be with her. And her home, I felt certain, would be safe from close observation; every rich person I knew valued privacy and security.

So I'd given her directions to the Slaughterhouse— actually, to the intersection of two well-marked streets nearby, the neighborhood being somewhat confusing and forbidding to a newcomer, especially after dark. Then I'd collected my night's pay from Jack, in fifties and twenties that I divided up between my gym bag and my wallet, and left. I had to resist the urge to hurry. No one in the crowd pointed at me or stared. These weren't the kind of people who checked the news on their smartphones.

Outside, the temperature had dropped to the high sixties. The streets were mostly empty. The occasional car passed, but I was the only person on the sidewalk. A newspaper skated past my feet. At the corner I stopped, shifted the gym bag on my shoulder. Beyond Tess's hospitality to depend on, I had six hundred in cash, two Vicodin, and the Browning. No change of clothes, but that was a minor annoyance. There were worse states of affairs.

Besides, wouldn't this be over in a day or two? Somehow the police had to figure out that there was a mix-up, that Hailey Cain wasn't their suspect. How could they not? I hadn't shot a cop or anyone else. I'd been in L.A.

One problem with that: I'd been off the grid a long time. No rental contract. No utility bills. No real job with a W-4 or a time card. Come to think of it, who could even alibi me that the police would take seriously? Serena? Diana? I hadn't even been hanging with CJ lately.

Oh, God, *CJ*. Had he seen the news yet? Would he possibly entertain the—

That was when I heard the sirens.

Don't assume they're for you, I told myself. *This is L.A., after all.* I looked around for flashing lights and movement and saw them. Two squad cars were heading my way.

I set the gym bag down, sat on my heels, and quickly retrieved the money from inside. I didn't want to run with the bag. I didn't want to run at all, because if there was any chance these squad cars were on an unrelated call, I didn't want to give myself away. Nothing gets a cop's attention like someone who runs away from the sight of him.

The two cars turned onto the street I was on.

Tess, dammit, I trusted you.

I abandoned the bag and sprinted, looking as I did so for an alleyway or any tight space I could disappear into. I didn't want to stay in the open. If I turned this into a footrace, with obstacles, maybe I could win.

The sirens grew louder behind me. Ahead I saw a narrow driveway between buildings and headed for it. When I dived between the buildings, I was almost in full dark while I ran about twenty yards, and then I emerged into moonlight again.

Dead end. I was in a paved area where several buildings backed up to each other. There were two Dumpsters and about several dozen cigarette butts from a legion of workers taking breaks, so many that the ghost of nicotine hung in the air. The doors that I saw were solid windowless double doors, almost certainly all locked. There were no open windows.

"Damn," I said. "Dammit." The sirens were growing louder. What now? Climb up on a Dumpster and jump for a low-hanging rain gutter, try to make the roofline?

The cop cars were so close that I could hear the engine noise under the sirens. I turned, resigned, to look back at the driveway I'd run along, saw a brief flash of black-and-white as the cars swept past. Then the sound of the sirens began to lengthen, stretching out in that Doppler fade.

False alarm. I took a breath and began to walk back down the driveway. The sound of the cop cars was still receding. Broken glass crunched under my boots.

Out on the street again, I saw nothing but a dark gray

Chrysler Crossfire, the little coupe with that funny, rounded European shape, parked at the curb. The driver's door was open, and Tess D'Agostino was sitting on her heels outside, examining the gym bag I'd left pushed behind a trash can.

"Hey," I said when I was close enough, my breathing back to normal. I bent down to pick up the bag. "Thanks for coming."

Tess straightened up. She was wearing a dark pea coat, heavier than the weather called for, over a collarless white shirt, black trousers, and black stack-heeled boots, the same kind she'd worn the first time I saw her. She'd cut her bronze hair back to chin length since I'd seen her last.

"Did you run when you heard the sirens?" she asked.

I nodded.

"I thought maybe I was too late," she said. Then she nodded toward the Crossfire. "Let's not linger here longer than we have to, shall we?"

7

Tess lived in Westwood, not far from UCLA, in a Tudor house set back from a quiet street. She led me to a guest room and left me alone to shower, but I couldn't wait to turn on CNN, to find out what the rest of the world thought it knew about me.

The police officer's name was Greg Stepakoff. His murder wasn't fresh news this Saturday night; a line-of-duty death had first been reported in a San Francisco Police Department press release on Friday night, in time for the late news broadcasts. Stepakoff had been thirty-five, with a wife and daughter, and he hadn't shown up for his midwatch shift as scheduled at four P.M. Friday. His colleagues had been concerned, as Stepakoff was responsible and punctual. Several hours later, responding to a citizen's phone tip, officers had gone to a St. Francis Wood address, where they'd found Stepakoff's car in the driveway and the officer dead in the house, shot twice in the chest. An ambulance had been called to transport a second person to the hospital. Pressed for details, the SFPD press liaison would say only that the second victim was a civilian, not an officer. This sparked early reports of a double shooting, which were erroneous.

By Saturday morning the second victim had been identified, and in turn that identification made the story catch fire in the national media. The second victim, who had died late Friday night at UCSF Medical Center, was Violet Eastman, heiress to the Eastman distillery fortune and—under the pen name V. K. Eastman—a science-fiction writer of some note from the 1970s and '80s. She hadn't been shot but had died of dehydration, and her tox screen showed high levels of an unnamed sedative.

At a five P.M. news conference, the assembled reporters and the SFPD had different agendas. The SFPD press liaison mostly wanted to stress how much manpower was going into the investigation and to talk about plans for a Stepakoff memorial. The reporters' questions were much more pointed.

They wanted to know whether Eastman's death was being investigated as an illness or a poisoning. They also pointed out that the first sign that Stepakoff was missing had been when he'd failed to clock in and that it was apparently his personal car that was found in Eastman's driveway.

In light of that, they asked, could he really be considered to have been killed in the line of duty? And if Eastman had lived alone and had been comatose, how had Stepakoff accessed the house? Had he gone in without a warrant?

And of course they wanted to know about the rumors of a young live-in caretaker at the Eastman house who now couldn't be located.

The press liaison said simply that the case would be treated as a line-of-duty death until further notice and that they didn't know how Stepakoff had accessed the house, but "we have no indication that he acted other than professionally." About the rumors of a young tenant/caregiver, she said again that "leads are being developed, and to comment further would be to jeopardize our investigation."

That didn't work as well as the department hoped. An hour later a radio station had reported the tenant/caretaker's name as Hailey Cain. Neighbors had seen her coming and going from the house, but only at a distance. A few had heard Eastman mention her by name. But no one had seen the young woman since all the official vehicles had convened in Eastman's driveway, the evening the cop was shot and Eastman was carried out on a stretcher.

The SFPD, apparently deciding that the door had been opened and that it was better to have the eyes and ears of the public working for them, had faxed another news release to the media confirming the tenant's name and adding a detailed description. That had been the source of the news report that Serena had seen. Now, at eleven, a reporter doing a stand-up outside the Eastman house was telling the world that I was to be considered armed and dangerous and that I was possibly driving a 1999 Mazda Miata.

I've never been in a goddamn Miata in my life.

More than anything it was the Miata—evidence of someone else's taste—that made this situation fully real. Since Serena had called me, I'd been thinking about this mess only as, *Hey, it wasn't me.* Now it was sinking in that a real, three-dimensional person had deliberately put on my identity like an article of clothing and presented herself to the world as me.

Everything about it spoke of premeditation. People had seen the birthmark, which meant she'd re-created it with stage makeup. Maybe she'd bleached her hair, too, or gotten brown contact lenses. She'd moved in with Violet Eastman, lived with her. This was no short con. It was a long-term plan, working toward a big score.

And despite the fact that I'd lived in San Francisco last year, this woman didn't seem to have been afraid of our crossing paths. That was very interesting. Did she know I was in Los Angeles? She couldn't have found out through public records, since there was no paper trail of my life in Los Angeles. If she knew where I was, that suggested a personal connection. Someone had told her. Someone who knew me had helped her. Maybe not maliciously, but unwittingly.

The hell of it was, I'd also unwittingly helped this unknown girl, the other "Hailey." Because while I hadn't died down in Mexico like I was supposed to, I'd gone home to Los Angeles and built a life so far underground it was suspect in itself. Who did I have to witness that I'd been in L.A. the past four months? Gangbangers and petty criminals, who could barely prove their own whereabouts on a regular basis. The hours just after Stepakoff and Eastman had been killed, I'd been in the desert, robbing a pair of trucks. What a great alibi *that* would make.

I'd thought I was so cool, dropping thoroughly off the grid, turning my back on the system with all its electronic trails and prying eyes. Now how screwed was I? Because just as I'd decided to shed my public self, someone else in San Francisco had been stepping into it.

From the doorway Tess cleared her throat, and I looked up. She'd changed into a fisherman's sweater and moleskin trousers, her feet bare. She was holding a bottle in one hand and two glasses in the other.

"I thought you could probably use a drink," she said.

"Yeah, I could," I said, muting the noise of the television.

She took a seat in a wing chair, setting the glasses on the nightstand and pouring us each about three fingers.

I took the square, heavy-based glass from her, tipped my nose down, and sniffed. "Gin?"

"Genever," she said. "A Dutch import."

"Wasted on me," I said. "I would have been happy with Coors Light."

I don't know what there was about her that made me want to play the working-class rube. Maybe because I could never have matched her sophistication had I tried. Everything around us spoke of her good taste. The room we were in was mostly Victorian in its furnishings; in addition to the bed and the wing chair, there was a writing desk and a lamp of delicately scrolled brass with a frosted-glass shade. The room's colors were light as a watercolor painting, touches of mauve and gold and mossy green against the off-white walls and carpeting. On the floor the scuffed black boots I'd shed looked like the corpses of crows in an English garden.

She glanced at the silent TV screen and said, "You haven't told me yet what you think is going on. Do you have any theories?"

"Not yet."

"Well, this woman's motives, when they come out, will be financial," Tess said. It wasn't a question. Tess's businesses had always been legal, but she knew plenty of people who didn't operate aboveboard, starting with her biological father. "Within a day or two, the papers will be reporting financial irregularities in Eastman's accounts, check forgeries or large-amount withdrawals."

"That'd be my guess," I said.

"Hmmm." Tess tucked one leg up underneath her. "It isn't hard to see why she'd target Violet Eastman. She had money, lived alone, and was vulnerable. The question is, why you? How did she choose you to impersonate?"

"I don't know."

"Do you think this girl is somebody you know?"

Like an old high-school classmate? I considered that. "I

doubt it," I said. "I haven't kept in touch with anybody from the old days. The connection might be looser than that. I was thinking earlier that this girl must know somebody I know."

"Why?"

"Because she seems to have inside information. She knows I wasn't living in or near San Francisco. It seems like she knew I was in L.A. or . . ."

"Or what?"

"Wait." I held up a hand. An idea was tickling the edges of my mind. Slowly I began to put it into words: "Or she thought I was dead."

Tess grimaced. "Why would she think that?"

"Because there were several guys in particular who last year believed that I *was* dead. The tunnel rats."

"Who?"

"Your father's guys," I explained. "That's what I called the guys he sent to Mexico to get Nidia Hernandez. They shot me in the tunnel, assumed I was dead, dragged me off the road, and cleaned up the scene. One of them could easily have set aside my driver's license and passport. Guys like that would know how valuable genuine identity documents are on the black market and how to find a buyer."

It was just a theory, but it was coming together fast, making a lot of sense. I'd thought of last year's ambush in the tunnel primarily as an attempted murder (mine) and a kidnapping (Nidia's), not a robbery. When I'd woken up in a Mexican hospital without any ID, I'd just assumed that my driver's license and passport were rotting in a swamp, along with my duffel bag and clothing and everything else Nidia and I had carried with us.

"Plus," I added, "whoever sold this girl my ID, he could have assured her that the real Hailey Cain wouldn't raise an alarm about identity theft, because she was a Jane Doe in the Third World morgue. At least that's what he thought at the time. It'd be a great selling point."

"Dead girls don't check their credit scores."

"Right. And that's only the half of it. In Mexico I was traveling with a gun. He had that to sell, too."

"Would she need to buy that from him? Guns are a lot easier to get a hold of than good ID documents. The gun might have come from elsewhere."

"Might have but didn't," I said, giving her a humorless smile. "I loaded that gun myself. That's how my thumbprint got on one of the casings, which is now being interpreted as ironclad evidence that I was the shooter."

"God," Tess said. "It's almost perfect. I mean . . . sorry."

I waved off her apology, thinking. I never learned the names of all seven guys from the tunnel. In fact, I just knew two: Joseph Laska, their leader, whom I'd thought of as "Babyface" for his soft, mastiff features, and a guy named Quentin, younger than Laska, with a live-wire energy and a foul mouth, and a sexual appetite that—

There really wasn't any point in dwelling on last December and the events of the projection booth.

Speaking of which, there'd been a third guy in on that little interrogation session, a man named Will, but I'd never been sure he'd been one of the tunnel crew. That gave me seven to eight suspects, only one identified by first and last name. Not good odds.

Tess straightened out the leg she'd had tucked under her. She said, "You know, the woman who committed these crimes would have to look enough like you to pass for you."

"I know," I said. "But my looks aren't unusual. Except for the birthmark, which she probably did with some kind of makeup."

"But your general profile—white, female, early twenties—isn't one that I'd associate with a well-planned financial crime. Or with murder, either." She drank again, then said, "This might not be funny to you, but if anyone asked me if I knew any woman in her early twenties with the nerve and initiative to carry out these crimes, I'd have said I know only one. You."

"You're right. Not funny."

"Sorry," Tess said. "But if there's a bright side to what I'm saying, it's that if this woman has arrests for similar crimes, she'll be in the system."

"That doesn't help unless someone looks for her, and the police won't. I'm their suspect. They don't need two."

Tess inhaled deeply and said, "They would look for her if you gave them reason to."

She seemed ill at ease. I said, "What kind of a reason?"

Her glass empty, Tess rolled it in her hand. She wasn't looking at me when she said, "I think you should get ahead of this and turn yourself in." She looked up and added, quickly,

"I'll go with you. You'd be safe with a respectable business-woman at your side."

"For a minute or two," I said. "But once they arrest me and take me behind closed doors, what happens, happens."

"Hailey—"

I raised a hand, stopping her. "The real problem is that I can't prove my innocence yet. And if no one else does, I could get tried, convicted, put to death."

"You've been living in Los Angeles for these last four months, haven't you?" Tess said. "Surely there are plenty of witnesses to that. I could mention seeing you socially, twice, since you've moved back here."

"That's two days out of more than a hundred and twenty."

Tess raised an eyebrow, but she said, "Hailey, they can't possibly find your fingerprints or DNA in that house. That's got to count for something."

"Maybe," I said.

She went on, "In the morning maybe I can make some phone calls for you. I still have contacts up in San Francisco, people who might have known Eastman socially. I'll just ask what they've heard, for things that haven't been released on the news. I won't say, 'Hailey Cain's right here sitting next to me.' "

"I know you wouldn't," I said. "But be careful, anyway. The last thing you need is police in Kevlar kicking down your door because someone tipped them that you might be harboring a fugitive cop killer."

8

I woke up the next morning at ten, to find a note taped to the bathroom mirror.

> Hailey—Have whatever you like from the refrigerator, etc., for breakfast. Also, you should check out the profile of Violet Eastman in today's LA Times, it's quite good.
>
> Whatever you do, please don't leave before I get back and go out on the streets by yourself.
>
> —Tess

She didn't say where she'd gone, and it wasn't until I saw the cheerful colored egg and the words *Happy Easter* by the date on the *Times* that I remembered it was Easter. Church? Tess had never seemed religious to me, but you never could tell.

The kitchen was so perfectly clean that I didn't feel comfortable cooking. I poured myself a large bowl of cereal instead, and sliced up a banana on top. The kitchen had a generous island with two stools, and it was there that I ate breakfast and read the profile of Violet Eastman.

Eastman's grandfather had been Johnny MacClain Eastman, the tenth-grade-educated Tennesseean who'd formulated Eastern Gentleman whiskey. By his death Eastman Distilleries had bought up several rivals and produced not only Eastern Gentleman but a costly premium blend called MacClain's Extra Rare and a line of ciders and hard lemonades favored by college students. After Johnny MacClain Eastman's death, his son, John Eastman Jr., took over the business for two decades before selling to a big umbrella corporation.

Eastman Jr. had had a single child, Violet. Her father's acquaintances remembered an always-tall-for-her-age girl who seemed perpetually to have a book in her hand or to be rambling the estate with her dogs, who'd shunned girlish pursuits like sleepover parties and shopping expeditions. But where conventional wisdom would call for a bookish heiress to be unprepossessing and awkward, Violet Eastman was remembered as confident and dryly funny when she did appear at parties. Photos from her youth showed good cheekbones and long-lashed eyes, and adolescence took her tall frame from the pejorative "skinny" to the approving "slender."

Though something of a tomboy, Eastman had a traditional coming-out and then went away to school at Oberlin. After college she'd seemed to be living the idle life of an heiress, settling down in New York City, working only part-time as a drama critic, traveling when she pleased. Only much later did friends learn her secret: She'd been steadily gaining a readership in science-fiction magazines, writing under the androgynous name V. K. Eastman.

A few paragraphs followed about her writing career, some of which was lost on me; I wasn't familiar with the names in science fiction to whom she was compared, nor the magazines in which she'd published. But her work was lauded as technically accomplished and more subtle and literate than could usually be expected of the pulp magazines of the time. Her stories were regularly chosen for year's-best anthologies. In the late eighties, she'd co-written the screenplay for a very successful film, one whose clever dialogue and subtle antiracism themes elevated it beyond the label of "space opera."

At age thirty-six, after seeming to commit to a life of single blessedness, Eastman surprised everyone by marrying a man twenty years her senior, a CDC epidemiologist for whom she moved from New York to Atlanta. The popular guess was that the marriage was one of convenience, between a man facing the discomforts of old age and a middle-aged single woman who feared a life of loneliness.

Again the easy supposition was wrong. They bought a house on the river and entertained there. They kept dogs. They traveled, often to exotic Third World locations instead of comfortable resorts. They moved together to San Francisco when he traded his CDC position for a department chair at UCSF Medical Center. In all, Eastman and her husband stayed together for twenty-two years, and she nursed him through more than a year of cancer treatments before he died.

Afterward Eastman stayed in the home they'd shared in the quiet, wealthy enclave of St. Francis Wood. She continued writing, though she published less frequently. Health problems were cited: a bad hip, vision problems that caused her to surrender her driver's license.

So last winter she'd advertised for a tenant to live in a semidetached private apartment in her home, offering free rent in exchange for light household help, errand running, and care of Eastman's elderly borzoi, the last of the four dogs she'd adopted with her husband. The horrible outcome of that venture was now well known. Readers were referred to a sidebar on the newest developments in the murder investigation.

The sidebar didn't have much to say. LONGTIME FRIEND RAISED THE ALARM, the headline read. The story explained that a Crescent City woman, Karen Adkins, had become concerned after Eastman failed to call Adkins on Adkins's birthday. It had been a longtime, never-fail tradition between the two friends, once classmates at Oberlin, that they exchanged birthday greetings by phone. Phoning the house, Adkins had spoken to a young woman calling herself Hailey, who'd said that she was Eastman's live-in personal assistant and that Eastman was too ill to come to the phone. Questioned about the exact nature of Eastman's illness and why she wasn't in the hospital if she was too sick even to take a phone call, Hailey had become vague and evasive. Adkins became suspicious. Something, she told the *Chronicle* reporter, was just "off" about the young woman she'd spoken to.

Adkins had tried to call Eastman again the next day and this time had gotten no answer at all. She was torn—worried about her friend yet feeling unable to justify calling the police. She'd compromised by calling Greg Stepakoff, a police officer and the son of another old friend, asking him to go by Eastman's house, unofficially, and check out the situation. Stepakoff had said this was no problem. It was when hours passed with no return call from him, and when he'd proved equally unreachable on his cell, that Adkins had been worried enough to call the SFPD main line and make things official.

This had cleared up the issue of whether Stepakoff's death had been a line-of-duty killing—it wasn't—but the SFPD saw the difference as merely semantic. Stepakoff's actions had been "clearly consistent with his sworn goal to protect and serve the public," the press liaison said. "We feel this investigation deserves the respect that a line-of-duty death would receive, and we're sure the public is in agreement with us on that."

•••

I'd rinsed my cereal bowl and started a pot of coffee brewing when I heard a key in the lock of the front door, and Tess came in.

"Is that coffee? Perfect," she said. She set a box down on the counter, with a woman in a glamorous, hair-swinging pose on the front. It was hair color. "I thought we'd change your hair a bit," she said.

I looked more closely at the box and the shade, a medium brown, about the color of a portobello mushroom. I said, "I'm a little disturbed by how quickly you've gotten with the fugitive program."

She was checking the progress of the drip coffeemaker. "Turning yourself in still gets my vote, but last night you closed the door on that, and next you're going to tell me that you can't stay in my house indefinitely. Right?"

"Probably."

"Then you need to be less recognizable." Tess took an oversize mug covered in bright polka dots down from a wall rack and poured herself a generous amount of coffee.

"You know," I said, "this'll help some, but my birthmark is the real problem. It's worse than having a name tag on my face."

"There's makeup for that," she said.

"Won't work," I said. "When I was younger, I'd get into my mother's cosmetic kit and try to cover it up with liquid foundation and powder. Then more liquid, then more powder. Makeup never quite covers it. All it does is draw attention to the fact that I've tried to cover it up."

Tess gave me an obliquely amused look. "That's not exactly what I had in mind. You need to start thinking like a movie person."

About ninety minutes later, I couldn't stop looking in the mirror with fascination. My hair was newly brown, and high on my cheekbone, covering the birthmark, was a deep bruise. Tess had created it from a mixture of mascara, eye shadow, a little mineral oil to blend, and then face powder to counteract the shininess of the oil.

"I wish I knew a makeup person I trusted to keep your secret," Tess said, speculative dissatisfaction in her voice. "A pro, with professional-grade stage makeup, could give you a bruise that would fool an ER doctor."

"Don't run down your own work," I said. "This is pretty good."

Tess was in her bedroom, and I was in the attached master bath, where we'd done the work. The chemical-perfume scent of the dye still hung in the air, rising in part from several stained hand towels and the disposable latex gloves Tess had used, now lying in the sink.

While I'd been sitting on the bathroom vanity with my wet, dye-soaked hair covered in a plastic bag, Tess had called two friends in San Francisco, politely fishing for news and gossip about the Eastman murder, but without luck. Neither woman had known Eastman personally, nor had either of them heard anything that hadn't already been reported on the news.

"You know," she said now from the other room, "I have Joe Laska's phone number. He took over several of my father's businesses up there."

I came to stand in the doorway, leaning against the frame. "Meaning he filled the vacuum in the organized-crime scene, too," I said. "Bringing heroin and undocumented Eastern European immigrant labor into California."

"Somebody was going to," Tess said. "I seem to remember you giving me a little lecture on the importance of it not being me."

I lifted a shoulder in a half-embarrassed shrug. "I was still in pain from my finger. It made me a drag to be around," I said.

"You weren't."

"Well, it doesn't really matter. I could call Laska, but if he knows which of his merry men sold my ID, do you really think he's going to tell me?"

"Actually," Tess said, pausing in the midst of smoothing the covers of the bed she was making, "I'm hoping he'll tell me."

"Wait," I said quickly. "I'm not sure you want to reopen an acquaintance with this guy. I've seen Joe Laska with his mask off. It's not pretty."

"So have I. I was in that projection booth, too, and I saw what he did to you," she said. "Then I successfully negotiated your way out of it, remember?"

I did remember, and I had to admit this situation was long-distance, and thus safer. "Just be careful what you say,"

I told her. "He's virtually the only person who knows that you and I know each other. You'd be best off leading him to believe that we didn't stay in touch. I wouldn't put it past him to drop a dime, if he suspects you're helping me."

"I'll be discreet," she said. "You can even listen in. There's an extension on the little table at the end of the hall."

I walked out into the hall, saw the table, and picked up the phone. "Ready."

I heard her pick up her receiver and dial. Three rings sounded, and then a male voice answered. "Hello?"

It was Laska, no question. I hadn't expected to be certain, to remember so clearly his voice from the defunct adult theater, the tunnel in Mexico, even the hotel in El Paso where he'd first spoken to me. Such a calm, reasonable voice.

"Joseph," Tess said. "This is Teresa D'Agostino."

"Ms. Skouras?" he said. "It's been a while." Then, "Is there something I can help you with?"

"This isn't really a business call," she said. "I just . . . I've been very busy and have only now caught up with the news from up north. Those two murders, isn't that the most extraordinary thing? I'm not mistaken—it *is* the same Hailey Cain, isn't it?"

"Yeah, it is," Laska said. "I saw her DMV photo in the *Chronicle*. It's the same girl."

"What do you make of it?"

There was a short pause. "People will do anything for money, I guess," he said. "She was pretty resourceful, so it doesn't surprise me that she was capable of something like this. How she was wired up psychologically, I never really got a good read on that. I never understood what made her do the things she did last year, with Mr. Skouras's grandson."

"Mmm," Tess said noncommittally. "I just thought there seemed to be such ill will between her and you and your men, that when I read the news, I did wonder—you guys didn't have a hand in this, did you?"

"Why would we help her kill an old lady and a cop?"

"Not help her," Tess said. "Frame her. Last year it struck me that she was rather obsessed with honor and doing the right thing. So it occurred to me that if she didn't do this, then someone else did and planned for her to take the fall. And no offense, but I thought of you and your colleagues. You people do have your vendettas."

Laska chuckled, unoffended. "I'm Greek. We don't have vendettas." He paused. "I'm telling you, she's been off my radar since last winter. I'm a businessman. I do what has to be done; I don't waste energy chasing my ego needs around. Quentin Corelli, he was a little more personally bothered by her, but I see him all the time, and he hasn't mentioned her at all."

"Interesting," Tess said.

"Can I ask why you're asking about this?"

"My own ego needs, perhaps," Tess said. "I rather liked that girl. I hate to think my judgment of her character was so far off. Listen, I'll give you my number. If you hear anything interesting that's not being reported on the news, can you give me a call? Likewise, if you're ever in need of some information in my sphere of things, down here in L.A., maybe I could help you out."

Hearing that, I winced.

"That's nice of you, Ms. Skouras. You never can tell when it'll be useful to have the acquaintance of someone in the know."

They exchanged final pleasantries, with Tess giving him her phone number before hanging up.

Walking back into her bedroom, I said, "You didn't have to give him your phone number. If he doesn't know anything now, he probably won't down the line."

"It never hurts to ask."

"It does if you're agreeing to trade favors with a guy like Babyface."

"I've swum with sharks before," she said.

I leaned against her dresser, studied her, and said, "You suggested to him that this was a deliberate frame-up. You and I didn't discuss that possibility last night."

Tess tilted her head slightly. "You think it's too great a logical leap? If this were only about your identity papers, I'd say maybe it was just a crime of convenience. The use of your gun, the failure to pick up the casing at the scene . . . It was simply logical to me that there was an aspect of this that was about you personally. Don't you think?"

I shrugged. "Seemed egotistical to assume that."

"But maybe it's not. Laska did say that one of his guys was 'personally bothered' by you."

"Quentin Corelli. He was one of the other two guys in

the projection booth." I played with a strand of newly brown hair, thinking. "He was making it kind of personal. We had a little history, from up in Gualala, where I took Nidia away from him."

"So that's not anything new, that this guy didn't like you."

"No," I said. "He has a grudge, and he was in the tunnel in Mexico, which would have allowed him to steal my identity papers." I lifted a shoulder. "I have to start somewhere. I might as well make that my working theory, that he's the one who sold my papers and gun to some female con artist. If he isn't, maybe he'll know who is."

"You can't go to San Francisco alone and brace one of Joe Laska's men. You don't even know where he is."

"Laska said that he saw Quentin regularly," I pointed out. "And Laska took over your father's businesses. It sounds like he doesn't just see Quentin, he also signs his paychecks."

Tess's face had darkened. She stood up. "This is insanity. The last time you opposed these men, you nearly got killed. If it weren't for me, you'd be dead now."

"I know," I agreed. "Have I said thanks recently? Thanks."

"Don't be flippant. You know what I'm saying."

"Actually, I don't," I said. "You just helped me change my appearance. You knew I wasn't going to the police and that I was planning to go back out in the world and straighten this out. Where'd you get off that train?"

Tess looked away, out the window. She said, "I knew

you were going to do something typically risky, but I didn't think you were planning something suicidal."

"Nothing's planned just yet," I said. "I'm still thinking through my options." I moved closer, put a hand on her shoulder. "If I go get my gym bag and walk out your front door, are you going to call the police? Tell them what I look like now, that I'm traveling on foot in the vicinity of Westwood?"

Tess shook her head silently.

"Then I hate to be a pest," I said, "but can you give me a lift?"

9

A half hour later, I was safely on the other side of the locked door of my Crenshaw place. Tess and I had carefully cruised past the building and then around the back, scoping up and down the street for anything that looked like police activity. Nothing had struck me as suspicious.

Just before getting out of the little Crossfire, I'd leaned back in the open door and said, "I already owed you before this, Tess, and now I'm in twice as deep." I'd looked away, into the sun, and then back down at her. "I pay my debts. I'll pay this one, too."

I'd expected her to say something characteristically

generous, like, *Just come back alive,* but she'd assessed me with serious gray eyes and simply nodded.

Tess hadn't been fooled by my little "Nothing's planned just yet" speech. I was going to San Francisco, because there were two people up there I needed to see, for vastly different reasons. One was Quentin Corelli, who had tortured me for Laska last year and would have been happy to kill me. The other was Jack Foreman, an Associated Press reporter, who had liked me and, I hoped, still believed in me.

The sky was clearing fast, and I shaded my eyes against the sun as I waited at the edge of the parking lot for a family returning from church to cross to their first-floor apartment. They were in the kind of Easter finery you didn't see much anymore, not in California: Mom in a wide-brimmed hat, father and son in clean-lined summer-weight suits, the little girl in a blue lace dress with a skirt splayed wide by an under-layer of tulle.

When they'd passed without seeing me, I climbed the stairs to my second-floor place, unlocked the door, and went inside.

My apartment always greeted me with the sort of spare quietness you felt when you'd been away for weeks. I wasn't there enough to make the kind of welcoming, personal messes that reminded you of what you'd been doing before you went out, nor had I put any effort into making the place look like it was mine. Here it was now, an unloved and unlovely place, with worn-out lime green carpeting, a heavyset Zenith TV, my few books on cheap secondhand shelves.

In the bedroom I threw my gym bag on the bed, unzipped it, and took out the things I wouldn't need: my fight clothes and mouth guard. Then I packed. I pried up the carpeting at the corner of the living room and retrieved my emergency fund, five hundred-dollar bills, to add to the six hundred I'd carried away from the fights. Then a change of clothes, the baby Glock and ankle holster, soap and toothbrush and tooth-paste in a Ziploc bag, as well as the makeup Tess had given me to re-create the fake bruise at will. A mini-flashlight and a little digital camera: I wasn't entirely sure I'd need those, but I was going to be doing some surveillance on Quentin, and they might come in handy.

My cell phone, lying on the center of the bed, buzzed, and I reached over and picked it up. I'd had this phone only since January, after losing the last one in my confrontation with Skouras's guys. I'd given the number to almost no one, which explained why I hadn't already been flooded with calls from people saying, *Hailey, have you seen the news, what the hell?* I expected that this was Serena, wanting to know where I was and what was going on.

Then I saw the number on the screen, and my heart stopped.

CJ was calling me.

Immediately, before he could speak, I said, "CJ, I didn't do what they're saying. I don't know what's going on any more than you do. Please believe me."

The voice that answered was male, and it was slow and calm and unhurried, like my cousin's. But it was clearly older, with a rasp at the edges. "Miss Cain," it said, "I'm sorry, I'm not your cousin Cletus. Please don't hang up. You're talking to one of probably two cops in America who don't think you killed those people up in San Francisco."

"Who is this?"

"My name is Magnus Ford."

The hair prickled on my arms and the back of my neck.

He cleared his throat. "This must be confusing. The call registered as from your cousin's phone because we got his account information from his cellular company and cloned a phone with his number."

"But how did you get *my* number?" I said. I had a cheap, pay-as-you-go phone and bought airtime cards at convenience stores. There shouldn't have been account information for him to access.

He said, "Before I answer that, Miss Cain, can I ask you one question? Are you missing a finger on your left hand?"

That was the last thing I'd been expecting him to ask, and that was how I knew the question was important.

"Yes," I said. "Can I ask you how—"

Then I stopped. I didn't like this. My phone might not have had an airtime plan with account information for Ford to access, but it did have a GPS system. As long as it was activated, Ford could track me.

"Miss Cain?"

I said, "Give me your phone number and I'll call you back."

10

I'd left the Aprilia parked near the Slaughterhouse last night, thinking it too much a risk to be on the roads on something with a license number traceable to me. Now I wished I had it, as I slung my bag over my shoulder and locked my apartment behind me. The helmet would have been ideal to hide my features behind. Or I wished that I lived back east, where in early April the weather was probably still cold enough to justify hiding under a cap, behind a scarf. Instead I was in L.A., where the mercury was climbing steadily toward a hundred degrees at midday. I touched my fake bruise for reassurance as I headed down the sidewalk, much as I used to touch my birthmark out of self-consciousness in my younger years.

A tall woman, addict-thin and with acne scars under her chestnut-colored skin, was doing some kind of personal business on the pay phone four blocks from my house, and she glared at me when I lingered too close, waiting for her to be finished. It was nearly fifteen minutes before she finally hung up and walked off without a backward glance at me.

The handset of the phone was warm and almost slippery where she'd been holding it. Ford answered on the first ring. Instead of hello, he said, "I'm not trying to track you, Hailey."

He was showing me he'd known that any unidentified pay-phone number was going to be me. *All right, you're clever, we knew that,* I thought. I also didn't believe him and knew I couldn't extend this conversation too long. Pay phones could be traced, too.

"Are you there?" he said.

"I'm here."

"I'm being up front with you, because I meant what I said about thinking you might be innocent. That doesn't mean I'm sure. It's a working hypothesis."

"How'd you come up with it?" I asked.

"You've been seen on several occasions in East Los Angeles, most recently the day after the Eastman and Stepakoff murders."

"By you?" I said. "Have we met and I don't know it?"

"No," Ford said. "This was an associate of mine."

I am a goddamn idiot. "The blind guy in the park, Joe Keller," I said. "He's one of yours."

"Yes."

"And he's obviously not blind."

He laughed, a short, rusty sound. "Are you kidding? Joel Kelleher was the best shooter in his academy class. Kid could hit the ten ring standing on a water-bed mattress."

That explained why he'd reacted so quickly to the prospect that I might reach for his sunglasses and try to look at his eyes. Even an experienced actor would have difficulty faking the sightless gaze of a blind person; a young cop would have known that it was beyond his skills.

It also explained how Ford had gotten my cell number: I'd written it right on the skin of a police officer.

"So it was your little joke," I said. "Your 'eyes' in the field, faking blindness."

"Not a joke," Ford said, "a tactic. Of course, we were looking for drug and gang activity—we never expected to net a suspect in a high-profile double homicide. But when the APB on you came in, Joel took one look at it and said, 'I was just talking to her in the park this morning. Something's not right here.' He said he'd spoken to you on two prior occasions within less than two weeks. Then your fingerprints came over the wire, and Joel said, 'This is screwy, too. There's ten fingerprints here, but this girl has only nine fingers.' I suggested maybe you were just one of those rare flukes, a dead ringer for someone else, but Joel said no. He'd seen your birthmark. And he said you'd told him that your name was Hailey." He paused. "Of course, that doesn't mean you weren't dividing your time between San Francisco and L.A."

"I wasn't," I said. "Mr. Ford, if you're serious about believing I'm innocent, try this: My DNA's in the Pentagon's battlefield registry. Ask the SF forensics guys if they found a single piece of DNA that matches mine. They won't have."

"What about the thumbprint on the casing?"

"It was a stolen gun," I said. "I should go. I'll call you again."

"No. No more game playing. You want my help, come in."

"I can't. Not yet."

"Hailey, do you want some nervous rookie cop to smoke you on the street? Because that's what's going to happen if you stay out there."

I hung up and stood a moment, thinking.

Magnus Ford, the Shadow Man, had a guy in the field doing his spying and his legwork. I needed someone like that on my side. I went to another pay phone and made a second call.

"Hello?" Serena said, cautious as always when the read-out on her cell said UNKNOWN CALLER.

"It's me," I said, "and I can't talk long. I think I know how I got set up. You want to ride on a mission with me?"

"I'm in."

"Wait, you need to understand what I'm asking. Yeah, I need you, but I don't like it. This could get dangerous. Remember last year?"

"How could I forget that shit?"

"This might come down to the same stuff: some surveillance, some lawbreaking, possibly a throwdown or two."

"I'm good with that," she said. "Warchild and Insula, kicking ass again. It'll be fun."

11

Serena marveled at my new hair color and especially the bruise: "That shit is tight, *prima*." She assumed I'd done it myself, and I didn't explain to her about Tess. CJ and Tess were the only really sane people in my life, and I took care to protect them from all the others, who, like Serena, were by necessity a little crazy.

She took me to where I'd parked the Aprilia and followed as I rode it to Chato's chop shop for storage. I wasn't happy about leaving it behind, but there's a big difference between a sport bike and a roadster. My Aprilia had no panniers, no storage. Neither Serena nor I traveled heavy laden, but this was a mission. We needed to carry gear.

By midafternoon, we were on the 101, heading north in her Chevy Caprice. I took the first shift driving. As I did, I told her what I'd learned and what I believed about it: that everything grew out of last year and my clash with Skouras's men.

"The mobster's crew again?" Serena said. "We shoulda killed those *pendejos* when we had the chance."

Serena liked to talk like that, as if she were as bloodthirsty as the gangsters of legend. I didn't know whether to believe it. There were a lot of years I hadn't been a witness to her life, though as far as I'd heard, she hadn't ever killed anyone.

I told her that among the things I was going to need from her was partly boring stuff, like going into mini-marts to pay for food, so my notorious face could stay off security cameras. She nodded and didn't complain.

Our relationship was flexible like that. Normally she was in charge and I was her lieutenant. But now my future, maybe my life, was at risk, so this was my mission, and I'd lead it. Serena knew that. We'd been friends too long to let ego issues get in the way. We'd hashed that stuff out long ago.

Then Serena said, "Hey, I got you some stuff. Extra cartridges for your piece and—" She dug in the black gym bag at her feet and came up with a small white pill bottle from which the label had largely worn off. She shook out part of the contents in her hand. Glancing over, I saw Dexedrines, Vicodins, Ambiens, as well as some plain orange-brown Advil tablets.

She said, "You mentioned stakeouts—that's what the Dex is for. The Ambien so we can sleep when we need to, between stakeouts. The Vicodin, who knows when that'll be helpful?"

"I'm not sure we should be traveling with this stuff."

She shrugged. "We're both carrying unregistered weapons, you're wanted for murder. . . ."

"So why sweat the details?" I finished for her.

A few hours later, we stopped in King City to eat. I didn't want to risk going into a fast-food place, so Serena went to buy takeout we could eat in the car. When she was gone, I went to a pay phone outside a grocery store, turning the "bruised" side of my face toward the wall. The ugly mark in itself might draw attention I didn't want.

The phone rang three times before he answered. "This is Ford."

"It's me," I said.

"Hailey?"

"There are some things I should add to our earlier conversation."

"Yes?"

"I'm going to give you the address of the apartment where I've been living in L.A. for the past four months," I said. "If your techs dust for fingerprints there, they'll find all of mine except the left little finger, the one I lost since I was fingerprinted for the Army's database." I paused. "That print is the only one that it's possible the San Francisco techs could have found in the Eastman place."

He absorbed that. "You're saying," he said, "that someone could have your amputated finger and be using it to create a kind of biological forgery?"

"I can't rule it out."

It was a theory I'd come to unhappily, thinking about it on the drive north. Last year I'd thought Quentin was likely to be the "fetishist" who'd needed a trophy from the torture session. If he was, and he was also behind the sale of my identity papers and my gun . . . well, maybe he was both inventive enough and disturbed enough to think of it.

"How'd you lose the finger?"

"That's a story for another time," I said. "Let me give you the address to my apartment."

After I'd hung up, I wondered if I was being paranoid in warning Ford about a biological forgery, as he'd called it. It was a theory that echoed Tess's question from earlier: How much of this was about me? The sale of the identity papers and even the gun I could write off as simple greed on Quentin's part. But if they found my fingerprint in the Eastman house, that would be personal. Quentin would have to know he was setting me up to go to death row.

I watched birds circle over the parking lot, looking for dropped french fries or bread crusts. The 101 was a cool roar not far off.

Was I creating a bogeyman in my head, building up Quentin Corelli into a master criminal when he wasn't? Adding up what I knew about him, it didn't come to much: a little older than me, a foot soldier for Skouras and now for Joe Laska, good-looking in that golden brown Italian way, tightly wound, kinetic, foul-mouthed, misogynistic. He was a nasty piece of work, but I wasn't sure he was capable of engineering a complicated frame-up. Neither did I know if his resentment of me burned that hot.

I picked up the receiver of the pay phone again. There was a second call I wanted to make, and again I thought it would be safer from a pay phone whose number wouldn't show up on caller ID.

I didn't know how Jack Foreman would respond to hearing my voice, that of a hotly pursued murder suspect, on the phone. Most journalists supported law and order, but at the same time they rejected a role as unofficial agents of the police. Some went to jail rather than turn over their informants, notes, or film to the cops. Jack Foreman, cynical and hardworking, struck me as likely to be in that camp. I didn't believe he'd automatically call the police after getting off the phone with me. If he believed I'd really committed the crimes, sure. But he'd known me. I had to believe that the idea of me as a double murderer wouldn't add up for him.

A year ago I'd had his home phone number committed to memory, but now I couldn't remember it. A quick call to directory assistance told me that there was no John or Jack Foreman in the published records. So I requested the number for the Associated Press in San Francisco.

I fed more coins into the slot—a long-distance phone card was clearly going to be in order—and dialed the number. After two rings a woman's voice answered: "Associated Press."

"I'm trying to reach Jack Foreman," I said. "Is he in?"

"I'm sorry, he's not," the woman said. "Jack's on sabbatical."

"Sabbatical?" I repeated. "Do you know when he's coming back?"

"I'm sorry, I don't," she said. "He's in Kiev, teaching investigative journalism at the university level. I wouldn't know how to get in touch with him. Could another reporter help you?"

"No," I said. "Thanks anyway."

I hung up, thinking that it was good that Jack was branching out and taking a break from the grind of being a newsman, but wishing that he'd timed it a little better. He'd been my only potential source of information and help in San Francisco.

Then I half turned, almost jumped in my tracks, and whipped my head around to face the phone again. Behind me, only six feet away, were a pair of uniformed police officers.

"—didn't mean it like that. Of course it's a tragedy, with a wife and kid, too," one of them was saying. "But how often do you get to be part of a huge investigation like that? It's something that really makes a department pull together."

"I'd rather not pull together, if that's the price of it, two lives."

Were they talking about San Francisco? Even as I tried to overhear them, I looked for something to do to justify my continued presence at the pay phone. I pulled the phone book off its metal shelf and opened it, as if searching for a listing.

The first cop was speaking again. "I'll tell you one thing, she's lucky she pulled that shit up in SF. I know some guys on the job down south. LAPD would eat her a-freaking-live."

"Maybe, maybe not." The second guy sounded older, and he spoke more slowly. "She killed a cop. Wherever she gets caught, I think she's gonna come to Jesus pretty quick."

I heard their movements as they passed behind me. Looking to the right without turning my head, I could just see a squad car parked nearby, clearly their destination. I began to slide the phone book back onto its shelf.

At that moment the cable that attached it to the phone snapped free. The book tipped in my hands, and I couldn't catch it in time. It fell to the pavement with a loud smack.

Quickly I sat on my heels to retrieve it, as the two cops stopped and turned around.

"You okay there?" the younger one said.

"Yeah. Fine." I didn't make eye contact.

His partner drew closer. "Hey."

I looked up. There was nothing else to do. Anything else would have been suspicious behavior.

The younger one was blond and blue-eyed, with a face that was hard-boned but innocent-looking, the kind of face that lost its freckles only a few years ago. His partner was more solidly built, with short-cropped light brown hair and a full mustache. His name tag identified him as Pratt.

"What happened here?" He lifted a finger to his own cheekbone, mirroring the bruise on mine.

"Oh, nothing. I was sparring at the gym." I shoved the phone book back into place and stood up.

"Really?" the younger guy said. "In town? Do you work out at—"

"No, I don't live around here. And I should get going. Be safe, now."

I turned and stepped off the curb, trying not to project haste. It was unwise to cut off a conversation with cops before they considered it finished. But neither was it smart to give them time to study my face at length.

"Miss! Wait." It was the voice of the older one, Pratt.

So sorry, didn't hear you. I kept going.

"Hey, *wait.*"

He wasn't going to let it go. Reluctantly I stopped and turned to face him.

He caught up to me at an awkward half jog. He said, "Listen, maybe I'm off the mark here, but if someone's hitting you, there are resources."

He reached into his pocket, drew out a billfold, and produced a card. "The top two numbers are local, but the bottom two are nationwide, since you say you don't live around here." He extended it.

"Thank you," I said, taking it from him. "Nobody's hitting me. But I'll keep it, just in case."

"Good." He regarded me uncertainly. "You know, you do look familiar."

"Really? But I'm from south of here. Outside of Lompoc."

"Oh, yeah? I know Lompoc. That's Air Force country."

"Right. I was just a townie, though. I didn't mix much with the military people." I fingered the card as if hesitant. "Can I go?"

"Yeah, you can go. Use that card if you need it."

Walking away, I decided not to go straight to the car. Should he look back, I didn't want him to see the vehicle I was traveling in, nor Serena when she approached. If the puzzle pieces fell into place for him, sometime later, I didn't want him to have any new information to pass along about Hailey Cain, other than about my new brown hair and fake bruise, which couldn't be helped.

I angled across the lot, heading for the delicatessen where Serena had gone, disciplining myself not to look back in the direction of Pratt and his partner. When I pushed my way through the door, Serena was at a self-serve condiment stand, getting napkins and straws. There were two white bags on the counter in front of her.

"Hey, I was just coming," she said.

"There's cops out there."

Her gaze shifted to the windows. "Where?"

"Up near the store. They saw me but didn't recognize me."

"So what do you want to do?"

"You get the car and come around. The less they see of me again, or us together, the better."

She nodded, put the napkins and straws into the bag, and left.

I stood inside the door, not too close, watching her

retreating form. I couldn't see Pratt and the other guy, but their car was still visible. A group of high-school-age kids came in, laughing together and briefly blocking my view. Then, when they were past, I saw a second police car crawling slowly up the far aisle of the parking lot, in the direction of the first.

This was probably a popular shopping center for coffee and lunch breaks. That was probably all there was to it.

Or Pratt could have called them.

Had he recognized me and just been playing me with the wallet card of abuse hotlines? Was he engaging me in conversation to get a further look at my face? It didn't make sense, unless he was a careful guy, too careful to confront a known cop killer in a public place, with an inexperienced young partner.

But I'd been looking at his face the whole time he'd been seeing mine, since I dropped the phone book. I hadn't seen anything change in his expression. Either he had the best poker face in the world or he'd been ignorant of who I was.

The Caprice reached the curb outside the deli at about the same time that the second squad car pulled in next to the first. Lifting my chin, I pushed the door open and ambled quickly but casually to Serena's car. Then I pulled the passenger-door handle, which snapped back against the door. It was locked.

"*Serena!*" I bumped the glass hard with the side of my fist, then lowered my head against the edge of the roof, face tipped down, out of view. Serena reached over and opened the door, the latch clicking free as she did so. I slid hastily inside.

"Sorry," Serena said. "That other five-oh car distracted me."

I slid down, out of view again. "It might be nothing. Don't panic."

It took a good fifteen minutes on the freeway before we were both satisfied it had been nothing. Serena had glided out into the center lane of 101 North and kept the speedometer needle at the posted sixty-five miles per hour, while I stayed in my uncomfortable position below the dashboard. Meanwhile she grilled me on my encounter with the police.

"How close did they see you?"

"Close. Like, normal range for conversation."

"You *talked* to them? Are you crazy?"

"I didn't have a choice," I said, and explained about Pratt seeing my bruise and his suspicions of abuse.

"Okay, so he didn't suspect anything."

"Probably not."

I straightened up, then reached down between my feet, to where I'd left the deli bags on the floorboard. I got busy unwrapping sandwiches and handed Serena's to her.

"Listen," I said, poking a straw through the lid of my Coke, "while we're on the subject of the five-oh, there's something I should tell you. I don't want you to find out by accident and think I was hiding it from you."

"That sounds heavy," she said. "What is it?"

"I've been talking over the phone to a cop about the Eastman case, a cop that thinks I didn't do the murders." I sipped from my Coke. "It's Magnus Ford."

Serena's eyebrows jumped sharply, though she didn't take her eyes off the road. "Ford, the freaking Shadow Man himself? You just called up and got through to him?" Then alarm broke through her surprise. "Hailey, you're not gonna roll over on me, are you?"

"Of course not, you goddamn know better," I said.

"I did, *prima,* but you've never been wanted for two murders before. You've got a lot to gain by trading."

"First, Ford doesn't know I'm Insula," I said, my tone matter-of-fact. "Second, even if he did, no one would go light on a cop killer just to get at a gangbanger, even a shot caller like you. Third, if I was going to cut a deal like that, I wouldn't be sitting here telling you I'm talking to the guy. How smart would that be?"

Serena nodded slowly. "I guess so," she said. Then, curiously, "So what's he like?"

As if I'd met a celebrity. After a second the absurdity struck both of us, and we started laughing.

12

Four hours later I was lying on a hotel bed, about five floors above Powell Street. Serena had registered for us; I'd waited in the car for her to come back with the keys before we'd gone up in the elevator.

She was in the bathroom now, and I was watching TV, though the Eastman case wasn't dominating the news anymore; it was relegated to the crawl on CNN. Lack of new information, I supposed, and a lack of reporters to cover what there was.

Until I'd met Jack Foreman, I hadn't realized that newspapers and TV stations, like most businesses, were short-staffed on weekends. In theory, Jack had explained, everyone acknowledged that news didn't differentiate between weekday and weekend. In practice, he'd said, any reporter with any amount of seniority had an "enterprise" piece in the can by Friday night and spent Saturday and Sunday at home with the kids.

I'd been surprised, told him that I'd thought reporters lived to rush out the door at any hour in pursuit of a good story. Jack had shaken his head. "A rare few," he'd said, "but you'd be surprised how many are willing to let a story *jell* for a day. That's what my old editor in New Jersey used to call it. Or editors say, 'We'll run a follow tomorrow.' " He'd laughed at my look of disbelief.

Tomorrow, Monday, the gears would begin to mesh in earnest. Whether that would be good for me or bad, I didn't know. I had to believe that eventually, under enough scrutiny, this case would render up a detail that would tell investigators I hadn't committed these crimes, despite the fingerprint on the casing, despite everything.

If that didn't happen, if things really went sour here, maybe I could join Jack Foreman in Kiev. Maybe he could use a bodyguard. Journalists got killed sometimes in the developing former-Soviet nations. Besides, we'd always gotten along fine together in bed.

Restless, I flipped away from CNN, around the other cable news channels until I recognized the exterior of the Eastman home, no longer under police barricades and crime-scene tape, closed up and empty. I turned up the sound, but not fast enough to catch the thrust of that report before the story changed to international news.

Serena came out of the bathroom, glanced at the TV and saw a commercial playing, and sat down on the corner of her bed. "Okay," she said. "What's the plan?"

I rolled over to lie with my chin in my hand. "Can you make a run to a drugstore?" I asked.

"What do you need?"

"Safety pins, in a couple of different sizes, and a little screwdriver."

"Lock-picking stuff," she said, understanding immediately. "You're going to the dead woman's house. Are you sure that's safe?"

"Reasonably," I said. "It's been two days. The technicians and detectives shouldn't need a round-the-clock presence anymore. I'll go late tonight and park a little ways off and walk to the house under cover of darkness. It's about the quietest residential area in the whole city. The neighbors will be sleeping, and even the most ambitious detective isn't going to be there after midnight."

"There are graveyard-shift cops," Serena said.

I shook my head. "Those are the kind of cops that mop up bar fights. Major-crimes detectives and forensics people might get called out to a fresh murder scene after midnight, but no one's going to be doing routine follow-up work at that hour."

"Okay, but what are you looking for?"

"Anything," I said. "Anything that'll tell me who this 'Hailey' chick was. If she left any clothes or shoes behind, I'll know something about her height and build. If there's red or pink swipes on the bedspread, I'll know what color she paints her toenails."

"Then we can stake out shoe stores and look at women's bare feet until we catch her."

"I'm just saying, she's a woman, I'm a woman. You think most cops know how often you paint your toenails sitting on the bed, and how you accidentally smear a little on the spread because you're moving around again before they're dry?"

She didn't look convinced, but said, "Give me some money, then. For the drugstore."

13

By twelve-thirty A.M. I was in the Caprice, driving the speed limit and obeying all traffic laws, heading south on surface roads toward the St. Francis Wood neighborhood.

Serena wasn't with me. It wasn't at all like her to fall asleep before midnight, much less without the use of Ambien or marijuana, but tonight she'd done both, dropping off peacefully in front of the quietly murmuring TV set we were both watching. I'd wanted her as a lookout, but couldn't bring myself to rob her of natural sleep. So I'd done a touch-up on my makeup bruise, gathered the tools I'd need and the car keys, and slipped out, leaving the TV on, lest the unexpected absence of its noise wake her.

Now, driving alone and cautiously, I flicked the turn signal and exited off Route 1 toward Mount Davidson.

Ask most people where the rich live in San Francisco and many of them will mention Pacific Heights or the Marina District. Outside the Bay Area, mention of St. Francis Wood gets you a lot of puzzled glances. It's a secret garden, guarded at its foot by a graceful white fountain and from above by the stark white cross on Mount Davidson, hilly and hidden and very rich, but rarely ostentatious. It was my bad luck—well, worse luck on top of bad—that the girl who chose to steal my face and name had ended up here, of all places in San Francisco. In a city that wedged even its millionaires in with a shoehorn, St. Francis Wood offered that rarest of luxuries—a little space and privacy. The other Hailey had never had to ride in an elevator with her neighbors. If she'd been careful to come and go from Eastman's home in her car, mostly after dusk, she would never have to be up close with her neighbors at all.

I didn't have Eastman's address, but the news reports had shown the house on camera, a narrow two-story of wood and brick, the wood painted a pale, creamy yellow and the brick aged and mottled with white, not the stark all-red kind of barracks and dormitories. English ivy climbed its edges, and April tulips bordered the slender strip of lawn.

When I spotted it, there was no sign of an ongoing police presence. I eased past at about fifteen miles an hour, then doubled back to park far enough away that the car wouldn't point to my location. Bad enough I had to park a car like

Serena's in this neighborhood at all. It was, in 911 lingo, a suspicious vehicle: a cheap sedan in a district of late-model imports and luxury SUVs. It stood out, but there was nothing I could do about that, except park it courteously flush with the curb and not leave it there any longer than I needed to.

The nearly full moon illuminated my surroundings to an almost uncomfortable degree as I walked back toward the house. I stayed in shadows until I could cross Eastman's dew-wet lawn, then unlatched a gate and went into the backyard. It was narrow, with several shade trees at the edges. Brambles that would produce blackberries in the summer overran the back fence, and the grass was native grass brought up by winter rains, not deliberate green turf. Protected from view by both the trees and the predawn dimness, I paused to consider my options. A pair of French doors opened onto a small porch, but of more interest to me were two steps that led up to a door on the east side of the house. The door and the way the roof angled downward there suggested to me a room with its own entry. Was this where she'd lived, the girl who'd posed as me?

The blinds were down on the window, so I couldn't peek in. But this made as good a place as any for my covert entry. I reached into the pack for my tools.

Serena had taught me lock picking earlier this year, after I'd had to do an artless pry job on a door as part of a break-in I'd considered merited, if not legal.

Last year a man I'd trusted, if not considered a friend, had sold me to Skouras for fifteen thousand dollars. I'd nearly died as a result of his betrayal. For that reason, I'd had no remorse about the mess I'd made of his back door, nor about taking the remainder of the fifteen grand that he'd hidden in his kitchen.

This time I didn't want to draw attention to the fact that someone had broken in, and thanks to Serena's teaching, I now had the skills to finesse the lock. It was mostly a matter of dexterity, one hand putting torque on the cylinder with a screwdriver while the other hand, wielding the safety pin, found and teased up the pins. Steady hands helped. Many people, in this situation, would be nervous. I wasn't.

The lock gave way, the cylinder rolling obediently under the pressure of my left hand. I straightened up and went in, closed the door quietly behind me, took out my flashlight, and looked around.

I was in a generously sized, clean bedroom with a standard setup: double bed in the center of the room, head against the wall, two night tables, a bureau with a large mirror perched on it and one framed photo, bookshelves, and a dog bed on the floor.

This wasn't where the renter had lived; this was Violet's bedroom. Two things told me that. First was the dog bed. An aged dog would want to sleep with its mistress, and vice versa. Second, the photo on the dresser was of Eastman and her husband. They were clearly traveling somewhere, standing in front of an open-air fruit market. She was maybe in her late forties or around fifty, hair pulled back under a straw sun hat. He was hatless, white-haired and lean-faced, and they were linking arms. They were, if not young, at least not yet touched by the depredations of old age. They looked good, straight-backed and serene, and I knew that the young grifter, no matter how stunted her conscience, wouldn't have wanted to look at that photo on the dresser. It would have indicted her every day.

There was a faint chemical scent in the air: The forensics guys had been here, dusting for fingerprints, though I couldn't see obvious signs that anything had been removed or rearranged.

Further inspection of the room bore out that it was Violet's: There was a pair of reading glasses on one night table, some large-print books on the bookshelf, and a faded yellow robe hanging on a hook on the back of the door. But beyond that I was surprised at how few markers of age there were in this room. There were no prescription bottles by the bed, nor over-the-counter meds. Other than the one photo, there was no clutter of memorabilia in the room, no framed pulp-magazine covers to attest to Eastman's writing career, no old photographs to remind her of her youth and onetime beauty. A vase held several wilting stalks that had once been bright sunflowers. The books on the shelf were a mix of nonfiction and fiction, but all of quality: no diet books written by celebrities.

Seen in daylight, without the scent of fingerprint dust and with the sunflowers in bright bloom, this would have been a pleasant place, entirely plausible as the room of a much younger woman. There was an ageless quality about it, or at least a sense of old age faced unsentimentally.

I went into the bathroom and opened the medicine cabinet. There were no prescription bottles inside. That made sense. Eastman had been fatally sedated. Probably the police had taken all her medications into evidence, in case one of them was the drug that had put her into a coma.

I walked out into the living room, where it became clear that the forensics people had been through. Here the chemical scent was stronger, and there were patches cut out of the light brown carpeting in the center of the room.

This was where it had happened. There were patches of carpet taken up because Stepakoff had bled and died here. This was where the grifter had found him, or he'd found her.

At least that was my assumption, that she'd been surprised by the young cop. I'd always heard that con artists tried to avoid violence, as did female criminals, and this woman was both. If she'd fired on Stepakoff, she'd felt she had no other choice.

That was interesting. If V. K. Eastman hadn't been able to open the door, and "Hailey" wouldn't have, had Stepakoff entered the house illegally, as the press had suggested? Maybe Stepakoff had been a bit of a hot dog, and he'd gone in through a window after seeing Eastman nonresponsive on the couch. San Francisco, like Los Angeles, had been in the throes of an early-spring heat wave the past week, so it was very plausible that a window had been open; many San Francisco homes, even expensive ones, didn't have air-conditioning, because intolerable heat was so rare.

I went around raising the blinds on all the windows, and when I had, the bright moonlight that had made me a little wary on the street now flowed through the windows and made my flashlight unnecessary; I switched it off.

Stepakoff going through a window was the answer that allowed for the renter taking him by surprise, which seemed certain. He'd made no call for backup, and his gun had been in its holster. He'd been shot without warning. And he'd died right here.

The living room was also where Eastman had spent her final hours, lying on this velvety, dun-colored couch. I saw a freestanding metal object by the sofa. Under closer inspection it turned out to be a quad cane, a cane with a more stable four-toed foot. So Eastman hadn't been very mobile. That was probably why she'd taken the downstairs apartment as her bedroom: no stairs to climb.

This all made sense. I could see how Eastman had ended up dying on the couch, not on her bed. She'd had some health problems, but she wasn't bedridden, and "Hailey" had been a personal assistant but not a nursemaid who brought meals to her bedroom. At least that was how the media reports had made it seem. So it was likely the first dose of sedatives had probably been administered in the living room, under the guise of a friendly drink together: *Why don't I make us some tea?* Then, after Eastman had succumbed to the first drugging, "Hailey" probably hadn't had the strength to carry her from the couch to her bedroom. Follow-up dosing had been done here.

I went into the kitchen and, still touching everything obliquely and never directly by the handle, found what you'd expect: plates and glasses and silverware, food in the cupboards. For a moment it seemed odd to me that so many everyday things remained here, but then the forensics techs who had gone through the place weren't a cleanup crew. Taking away the clothing and the canned foods and the books, that would fall to Eastman's heirs or friends.

There was no second bedroom downstairs, meaning the grifter had lived on the second floor.

The first room upstairs was a home office: a heavy, old-fashioned banker's desk and a metal filing cabinet. The cover to the rolltop desk was up, but little remained on it: pens and pencils, a notebook, a dictionary. I picked up the notebook and opened it, but it was blank. That didn't surprise me. Likewise, if there were manila folders left in the filing cabinet, they'd be empty, unused spares. Whatever the young grifter hadn't taken in her predatory searches of Eastman's office, the police would have taken as evidence. It would do me little good to poke around in here.

Yet I couldn't help but think, before I left, *Why did Eastman trust her so much?* It seemed that Violet's tenant had had easy access to this office, and thus to everything—applications for savings and brokerage accounts, with Eastman's Social Security number on them, bank statements with balances, stock certificates, the title to the car. . . . If Eastman couldn't climb the stairs, the grifter wouldn't even have had to worry about getting caught looking for these things. She could have done it at her leisure.

Maybe Violet had trusted the young woman simply because she'd had to, because she was ill and too low on energy to do a thorough background check. Old age was frightening, the vulnerabilities it brought.

I crossed the hall to the other bedroom. It was on the backyard side of the house and didn't get the same generous moonlight as the front, so I switched on the flashlight once again.

The room was big, obviously once the master bedroom. What caught my eye was not the bed but the piano. That took me by surprise. I hadn't even known that Eastman could play. She must have been good. Nobody pays movers to bring a piano up to the second floor without a serious commitment to the instrument.

Beyond that, the room was furnished in Twenty-first Century Girl: cream and pale blue, with several fat scented candles on the dresser, as well as a wicker basket full of small seashells. This was where she'd lived, the other "Hailey."

Please let there be something personal. Clothes, shoes, anything.

The ceiling was high in here, as in the rest of the house, and a shelf ran over the door, but its individual cubbies had been cleaned out. The closet was a walk-in with no door on it, and it took me only a glance in that direction to realize there was nothing in it but hangers and an ironing board leaning against the back wall. The drawers of the bureau were empty.

Either she'd taken her things with her—the likeliest scenario—or the police had taken what she'd left as evidence. I felt deflated. If nothing else, I'd hoped to get a sense of her height and weight compared to mine. I already knew she was Caucasian and close enough in age to me to pass as me. I sat down on the bed, thinking. Surely there had to be something else here I could learn from.

That was when somebody shut the front door downstairs. Not covertly, like I'd pulled the door to V.K.'s bedroom softly closed behind me after breaking in. This was a declarative, I-belong-here sound. That meant a cop.

I clicked off the flashlight immediately, then got silently to my feet and stood in the bedroom doorway, listening. The downstairs footsteps were as confident-sounding as the door's closing—unhurried but not tiptoeing. Then I heard him climbing the stairs. Dammit, this was happening too fast. Why couldn't he have needed something from Violet's bedroom or the living room, where most of the forensic work had been done?

The bedroom window was a single pane of glass; it didn't open. The closet offered no refuge. It didn't have a door, and there was nothing inside it to hide behind or under.

The footsteps were still coming.

I studied the sturdy-looking shelf that ran over the door. It was wide enough for me to crouch on, if I put my hands against the ceiling for balance.

I took my gun from my runner's pack, checked the safety, and tucked it into my jeans at the small of my back. Then I carefully got up on the dresser, braced one foot on the doorway's edge, and pulled myself up. *Easy, easy, okay, good.* I got my legs under me properly, crouching, both hands braced against the ceiling, because there wasn't any place in front of me to put them for balance. It wasn't a comfortable position, but I wouldn't be here long.

I had one thing on my side: I could hear only one set of footsteps, and no voices. That meant a lone policeman, not a pair.

Why the hell was a cop here alone, though, and at one in the morning?

I didn't have any more time to consider that. The overhead light came to life, and then he walked in, a tall young cop with his handcuffs looped over his belt in back, the tan leather straps of a shoulder holster coming together between the shoulder blades, a utility bag like a photographer's over the left shoulder. As he passed right under me, I could have reached down and touched that familiar curling red hair, worn today in a neat ponytail at the nape of the neck.

"Joel," I said lightly, and before he'd even fully turned around, I jumped.

He took it better than most people could have. We went to the floor hard, but it didn't knock the wind out of him. I stuck the muzzle of the Browning against his jawline and clicked off the safety.

"Hailey?" he said, seeing past the new brown hair.

"Be smart," I said. "I'm going to take your piece now. *Let me.*" Without lifting my body weight up off him, I reached for his gun, eased it out of the holster, and tucked it into the place where the Browning had just been.

"Hailey, think about what you're doing."

I ignored that. "Do you carry a backup weapon?"

"I've got a knife in my boot."

"Which boot?"

"The right."

To reach it I'd have to turn facing away from him and reach down, which would put me off balance. I didn't like that. "Okay, we'll let that go for a moment," I said. "Don't make any sudden moves. It's not my intention to hurt you, but remember you're dealing with a very nervous wanted criminal who's facing death row."

At his size he would win a wrestling match, so I didn't want him to try.

I sat up to a straddling position on his hips and pushed the bag he'd been carrying out of his reach. Then I said, "Arch your back a little bit, I'm going to reach under you for the cuffs."

His jaw tensed, but he cooperated. I leaned forward slightly and slipped my free hand under his lower back until I felt metal. I pulled the handcuffs free.

"Where's the key?"

He didn't answer, but I saw his eyes go to the bag. I pulled it to me, keeping the gun on him with my other hand.

He said, "I don't think you want to do this. You've

already committed assault on a sheriff's deputy. If you handcuff me, legally that carries the weight of kidnapping, which—"

"Stop," I said. "I've already got two murder charges on the books against me. I'm through sweating the details." I felt a round nub of metal under my rummaging fingers and pulled out the handcuff key.

"Okay," I said, "very slowly, you're going to sit up—not stand—and slide backward until you're sitting against the leg of the piano. My gun's going to be on you the whole time."

I climbed off him into a crouching position, holding the gun in front of me, still pointed at him.

Joel obeyed me, easing himself slowly backward, but as he did, he said, "Magnus believes your story. So do I."

"Put your arms back so that one hand is on either side of the piano leg."

"Please let me take you in. Magnus has some weight. He can run some interference for you in the system."

"That much? I doubt it. I'm a suspected cop killer. Put your hands where I said."

He lowered his face as he did so, nearly closing his eyes. I knew what he must have been feeling, but I couldn't afford the distraction of empathy. I moved behind him and locked the handcuffs around his wrists. Then I leaned back a little and put my hand on his leg. "Relax," I said, slid my hand inside his right boot, and took out the knife he'd said would be there. I flicked it open.

"Pretty," I said, examining the curved blade. "Most cops would prefer a gun as a backup piece, a little .380 with an ankle holster."

"I've always liked edged weapons."

"Really? Magnus told me you were a real marksman. 'Kid could hit the ten ring standing on a water-bed mattress' was his exact expression."

"He said that?" For a second, Joel seemed pleased, but then his expression darkened again. I knew why. Whatever respect he'd won from the veteran Ford, it was lost now, after he'd let a fugitive get the drop on him and chain him up with his own handcuffs.

I stood up and surveyed him thoughtfully. "You may be a lights-out shooter, but you've got some things to learn about being on the other end of a gun," I said. "Like, a gun's not dangerous at all if the person holding it isn't willing to pull the trigger."

"You're saying you weren't?"

"I had my finger outside the trigger guard, that's how worried I was about accidentally shooting you."

"I didn't know that."

I turned my attention back to the bag he'd been carrying, opening it again to examine the contents. Among them: a digital camera, a sketch pad, a narrow notebook like the kind reporters use.

I said, "Magnus sent you to get some photos and drawings of the scene? To make some notes?"

"Yeah."

So he was here to do essentially what I was here to do. Interesting.

He said, "You could've broken my neck, jumping on me like that."

"But I didn't."

"I could've shot you."

"But you *didn't*. These kinds of conversations bore me. They're pointless." I started pacing. "Listen, we're both a little jammed up here," I said. "I can certainly call someone and tell them you're here, but you're way out of your jurisdiction, and I'm guessing you didn't give SFPD a courtesy call about your visit."

His guilty, irritated expression told me I was right.

"When Magnus Ford hears about this, I don't think he's going to be happy. And me, once your colleagues hear about this, I'm facing those added assault and kidnapping charges you mentioned."

Joel said nothing, but his expression was dark.

"But I think there might be a way out for both of us." I reached inside my pack and dug out the aspirin bottle, with Serena's pills inside. Shaking out a handful, I separated several small white tablets and scooped the rest back into the bottle. Then I sat on my heels in front of Joel and showed him.

"Ambien," I said. "Two of these should put a guy your size under."

"No way," he said. "I'm not letting you drug me. I don't use. I hardly even drink."

"Hear me out," I said. "You take the pills, you fall asleep, I take the cuffs off and leave. You wake up, grab your weapons and cuffs, and go. Ford never knows what happened here tonight. I'm certainly not going to tell him."

There was conflict on his young, open face. He saw the merits of it, but at the same time he hated the idea. Cops, soldiers, firefighters . . . they trust their bodies, rely on them. They hate to lose control of them, even temporarily.

He said, "I've never seen Ambien before. How do I know—"

"That it's not something dangerous?" I said, impatient. "Because A, I'm not a killer, and B, if I wanted you dead, I would've shot you as you walked right under me. I wouldn't chain you to a piano and make you poison yourself."

He sighed. "All right."

"Good. You could probably dry-swallow these, but I'll get you some water. Don't let me hear you fooling around up here while I'm gone."

I wasn't really worried about that; there was nothing he could do to get loose in such a short period of time.

When I came back with the water glass, I knelt, put the tablets in the palm of my hand, and held it out as if I were feeding a horse. He lowered his face to my palm, and briefly I felt him use the tip of his tongue to get the pills out of my hand. Then I held the water glass to his mouth and he drank.

He didn't seem like the devious type, but just in case, I said, "Open your mouth and lift up your tongue."

He sighed again, irritated, but complied. There was nothing there. "Okay," I said.

Then I reached around to the back of his neck, felt for the rubber band holding his ponytail, and pulled it out, then shook the loosened hair free with my fingers.

Joel gave me a curious look. "What was that for?" he said.

I shrugged. "I get uncomfortable when my hair's pulled back for too long."

"I never noticed," he said. "Since I've had to wear mine long, I pull it back every chance I get. I can't wait to cut it off."

He wasn't like CJ, then, who'd grown out his hair despite his mother's frequent sighs and rarely so much as pulled it back.

I said, "Magnus made you grow it out? To work undercover?"

" 'Work undercover' is putting it too strongly, but yes, to be a decoy in the park. He wanted me to look less like a cop."

"It worked."

"You have hard feelings about that? That I fooled you?"

I shook my head. "No," I said, being honest. "That was your job. It was a good trick, and you were good at it."

"My father is blind. I grew up around it."

"Yeah?" I said.

"I think that's how Magnus got the idea. He didn't come up with it until after I mentioned my dad."

"I'm kind of surprised you guys really expected to get anything out of you sitting in the park watching people."

"I had my doubts, too, but we didn't use a lot of hours on it. Magnus just wanted some boots on the ground in that neighborhood. He's a patient guy, and his methods can be unusual."

We were quiet a moment. A lot of people wouldn't have understood it, I thought, the two of us having a civil conversation. But Joel wasn't revealing anything that would hurt their investigation, and he knew I wouldn't give him any information that he or Ford could use against me, either.

Then, apropos of nothing except for the fact that it'd just crossed my mind, I said, "How'd you get in here, anyway, if the SFPD didn't let you in?"

"Pick gun," he said. "Magnus gave it to me."

That was something I'd only heard about, never seen for real, that greatly sped up and simplified the process of lock picking. Trust Ford to have all the cool toys.

Joel said, "My shoulders are starting to hurt a little."

They shouldn't have been, not this early. "First time in handcuffs?"

"No, we practiced on each other at the academy, to learn—"

"That doesn't count," I said dismissively.

He tilted his head, assessing me. "You're saying you've been? I didn't see any arrests in your history."

I didn't answer, looked away, remembering last December. What would this kid say if I told him the truth? *Yes,*

I've been handcuffed. Last year I fellated a man while I was handcuffed and at gunpoint, and when he was finished, he dropped me on my face and I couldn't break my own fall. That probably distracted me from a minor pain in my shoulders.

Don't think about this, I warned myself, but already I was back there, hearing Quentin saying, *The first thing I do, with a woman, is see what group she falls into.* Hearing Joe Laska say, *This is taking way too long. Get her back up on the table.*

I heard a cracking noise and saw that I was still holding the water glass, but now it had a fine line running up its side from the pressure of my grip.

"Hailey? What's wrong?"

"Shut up. Don't talk to me."

It had been months since the projection booth, and memories of it had caught me unexpectedly before, but I'd never felt a shaking red rage like this until now. Even the sound of Joel Kelleher's voice threw fuel on it, as Quentin's or Joe Laska's might have. I closed my eyes.

No, don't touch Joel—he didn't do anything, he's nothing like them. Think of walking with Tess afterward, think of North Beach on Christmas Eve, the lights in the window displays.

That was better. I took a deep breath, felt the events of last winter recede.

"I'm sorry," I said. "I'm all right."

"Are you bleeding?"

"No," I said shortly.

He tilted his head, watching my face. He said, "Something bad happened to you, didn't it?"

I gave him a sharp glance. "Like what?"

"You tell me," he said. Then, "I heard something about a traffic accident on Wilshire—"

"*Don't* go there."

He fell silent, chastened. Then, after a moment, he said, "You wouldn't tell Magnus how you lost the finger, either."

"Does it matter?" I said. "No, it wasn't an accident; yeah, it hurt. Who cares? Thieves get rich, saints get shot, God don't answer prayers a lot."

He didn't have anything to say in response to that. When I looked over at him again, I saw that the Ambien was taking effect. It was visible in his relaxed face, his heavy-lidded eyes. "You're circling the airport," I said.

He shook himself like a horse feeling a fly on its skin. "No," he said.

"Don't be stubborn about it. The sooner you fall asleep" —a safer-sounding term than *go under*—"the sooner we can both get on with our lives. Okay?"

"Mm-hmmm." His head tipped forward, but he felt it and shook himself, like a student trying not to fall asleep during a lecture.

"*Joel.*"

"S'hard, I'm sitting up, I can't just go to sleep this way."

"What if," I said slowly, "just to speed this along, I sit next to you, so you can lean on me?" I went to settle down at

131

his side, carefully keeping the Browning on the far side of my body, just in case. "Here," I said, "slide your hips forward a little, if you can, so you're kind of leaning back, and then rest your head on my shoulder. That might help."

Joel shifted in place, doing as I asked. "Your shoulder's bony," he complained quietly.

"Sorry."

For a few long moments, he didn't say anything, and I hoped he was finally dropping off. But then he spoke again. "Can I tell you something? On the job, I . . ." Then he stopped.

"You what?"

"No, I shouldn't be telling you this."

"Telling me what?"

He said, "The job . . . I think I do it pretty well, but I have to swallow a lot of fear. There's no one I can tell. On the job nobody talks about being afraid. S'like I'm the only one."

Whatever he'd been about to tell me, this wasn't among the possibilities I'd considered.

"Uh, you're not," I managed finally. "I mean, everyone feels afraid sometimes."

"No. Not like this."

"I, uh . . ." How big a hypocrite was I, trying to address this? "Sure they do." It sounded unconvincing even to my own ears.

Then I noticed that Joel's respiration had become slow and steady. I carefully pulled away, letting his head drop to his chest.

I took the handcuff key, unlocked his wrists, and lowered him gently to the floor. Then I took his right arm in my hand, two fingers on the radial artery, checking the pulse against his watch. It was fifty-two. Low, but not dangerous. He was probably a runner. He could probably get down to the fifties every night in normal sleep.

Before I left, I went through his bag again and found the pick gun that Joel had been telling me about. It didn't look like a gun, really—more like a price-tag applicator in a supermarket, except made of metal, with the slender pick protruding from the business end. I slipped it into my pack. Magnus was going to be pissed at his young assistant, but I was working with a lot more disadvantages than they were, and I needed all the help I could get.

14

Sometime in the night, the media had discovered what Ford and Joel Kelleher already knew. When I woke up, Serena was reading the story in the *Chronicle:* SLAYING SUSPECT WAS USMA CADET.

"You're getting more famous by the day," she said, wet black hair pinned up atop her head. She'd already taken a shower; scented humidity hung in the air.

"Looks that way."

"And," she said, "you ditched me last night. *Pendeja.*"

"You were sleeping."

"I was supposed to be your backup."

"You were *sleeping,*" I repeated. "You can't actually be

complaining that I left you in a warm bed at midnight instead of taking you across town to stand around in the dark."

Actually, she was right. Leaving her had been a big mistake. If I'd had a lookout last night, I would have gotten out of the Eastman place before Joel was in. Now Ford's right-hand man knew I was up here in San Francisco. Was I going to have to look over my shoulder for him everywhere I went?

"What?" Serena said. "You look kinda funny."

"Thinking," I said, dismissing that train of thought. "Let me see the paper."

Details were pretty thin about my West Point career; the Army's famous dislike of dealing with civilian reporters was working in my favor.

Of more interest, at least to me, was a related story on CNN: With banks once again open for business, details were coming out about Eastman's accounts. As Tess had predicted, there had been "irregularities." Apparently "Hailey" had written herself four checks on Eastman's account on Thursday and Friday, cashing them at different bank branches. Each of the checks was for an amount just shy of five thousand dollars, the level that triggered bank oversight. In addition, there had been large purchases made with Eastman's Visa and American Express cards those same days, at Neiman Marcus and Macy's and a lower–Market Street jewelry store.

I kicked off covers and went to pour myself a cup of coffee from the little machine on the counter.

"So how did it go last night?" Serena said. "Was it interesting?"

"You can't imagine," I said dryly, tipping my face down into my cup.

"Yeah? What'd you learn?"

Shit. I didn't really want to tell her about Joel; it'd freak her out. I sipped coffee and backtracked. "I was being ironic. It was a wash. Everything interesting has been cleaned out."

"Mmm," she said, and then, "So what's the plan today?"

"Surveillance," I said. "If Joe Laska is working out of Skouras's old offices, we might be able to catch my good friend Quentin coming and going from there. This is going to be the boring part, surveillance."

"That's okay," Serena said, "as long as I get to be there when things do get interesting. Like when you're ready to throw down on this guy."

"Sure thing."

"I mean it, Insula. No 'This part's too dangerous, go wait at the hotel' shit."

"Be careful what you wish for," I said. "You remember who these guys are. They're heavy. If we don't have to mix it up with them, we shouldn't." I drained the last of the coffee. "Let me take a shower, and we'll head out."

That's how we spent the rest of the day: at a discreet distance from Laska's office not far from the Port of San Francisco, watching people arrive and depart. I saw Babyface himself and pointed him out to Serena. Quentin did not appear. At one point I found some scratch paper and tried to draw him from memory, an exercise that reminded me I couldn't draw at all. Serena smoked cigarettes and fielded occasional phone calls and slipped away to talk in private; Trece business, I knew.

By seven that evening, we were back at the hotel, eating Indian takeout and watching cable news. I'd been hoping that by the time the prime-time shows were on, I'd have been supplanted by a missing child or a homegrown-terror plot. That wasn't the case. On CNN's marquee crime-news show, generic footage of West Point cadets drilling was intercut with my military ID photo, footage of police activity outside the Eastman house on Friday night, and a brief snippet of Lucius "Luke" Marsellus getting out of a black Escalade and walking into the offices of his record label in L.A.

Marsellus? I set down my plastic fork and looked at the banner at the bottom of the screen. It read, BREAKING NEWS: MURDER SUSPECT HIT, KILLED CHILD IN TRAFFIC ACCIDENT.

"Oh, great," I said.

The show's host was saying, "This *terrible* story, these two murders up in San Francisco, the story just keeps getting more *tangled,* everything we hear just keeps getting *worse.*" She spoke not in sentences but in strings of clauses, with drawling emphasis on the key words. "The news late today out of Los Angeles about a *traffic fatality* in which—"

"Well, you knew that shit was gonna come out," Serena said philosophically.

"Yeah, I guess," I said.

On the screen the host was now talking to a remote guest, identified as a "psychologist and popular author."

Serena was about to speak again, but I held up a silencing hand.

"Now, Dr. Schiffman," the host said, "what we're hearing about this young woman, this *suspect,* more and more we're seeing a picture of someone whose life has gone very *wrong,* who set herself this very high goal of going to the U.S. Military Academy and then failed at *that;* she later, for whatever reason, is responsible for the death of a small *child.* . . . Dr. Schiffman, what kind of effect would this string of, I guess you'd say missteps and failures, have on the psyche of a young person like Hailey Cain?"

The psychologist, a man with very short, curly hair and round glasses, cleared his throat. "Well, I think it's important first to remind everyone that Cain is still a suspect, she hasn't been tried or found guilty—"

"Of course, of course."

"—and that the Wilshire Boulevard accident was found not to be her fault. But with those . . . uh, caveats, you'd have to say that the failure to complete West Point and then the death of this child, those kinds of life events at a fairly young age, could have a potentially devastating effect."

"Certainly."

"You could potentially be looking at someone who's saying, 'I've tried hard, I've failed, what's the use?' I mean, particularly someone being the agent of a child's death, and completely by accident, that's someone who could be saying, 'Society's going to look at me like I'm some kind of monster no matter what, so I give up, I'm just going to be as bad as

I can be.' I'm not saying that's what happened here, but it could be."

"So you're saying that this could be someone who just *snapped*."

"That's entirely possible."

West Point and Wilshire Boulevard—they were the two turning points of my adult life, the two points that allowed these people who'd never met me to triangulate, to plot out my psyche like they were laying out a map.

"For God's sake," I told Serena, "the Eastman thing was obviously a planned-out, long-term crime, moving into an old lady's house and embezzling her money. That's not 'snapping.' "

"They gotta make it interesting," Serena said.

Finally the news shifted to an update about a missing woman in South Carolina. Serena muted the TV and turned her full attention to her food. I tried to do the same, but I wasn't very hungry.

I went to bed early that night, to make up for the sleep I'd missed the night before, in St. Francis Wood with Joel. But instead I fell into that dark, dreamless, not-quite-asleep state for I don't know how long, coming fully to consciousness at the sound of Serena shaking an Ambien out of the bottle I'd left at bedside.

Eventually I succumbed, dreaming that I was far from California and my troubles. Instead I was on an African beach, alone with CJ.

15

The next day we sighted Quentin Corelli, driving a dark sedan that he parked outside the Laska offices. I'd almost forgotten the way he moved, light on his feet and cocky. And I hadn't expected the extent to which I bristled on seeing that, an almost literal hackles-of-the-neck feeling. *Bastard,* I thought, *you haven't changed.*

"Asshole," Serena said next to me, as though she saw as much to hate in him.

Around midday he left Laska's offices, and we followed him, Serena at the wheel. We tailed him to the south part of San Francisco, near Candlestick Park. It was a mixed-use neighborhood, residential and light-industrial, where there was so little traffic on the streets that Serena dropped back for fear he'd make us. Then Quentin's dark sedan turned left down a narrow driveway that ran alongside a pale blue stucco house. Serena was forced to drive on or be conspicuous in stopping, but I turned in my seat to keep an eye on him. I only saw him getting out of his car, which was sheltered under a carport, before we'd rolled past.

"Go around the block," I told Serena. "We'll scope things out from one street over."

"I can't, it's a dead end."

I looked ahead and saw that she was right; before us was a low fence and some scrubby bushes. "Then go back," I said.

"He's gonna see us."

"Dammit. Stay here a minute," I said.

It was true, he might see us if we turned around right away. But if we stayed idling at the street's dead end, I hoped, he'd go into the house, at which point we could safely backtrack.

I waited, watching the side mirror to see if Quentin or his car emerged from the driveway. Neither did.

"Find a place to park," I said.

Serena made a three-point turnaround and pointed her car back down the street. I studied the house as we went by again. What looked like the main entrance was on the side of the house, facing the driveway, not the street. It had a double-door system: A security door of tightly scrolled metal allowed access to a cavelike entry area, where the resident could stand and unlock his real front door in safety.

"Do you think he lives there?" Serena said, voicing my thought.

I frowned. "I would have thought he'd live somewhere better." Quentin had dressed well every time I'd seen him, and for his home I'd envisioned something downtown and coldly modern, with a neo–Rat Pack design aesthetic without signs of genuine individual taste.

Serena eased along the side of the road and killed the engine, then fished out her cigarettes and lit up. "So?" she said, exhaling. "What are you gonna do? Wait until he goes out again and search the place?"

"No," I said, almost to myself. "No."

I'd gone to the Eastman place with some stupid, vague idea that I'd find a trace of the grifter, something to help me intuit her identity or her direction. Instead I'd found nothing and nearly gotten caught. I was done with passive searching for hints and traces. Everything I needed to know was between Quentin Corelli's ears.

"Can I use these?" I pulled a pair of sunglasses, square and glossy black, from the narrow side compartment in the passenger door.

"For what?"

Sunglasses on, I opened the door and bailed out into the street, Joel's pick gun in my hand.

"*Hailey!*" Serena complained behind me.

I ran across the street and knelt in front of the security door, sliding the pick in, narrow screwdriver in my other hand, twisted like a tension wrench.

The lock didn't give. I blew hair out of my eyes, impatient, tried again.

He's going to hear you. Fine, let him.

The lock on the security door sprang, and I was into the entry alcove. I banged on the door with my fist. "Quentin, it's me," I called, giving my voice a sound of familiarity and entitlement. "Open up, I need you."

When he opened the door, I had only a second to register his expression—slightly irritated, not recognizing but clearly not threatened by this young brown-haired stranger— and then I said, "Thanks," and swung the pick gun as hard as I could into the bridge of his nose. His eyes crossed, and his body flopped down to the floor like a shark on the deck of a fishing boat. I cocked my arm for a second blow, but it wasn't going to be necessary.

"Holy shit, Insula," Serena said, coming up behind me.

"Shut the door," I said, "and check around to make sure there's no one else here."

16

I think Quentin was living off the books, like I did back in Los Angeles. It was the only way to explain the difference between the run-down neighborhood he lived in and the inside of the one-bedroom apartment that apparently was his. It looked better inside than out, furnished almost as I'd imagined, with a black leather couch and a glass coffee table on the warped wooden floor, and on the coffee table a razor blade and a few telltale whitish grains to attest to Quentin's bad habits. There was a table with two straight-backed chairs in the dining area, under a hanging lamp, and a forty-inch TV stood on a black, nearly empty bookcase along the wall. Other than that, the room was spartan and unadorned, unless you counted, at the moment, Quentin Corelli himself on the floor, hands and feet lashed with telephone cord and a narrow leather belt, respectively. There was a trickle of blood that ran from his left nostril to his upper lip, but it had stopped flowing on its own. I hadn't stanched it. I didn't particularly want to touch him. I didn't fear him, but I didn't want to touch him.

Now he was awake and looking at me, and it was clear he still didn't recognize the stranger with the bruise on her cheek.

Serena came out of the bedroom. "We're alone," she said.

Quentin looked from me to her, back to me, and got it. "You," he said. "Fucking A."

"Hi, Quentin," I said. "Seems like old times, doesn't it?" Like Gualala, where I'd gotten the drop on him once before.

His shoulders jerked as, for about ten seconds, he tried to get his hands free. Then, frustrated, he sank back down on the floor. I wasn't surprised that he didn't start yelling. Anyone near enough to hear would call the cops, and people like Quentin didn't do cops.

I said, "Did you think I wouldn't figure it out and come visit you?"

This is where, if he were innocent, Quentin should have said, *Figure what out?* He didn't, and that made me smile. I said, "Where is she, Quentin?"

"I don't know what you're talking about, bitch."

I picked up his coat, a good-quality leather jacket, from the couch. It was the only item he'd taken off; otherwise he was still crisply dressed in his work clothes—charcoal trousers, white shirt with a fine gray stripe, square-toed black leather shoes. He hadn't even gotten blood on his shirt. Yet.

His coat yielded a cell phone and a key ring; I already had the gun he'd dropped in our brief fight.

"Glock makes a nice gun," I said, holding it up. "I hope you wore gloves when you loaded it. It'd be a really bad thing if I walked out of here with this gun and later I shot someone with it and your prints were on the casings, eh?" I paused. "I guess you know how I know that."

Quentin's golden eyes flickered briefly with an emotion I was pretty sure was malicious pleasure. Even in his precarious current situation, he was happy I was so badly jammed up.

I toed him in the ribs, not hard.

"Pay attention, Q," I said. "The more immediate point here is that both I and my associate are heavily armed"—I nodded to Serena, who was sitting on the spine of the couch, with Quentin's discarded coat, wallet, and cell at her feet—"and you're not."

He looked at Serena and said to me, "What is it with you and Mexicans? Can't you get any white people to hang out with you?"

Serena didn't say anything, not rising to the bait. I sat on my heels and put the muzzle of the Glock against his face. "I got no love for you, you know that," I said. "But I've got bigger things to do than mess with you, so if you just answer one question for me, you're gonna be home free. Here it is, for the washer-dryer set and a chance at the bonus round: Who'd you sell my ID and gun to?"

"Fuck you, bitch."

I'd figured it wouldn't be that easy. Time for Plan B. "Hand me his phone," I told Serena.

She did, and I brought up the call log. "Look at this," I told Quentin conversationally. "Missed calls, received calls, dialed calls. What am I gonna find in here, Q? Anything interesting?"

His face was stiff and angry, but that didn't tell me much. I turned my attention back to the gray-green readout.

He should have deleted this stuff more often. His call log went back well over a week. I scrolled backward. I recognized the number for Skouras Shipping—"work" to Quentin—and also Joe Laska's private cell, identified as "JL." The other names and numbers meant nothing to me.

I kept scrolling back until I got to the window of time that interested me: Friday afternoon after three-thirty. Stepakoff's death could have been no earlier than that, according to the SFPD's timeline. Sometime in the hours afterward, the grifter had collected all her things and vacated the Eastman house. Around that time, I thought, she might have called Quentin. If he'd given her the ID papers and the gun both, then maybe he would be her go-to guy, the one she'd call when the plan went to hell and she was looking down at the body of a dead cop.

That afternoon, at 4:07 P.M., Quentin had missed a phone call from someone identified just by a nine-digit phone number, not by name. Seven minutes later that same person had called again, and Quentin had picked up.

I scrolled back. The other phone call from that number had come in on the next day, Saturday. Nothing since then.

I nudged my chin at Quentin. "Watch him," I told Serena. "I'll be back in a minute." I didn't want Quentin overhearing this conversation. Certainly I didn't want him to be yelling in the background.

I walked out Quentin's front door and glanced around. No one else was visible nearby. I emerged from the entry cave and sat on the front steps, largely out of view of the street.

A gray cat sprang to the top of the fence alongside Quentin's building. It gave me an insolent stare, decided I was no threat, moved on. I looked down at the phone, still registering the suspect phone number on the screen. I pressed the key with the green telephone receiver on it, and the screen flashed the message CALLING.

On the second ring, a woman's voice answered. "Quentin? What's up?" She sounded young. There was a little edge of caution in her voice; it wasn't flirtatious.

I, though, took care to make my voice quick and light as I said, "Hi, sorry, this isn't Quentin, I'm Jenny, from Joe Laska's office. Who have I reached?"

I said all that in one breath, trying first to set her at ease with a name I thought would be familiar to her, Laska's name, then not giving her time to think before making my officious request.

"This is Brittany," she said. She sounded uncertain but not yet suspicious.

"Oh, good. Quentin asked me to call and ask you a

question. He wants to know if you've gotten rid of everything that links you to—this is what he said—'Hailey and Violet'?"

There was a long pause. As the seconds stretched out, I felt something hopeful rise in my chest.

She said, "Who did you say you were?"

"I'm Jenny, from Joe's office." I wanted to ask her if she was still in San Francisco or nearby, but that would clearly give this away as a fishing expedition.

She said, "I think I need to talk to Quentin personally."

"I'll have him call you," I said.

"Why did he—"

I broke the connection but didn't immediately go back inside. I stood up for a moment, breathing a little quicker than usual.

People who believed in astral projection sometimes referred to something called the "silver cord," a line of energy that connected the unconscious body to the traveling spirit. Some said the same cord, faintly visible to the truly aware, connected people whose lives were deeply intertwined. For a brief moment, while I'd had her on the line, I'd almost felt that same thing, a nearly tactile connection. Our lives were linked because we'd briefly shared the same identity, and now we faced the same potential fate: a death sentence.

And for about twenty-eight seconds, according to the log on the screen of Quentin's phone, I'd created a cord between us. I'd had her on the line, giving me information. It wasn't Magnus Ford who'd done that or any of the cops in the Eastman-Stepakoff task force. It had been me.

Quentin's phone rang in my hand, shaking me out of that reverie. Ignoring the phone, I went back inside.

"Guess who that is?" I told Quentin brightly, holding up the phone as the ringing continued. "Brittany's very anxious to talk to you." I moved closer, stood over his supine form. "I know her name and her cell number now. I know you were helping her with this. Tell me the rest and I'll leave. You'll never see me again."

Quentin glared. "Oh, you're definitely going to see me again. You're gonna die screaming, bitch."

I lifted a shoulder. "Last year you said I'd be dead by Christmas. What are we shooting for now? Easter's over." I watched his face. "So tell me what I need to know."

He was silent.

I hadn't expected this to be easy, but I sighed aloud for the sake of dramatics. "Quentin," I said, as if weary, "you hate women. You know it, I know it, little girls on bicycles with sissy bars probably sense it when they ride past you on the street. Why protect this one chick? Just give her up and this doesn't get messy. I'll call Laska, and he'll come and cut you loose. No harm done."

Except to his ego, and to guys like Quentin, ego was a lot. Particularly when its bruises came at the hands of a female.

"Go to hell," he said.

Since he'd woken up to find himself at the mercy of an old enemy, Quentin just hadn't seemed as scared as I'd have hoped. Even now he was glaring, resentful, but it was a frustration with a sly edge. He was sure we wouldn't really hurt him and, more than that, sure that we'd make a mistake and he'd get the upper hand soon enough.

"Serena," I said, "can I have a cigarette?"

She dug them out, the pack of Marlboros and the lighter. I tapped one out of the pack, lit up, exhaled a cloud of start-up smoke. I held out the cigarette to Quentin but yanked it away when he tried to snap at my hand.

"I had that move scouted, didn't I?" I said. "I know you, Quentin. And you probably think you know me. You think, because of last winter, that I'm hung up on doing the right thing, yeah? But that was then." I took the cigarette in my right hand and then, watching his eyes, slowly stubbed it out against the stump on my left hand, where the nerves still hadn't grown back.

"This is now," I finished.

Quentin's eyes showed white at the edges; for the first time, I had his full attention. I thought I'd reached him.

Then he said, "That's not what I remember about last winter." He smiled. "I remember you weren't such hot shit then. You were down on your knees sucking on my crank like it was sugarcoated. You—"

I really don't remember much about what happened next. I think I heard a sound inside my head, a faint crunch like when you bite into a particularly crisp apple, and then my vision swam red except for a narrow window through which I could see Quentin's face and the knuckles of my own fists, white with fury.

17

"I'm feeling a lot better," I said meekly.

I was sitting in Quentin's bathroom with my back against the hard curved ceramic of the tub. My arms rested on my knees, my knuckles skinned. Cold water dripped down my spine, water that Serena had squeezed from a wet hand towel down the back of my shirt. Oddly enough, it did have a calming effect.

Serena, unimpressed with my claim to be recovered, was leaning against the closed bathroom door. On her wrist I could see the marks from where I'd fought her attempt to pull me off Quentin. I hadn't drawn blood, though I had broken skin—there were long pink lines edged with torn white skin where my short, blunt fingernails had clawed at her. On my shoulders, the tendony midpoint between neck and shoulder, I could feel where I'd have light bruises from how hard she'd initially grabbed me.

"Sorry," I told her, maybe not for the first time. Like I said, a few minutes were a blur, lost to me.

"Nothing to be sorry about," she said flatly. "He's a waste of oxygen. But he wasn't going to tell us nothing from a fucking coma."

"Well," I said, "he'll talk to us now."

But Serena's next words surprised me. "I don't think he will."

I gave her a quizzical glance.

"I know his type. He's had beatings before. That's part of what he gets paid for, not folding at the first threat of a little pain. Plus," she said, "now he's seen you lose it. Yeah, you got in a few licks, but you lost it. He's gonna keep jerking you around." She lifted her weight from the door and came to sit on her heels in front of me. "Give me my cigarettes back, okay?"

I handed over both the matches and the cigarettes. She tapped one out of the pack and then struck a match and lit up. As I watched, she inhaled until the cigarette's end glowed, then exhaled smoke, then handed the cigarette to me.

"Come on," she said, standing. "We're gonna get it outta him. But you've got to give me the lead on this."

"Meaning what?" I said, getting up from the floor.

"Meaning I'm going to do what we've gotta do to get it out of him," she said.

"Yeah, but how?"

"Just trust me."

I'd tried, I really had, to shed the way of thinking that West Point had trained into me. But now my first thought was that an officer never turns his or her back on what his or her troops are doing. *Deniability,* one of my COs at West Point had said, was a cowardly term for a cowardly age.

Serena read my mind. "Hailey," she said, "don't be thinking what you're thinking. Not now."

"What am I thinking?"

"Duty and honor," she said.

"Give me another chance. I can get it out of him," I said.

"No, you can't. And if you did, you couldn't live with yourself." The cigarette was still smoldering in her hand. "Come on, Hailey. What do you think you brought me along for? Just to pump the gas and buy the food so you could stay out of sight? You knew this mission might come down to something like this, something I can do and sleep at night afterward and you couldn't."

Serena opened the bathroom door. I followed, still holding the cigarette she'd given me.

Quentin eyed us both sourly as we came back into the living room, but he said nothing.

Serena nodded toward the table. "Get a chair over here, and let's get him up in it."

"You touch me again, you're gonna die, bitch," Quentin said. I ignored him and pulled one of the straight-backed chairs into the center of the room. Avoiding his angry eyes, not looking at the red pre-bruise marks on his face that I'd made, I grabbed him by the collar, Serena grabbed his hips, and together we wrestled him up into the chair. He was quieter than you might expect for someone in his situation, and he didn't put up a fight, but I understood why: ego. Even if some of his neighbors were at home at midday, he wasn't about to scream for help like some civilian. He didn't want help from upstanding normal people, and he certainly didn't want cops. Quentin was waiting for us to make a mistake—like weak, stupid females inevitably would—and then he'd make us pay.

But for now Serena had found extra electrical cords and a few of Quentin's belts, and she was tying his ankles to the chair legs, then strapping him to the chair.

He looked up at me. "You hit like a girl," he said. "I've been hit harder by interesting ideas."

"Hold that thought, Q," Serena said, straightening up. She went into the kitchen, then the bedroom. We heard her rummaging noisily. Her disembodied voice, from the bedroom: "Gross."

"What?"

"I found the porn."

"I'll take your word. I don't want to see it."

Quentin snorted.

Serena returned to the living room, carrying a red metal

tool chest. She set it down on the floor and snapped it open. "Gangster toolbox," she said, sifting through the items inside. "Lock picks, extra cartridges for the gun, handcuff key but no handcuffs—and what's this?" She raised her face to Quentin's and smiled. "You ever hear the expression 'What goes around, comes around'? Time for you to pay for what you did to my friend last year."

"Yeah? You gonna make me lick your greasy Mexican—"

She cut him off: "*Right,* I'm sure that was going to be a *terribly* demeaning racial comment, Q, but that's not what I had in mind. Does this freshen up your memory?"

She lifted out a pair of heavy shears, much like the tin snips that Babyface had used to take off my finger in December.

He scowled. "You haven't got the stones to take off a finger."

Serena tilted her face up toward me. "You think that's true, H? Maybe he's right." She moved around behind the chair, where Quentin's fingers made a downward-splayed bouquet from his bound hands. "I actually think I do have the stones for that. And I could get into the whole eye-for-an-eye thing. But I'm feeling creative." She walked back around to the front of the chair, sat on her heels, and pried off one of Quentin's good leather shoes, then peeled off the sock underneath. His foot, exposed, looked reddish and vulnerable, toes compacted together from being inside the shoe.

Serena said, "You guys want to hear a fun fact about anatomy? Lots of people don't know this, but the big toe is really important for balance. Once it's cut off, you never really stand or walk right again. And if you lose both of them? Then things get just crazy. You balance like one of those goofy balloon people they put up outside grand openings of stores and shit."

For the first time, there was uncertainty—maybe fear—in Quentin's face. He said again, "You don't have the stones."

Serena shrugged. "Maybe not. Maybe I should start with a smaller toe, work my way up. I'm sure it's easier the second time."

Quentin tried to jerk his foot out of her reach, but it was tied by the ankle to the chair. Serena easily put her hand on the top of his foot, holding it down, and then wedged the two jaws of the shears around his third toe. Quentin breathed raggedly.

Serena, I thought, but kept myself from saying it. No weakness now.

Then her hand tightened on the shears, and the bones of her hand stood out slightly under the skin. *She's really, really going to do it—*

"*No!*" Quentin's voice was a howl. "Stop! I'll tell you, you bitch! What the fuck, I don't care."

Serena had withdrawn the shears, but blood was springing up where they had been; he'd truly stopped her at the last minute.

Her voice was cold. "Fine, but consider this a temporary reprieve. You start holding out on us, or if we think you're lying about anything, that toe's coming off."

"I don't got to protect her," Quentin said. His face was flushed, and he was still looking down toward the toe he couldn't see beneath his lap and knees.

"Her?" I said. "You mean Brittany?"

"I don't owe her anything. She was just some chick I picked up in a bar and did a couple of times." His voice was gaining conviction and bravado. Now he wanted to act like it was all his idea to tell me. Fine. Easier all around.

I stepped in as Serena sat back on her heels again. "What was her last name?"

"Mercier."

"Which of my guns did you sell her? The Airweight or the SIG Sauer?"

"The SIG."

"That's what I thought," I said. "Tell me the rest. This girl's more than some chick you 'did a couple of times.' She reached out to you for help after the cop died. Tell me who she is, how you came to sell my things to her, all of it."

"It was like I said. I met her in a bar. She was just this chick up from L.A., looking for a rich guy to be her boyfriend and support her." His voice and breathing were returning to normal. "I wasn't about to do that shit, but we went home together. She's a little younger than you. A lot hotter, too. We hooked up a couple of times. She liked to think of herself as a con artist. The stuff she did was just nickel-and-dime crap, like the broken-package scam or hanging around outside the bus station pretending she was trying to get out of town and away from an abusive boyfriend. Bleeding hearts fell for that crap a lot, gave her a lot of money for bus tickets she never bought."

"And she could tell you were nonjudgmental about the way she lived."

"I didn't give a shit that she did that kind of crap. Girls have to—they don't have the nerve for big crimes like robbing banks, stuff that takes planning and guts. So they've gotta do little shit."

I didn't respond to that. If making sexist comments was what he needed to do to soothe his ego and justify telling us this stuff, fine.

He said, "We didn't hook up long-term. But later I had stuff to sell, the stuff from Mexico."

He didn't say, *your* stuff, and that irritated me, though I knew it was typical of career criminals. They stuck a gun in the face of their victims and said, "Where's *the* money?," not "Where's *your* money?"—psychologically divorcing the victims from what was theirs.

"The problem was, both the driver's license and the passport had your photo on them, and there's not a lot of people who look like you that're also in the market for ID papers. So I had this stuff and no one to sell it to, and then I remembered Brittany. She could pass for you. So she bought the stuff. I didn't offer to sell her the gun. Her tricks were all nonviolent. I figured she'd be scared and say, 'Oh, no, I hate guns,' like most girls do."

"Yeah, whatever," I said, feigning irritation. If thinking that he was getting under my skin would make him run his mouth more, I could do that. "But at some point, you changed your mind about the gun."

"Yeah, in February I sold her the SIG."

"What happened that made her want a gun?"

"I don't know."

I looked at Serena. "I sense bullshit."

"Fine with me." Serena put her hand on his foot again.

"Okay, okay," Quentin said. "It was kinda me. We didn't really keep in touch, but in February I saw her outside a bar. I thought she was you at first. She even had that ugly thing on her face, like you've got. When I saw who it really was, I got it: She was using your ID to do a real con. This wasn't just that she'd gotten a credit card in your name—she was really *being* you, in public. I thought that took a lot of balls, so I went and talked to her. We had a beer together, and she started telling me about this long con she was doing. She'd moved into a rich old woman's house, a woman who couldn't see well enough to drive anymore. Brit was running errands for her, getting groceries, taking the dog to the vet. The old lady liked dogs, so Brittany was pretending that she wanted to be a vet student at Davis someday. She even got a city-college ID card to make it look like she was in school. The old lady was completely snowed. Meanwhile Brit's getting access to everything—all her account numbers and paperwork, everything."

I said, "What was she really living on? Was the old lady paying her so much that she didn't have to work at all?"

"Credit cards. She took out four in your name. She was just paying the minimum so they wouldn't cut her off."

"Great." Now my credit was going to be wrecked, on top of everything else. "Get to the part about the gun."

"When I saw what she was doing, I told her that someday there might be a relative or old friend that drops by unexpectedly and figures out the situation. What if it's a guy, I said, and he gets angry, and the situation turns physical? I told her she needed to be ready to defend herself. Just in case."

"You knew it might be a lot more serious than that," I said. "You knew it might be the cops."

"I didn't want to scare her."

"How much money did she pay for the gun?"

Suddenly Quentin looked uncomfortable, more than he had before. Then I understood why: because this was where the story took a turn from being about simple greed to setting me up for death row.

"It was free, wasn't it?" I said. "You just gave it to her."

"Yeah."

"Because you knew if I'd loaded it, my prints would be on the casings. Did you tell her not to clean up the brass if she had to fire it?"

"I might've said something like that." He looked uneasy. "It wasn't like either of us thought this would ever happen."

But if it did, so much the better, from his point of view. I said, "Let's get to the day Brittany shot the cop. What'd she tell you happened?"

"She'd heard someone at the door, but she didn't answer. She didn't even look. She was so close to being done with . . . with what she was doing, that she didn't want to mess around with any visitors who might get suspicious." Quentin paused. "But then she heard these noises from the living room. That idiot cop climbed in through the window. Brit was coming downstairs. She was about to go out shopping, so she had her purse, and the SIG was in there. Then when she went into the living room and saw a cop seeing the old lady like that . . . bang! That was it."

"So Brittany called you," I said.

"Yeah. She was pissing herself, she was so scared. I came over and helped her out. She wanted to try to clean up her fingerprints and maybe loose hairs, for DNA. I knew you can never really get rid of all of that shit, but I did the best I could while she was throwing all her stuff into bags to split."

"Where'd she go?"

"Los Angeles," he said.

"Quentin," I said, "this is the other million-dollar question: Where, exactly, in L.A. did she go?"

"To a friend's, that's all she said. I fucking swear."

"Fine," I said. I paced a little, trying to decide if there was anything else I needed to get out of him. I couldn't think of anything.

Serena said, "So now what?"

"Now he takes a little nap while we split for L.A."

If it had worked with Joel, it'd work with Quentin. I needed some lead time in my search for Brittany Mercier. As soon as he could, Quentin would call her and warn her I was coming to L.A. No matter how little he might care about her, he hated me, and he'd help her out for that reason alone.

But when I shook out the pills from the bottle into my hand, I had only one Ambien left. I'd given two to Joel yesterday, and Serena had taken one the night before. One would make Quentin sleepy, but it might not knock him out.

I told Serena, "Go see if he's got anything like sleeping pills in his medicine chest."

"I don't," Quentin interrupted.

"Check anyway."

She said, "Come with me. I need to talk to you."

"Yeah, okay, in a second." To Quentin, "Don't let me hear you fooling around out here, trying to get loose. You don't want to make me mad right now, because you have no idea who my friend really is. She doesn't work for me, I work for her. And right now she wants to kill you, and I have to go try to talk her out of it."

I'd known that was what Serena intended when she'd asked to talk to me out of his earshot. She was cold, but not cold enough to discuss Quentin's murder in front of him. She wanted to put a round in the back of his head, execution style, before he even knew what was happening. That was the quality of her mercy: quick and from behind.

For once Quentin didn't have anything to say, so I stood up and went into the bathroom a second time, where Serena was waiting for me. I shut the door behind us. There were no windows, and the overhead light was harsh. I thought of hospital physicians making a quick, private consult.

"We're not killing him," I said flatly.

"He's gonna tip her off," Serena said.

"I know, but we can buy ourselves some lead time. There's no sleeping pills in the medicine chest?"

"No."

"Dammit." Of course he didn't have any. Bastards are the only people who never have any trouble sleeping. "I wanted to put him down for a good seven or eight hours." I reconsidered. "Okay, we'll get him in the closet, tied up, brace the closet door with the couch. It'll be a while before he gets out."

" 'A while'? You know how long a phone call takes? We'll be driving through Salinas and she'll already be out the door. We'll never find her. Not to mention, he's not just gonna let today go. He'll look for you. Me, too. He'll want to kill both of us."

She was right, and I knew it. "I don't care. We're not killing anyone."

"Why not?" she demanded. "For God's sake, Hailey, look what he did to *you*. You never told me about that, that last year he made you—"

"I remember, I was there," I said sharply. "Maybe we're thinking about this wrong. We could take him with us. Late tonight, when everyone's asleep. We'll put him in the trunk of the car, and he'll be with us the whole time, until we find Brittany. He won't have a chance to—"

"*Hailey.*"

It was the exasperation in her voice, more than anything else, that shut me down. Serena didn't even sound angry anymore, just frustrated with my lack of logic. Of course it was a ridiculous plan. The long-term kidnapping of an adult male, one who was strong and crafty if not particularly smart . . . it would be a logistical nightmare. What were we going to do, drive to L.A. and go around looking for Brittany with Quentin in the trunk of the car? Ludicrous.

Yet something tickled the edge of my mind. *Riding in the trunk of the car.*

"Wait," I said.

"Wait for what?"

He's not just gonna let today go. He'll look for you.

"I have an idea," I said. "Go keep an eye on him. Don't, whatever you do, kill him. Quentin being alive is the key to everything."

"How?"

"Just go watch him. Let me think about this, and I'll tell you later."

After she left, I put my hands on the sink, arms braced wide, head down, thinking. It was a crazy idea. The odds were against it all working the way I hoped. But it was the best plan I had.

I used the toilet, then rubbed the sore spot on my shoulder again, where Serena had yanked me off Quentin. Then I emerged from the bathroom and looked at him. His face was reddened again; clearly he'd been fighting to get loose of his bonds, but he hadn't made any headway. I gave him an assessing look.

"Quentin," I said, "you want to know the difference between you and me? No, scratch that. If I started to list the differences, I'd have two problems: I wouldn't know where to start, and I wouldn't know where to stop."

Serena, sitting nearby, tilted her head, surprised at the brisk ease of my tone, after our hushed and frustrated planning session.

I went on, "Let me put this another way: You want to know the reason I'm not going to kill you? Other than morals?" I stepped closer and leaned over him, looking down into his dark, mutinous face. "I don't *care* that you're going to tip Brittany off. If she runs, so much the better. A moving target is easier to spot than one that stays still."

Then, to Serena, "Check the knots, make sure he can't get loose."

18

When we left, Serena and I smoked a cigarette each, sitting in her car.

"So now what?" she said.

"Now I call Joe Laska and have him send the cavalry, to let Quentin out of the closet."

"Let him *out*?" Serena said.

"The sooner the better."

Recognition dawned. "You don't think Quentin's going to call this girl," she said. "You think he's going to go to where she is."

"Yeah. Not really to protect her, but to be there when I show up. I know that to you and me it doesn't seem likely that I can find her with the information I have, and that's true, but look at it from Quentin's point of view. I wasn't supposed to figure out how Brittany passed herself off as me, but I did. I had no way of knowing where he lived, but somehow I turned up here. It's easy to start overestimating your enemy when they've scored a couple of victories off you. He'll believe I can find Brittany."

"So we're going to tail him."

"No. As soon as we're off the freeway, he'll spot a tail."

"Then what?"

This was going to be the hard part, getting Serena to accept this part of the plan. "I'm going to be in the trunk of his car the whole time."

Serena almost dropped her cigarette into her lap. "No. No way. That's just crazy. I'm not helping with this."

The truth was, I could almost carry out this plan by myself. When I'd left the house, I'd taken Quentin's keys. So I could open the trunk, get in, and hide myself as much as possible in the back. But I couldn't slam the trunk lid from the inside, not hard enough to make it latch.

"It's the only way," I said. "He's my only link to this woman. He'll go to her because he thinks he's chasing me there. My only way to find her is to go to the back of the line."

"I know, but we can follow him. You don't have to get in the fucking trunk of his car."

"It's the last place he'd look for me," I said. "There'll be a trunk release for when it's safe for me to get out, and if he opens the lid before that and sees me, I've got this," I said, showing the Browning.

"You don't even know he'll go down there."

"No, but there's a good chance," I said. "Think about it: If Brittany gets arrested, she'll implicate him as a co-conspirator, both before and after the fact. That can carry a sentence as stiff as the original offense, which in this case is murder." I let that sink in. "Quentin will tell Brittany that they need to kill me because the one thing that'll close the Eastman-Stepakoff case with a certainty is if I turn up dead. The confession by suicide—it's a classic."

"How would he get your handwriting on a confession note?"

"You're thinking way too elegant. Quentin's idea of sub-tlety will be to walk me into an abandoned building, stick a gun under my chin, pull the trigger, and spray-paint the words *I'm sorry* on the wall." Then I said, "Besides, he said he was going to kill me. He doesn't mean someday years from now, when I've dropped my guard. He's not a chess grand master. He wants to settle accounts now." Then I played my trump card: "*¿Cómo vivimos?*"

She stared straight ahead, through the windshield.

"Serena. *¿Cómo vivimos?*"

"*Ad limina fortunarum,*" she said, capitulating, under-scoring her frustration by grinding her cigarette harder than necessary into the pullout ashtray.

It was our old affirmation, in Spanish and Latin. *How do we live? To the limits of our fate.*

Then Serena blinked, and for a moment her face looked so sad I thought she might cry. Now, that really was crazy.

She shook it off and said, "What if he flies?"

"He'll drive. He'll need a car once he gets down there." I didn't add that he wouldn't rent a car, either, because he wouldn't want to leave telltale blood or hairs in the trunk of a rental car.

"How's he going to drive if we've got his car keys?"

"Hopefully he's got a spare to the car," I said. "But just in case, you need to tiptoe back and drop the keys somewhere near his front door."

"Like we dropped them by accident?"

"Yeah. He won't figure it out. The guy's not the world's deepest thinker, like I said."

This part of the plan would have been easier if I were dealing with Joe Laska. I wouldn't have to wonder if Laska had a spare key to his car. He would, and he'd remember exactly where he kept it. Quentin couldn't be counted on to be that organized.

I held the smoke from the last of my cigarette in my lungs, then exhaled and squashed it in the ashtray. Then I took out Quentin's cell phone. I'd taken it from his house because it would be useful to read whatever text messages Brittany might send him, at least until he got in touch with her and told her not to use that phone number anymore.

"Call that Laska guy," Serena said. "I'm going to walk over to the car, make sure there's a release in the trunk. Give me the keys."

When she'd gone, I took out Quentin's phone, scrolled to Joe Laska's number, pressed "Options," pressed "Call Number." He picked up on the third ring. "What's going on?" he said.

"This isn't Quentin. It's Hailey Cain," I said.

"Last year's girl," Laska said, his voice mild and unsurprised. "What can I do for you?"

"Your man Corelli, the fellatio enthusiast, is in a closet in his apartment, tied up. I don't think he's going to get free by himself, so you'd better send someone to help him."

"Your resourcefulness never fails to amaze me."

"I'd love to play the banter-between-adversaries game," I said, "but I'm short on time. Let me ask you one thing: Last year did Quentin keep my finger as a trophy?"

"What?" he said. "No, I dropped the finger down a sewer grate, because it would have been just like Quentin to keep it, even though it linked him to a violent felony."

"Why do you even keep that guy on the payroll? He's a loose cannon, and I've punked him twice now."

"Maybe you should have killed him."

"Nice talk, especially from his friend and employer."

"Let's just say employer," Laska said. "Quentin's a bad guy to have angry with you, especially if you're a woman. That's all I'm saying."

"Why do you care what happens to me?"

"I don't."

Serena betrayed her nerves only by lighting up her second cigarette in five minutes as she and I crossed the street. Otherwise her face was set, cool. I didn't have to catch my reflection anywhere to know that mine was, too.

"We've gotta do this fast and casual," I said. "Once we've started, don't scope around for anyone who could see us. Be as casual as if you were unloading groceries from the trunk. Don't act guilty."

"I know," she said, stepping up onto the sidewalk.

It would have been much better if Quentin kept his car in a garage, but at least the long side driveway, shielded by two-story buildings on each flank, was nearly as good as a carport.

We walked down the alley and reached the car.

"What if there's already a body in there?" Serena asked, and we both started laughing.

"Shut up," I said. "Turn around, look around real casually. You see anyone?"

So far it hadn't really mattered if one of Quentin's neighbors saw us; all they would have seen were two young women entering and leaving Mr. Corelli's place. But if anyone saw me climbing into the trunk of his car and Serena closing it, that'd be too strange to ignore.

I slid the key into the lock and opened the trunk, looked

underneath for a release, and saw it, glow-in-the-dark yellow-white plastic tag on a cord. Good.

Beyond that was a mostly clean space, except for a tangle of jumper cables, a gallon of antifreeze, and a set of golf clubs.

"Golf clubs?" Serena said, echoing my own thought: *Quentin Corelli golfs?*

I said, "Maybe he's on the executive track for thugs." Then, "Come on, we'd better do this before someone comes along."

She lifted out the golf clubs and pushed the jumper cables to the side. Gingerly I climbed in and edged all the way to the back, where the body of the car, not the trunk lid, overhung the storage space. It was a generous, deep trunk. Thank God not every car maker in America went for fuel economy. I'd slid Quentin's cell phone into my pocket, switched off, and now I took out the Browning, to hold it in front of me. Quentin wouldn't pack elaborately—he wasn't going on vacation—so I hoped that what little he took with him he'd throw into the cabin space of the car. If he did open the trunk, I was hoping he'd just toss his bag in without really looking, the way an angry and distracted guy would.

If those two plans failed, though, I'd have only a short time in which to defend myself. I needed the gun ready.

"Come on," I told Serena. "Cover me up."

She leaned in, holding the blanket she'd taken from her own car in her hands, then stopped. She said, "I don't like doing this, as if you're a body already. It feels like seeing the future."

I knew that Serena believed in past lives; she had never suggested before that she believed in premonitions. I made light of it. "Think about him," I said. "Think how stupid he's gonna look, racing down the freeway to catch someone who's only four feet away."

She nodded, but not with a lot of conviction.

"I'll be fine," I said.

She arranged the dark brown blanket around me, and then I felt her push the bag of golf clubs back against me, leaving space for Quentin to easily toss in a bag. Then she said, "*Tú estás en mi corazón*, Insula."

"*Semper in corde meo*," I said.

Serena closed the lid, and I flinched as the pressure differential pushed against my eardrums.

19

This is your life: You were your parents' only child, the light of your father's world before he died much too young. You wanted to honor his memory, and to do so ran a gauntlet of challenges to get into one of the nation's most elite institutions, the United States Military Academy. You'd spent the first eighteen years of your life mostly in places where trash blew up against fences and no one cared, so you decided that you'd live the rest only in the cleanest, brightest places, with people who made you better just to be around them.

And now, at not yet twenty-five years old, this is you: in the trunk of a car with an unregistered gun in your hands.

When you get where you're going, someone might try to kill you. Or you might have to kill someone.

I don't know where I was when I started thinking about these things. Soledad maybe, King City. The confinement was making me stiff, sore, hungry, and increasingly reflective. That wasn't a label you could often hang on me, but being in the dark, alone, with absolutely no distractions, that probably counts as special circumstances.

Things had worked out about as I'd hoped. I'd been in the trunk a little over an hour when I'd heard Quentin's fast, angry footsteps on the pavement. He'd opened and slammed a passenger-side door—throwing in his bag, I assumed—and then the driver's-side door. He did not open the trunk. My hands, on the Browning, had relaxed.

As the time wore on, I tried to imagine everyone I knew, where they were and what they were doing. Serena was easiest: She was on the road, maybe a little ahead of us. She'd had to return to the hotel for our things, but then Quentin had had to wait for whoever Laska sent to come and untie him, and then he'd had to throw at least a few things into a bag for his trip, so I was guessing Serena had gotten on the road a bit ahead of us. CJ was hardest: Was he still in Africa, or had he come back to the States by now? Was he alone or with friends? I couldn't know.

My mother, Julianne, was living in San Diego now. With a man; there's always a man. She and I hadn't been in contact for months. Not an estrangement per se. Just very little in common.

My real family, as I sometimes thought of them, were CJ's parents, sister, and brothers. Julianne and I had moved in with her sister Angeline and brother-in-law Porter, and their big, ramshackle house outside Lompoc was for me, after a lifetime of Army posts, my first real family home, with a sprawling yard and the smell of baking clinging to the kitchen wallpaper and arguments about who was spending too much time in the bathroom.

Angeline and Porter had since sold that place and were living in Washoe County in Nevada. Porter was retired, though Angeline, a homemaker, was still earning extra money the way she always had, giving piano lessons and selling flowers from her garden at a farmers' market. Their children, the brood of four they'd transplanted from West Virginia, had all stayed behind in Southern California. Moira, their daughter, was a teacher now. Both Constantine and Virgil, CJ's brothers, had inherited their father's gift with machines and worked as mechanics.

Magnus Ford was probably at work, among the people who knew his face and found the sight of the Shadow Man unexceptional.

That brought me to Joel Kelleher. Was he still in San Francisco or back in Los Angeles already? Or en route? He could be driving on the 101 like Quentin and Serena, or he could be overhead, studying his notes and diagrams on a short flight back to Los Angeles.

I'd screwed up with him. He'd revealed a bit of himself to me—the thing he'd said about fear, about feeling like the only one who was hiding it. Even though it was just the Ambien that had brought his defenses down, I felt like I'd mangled my answer, that generic, useless line about everyone feeling afraid sometimes. I wished I'd said something better, though I wasn't sure exactly what that would have been.

Joel probably would have envied me my severely blunted capacity for fear; Serena had already implied that she did. And as insensitive as their attitude might have seemed—I mean, my lack of fear came at a very high price, which I would pay sometime in the not-too-far-off future—I understood it. Because who really wanted to feel afraid? Who, being freed from fear, would deliberately re-create its smothering demands? A severely compromised ability to feel fear had been of obvious advantage when I'd been a bike messenger in San Francisco, where couriers are paid on commission, and speed and traffic-law breaking mean more runs a day and higher tips from satisfied customers.

And later, in the gang life? Don't get me started.

But deep down, part of me envied Serena, and now Joel, too. People like them, who felt fear and acted anyway, they could know they were brave. I couldn't say the same.

20

Another liability that comes from not feeling fear properly: It's too easy to fall asleep when no sane person would. Like in the trunk of a car.

Now I'd lost what little sense of time, and therefore distance, I'd had. I'd come fully awake with a memory of hearing and feeling the car door slam, shaking the sedan's body. The engine was off, and Quentin's footsteps were receding outside. I groped for the Browning in the darkness; it had slipped from my hands. Then I raised my head and tried to listen for the sounds around me.

Was this a pit stop, or had we arrived? If it was the former, I couldn't afford to open the trunk. People might see me, among them Quentin, if he was merely paying a gas-station clerk in one of those glass booths. And once I opened the trunk, that was it. I couldn't simply flag down a passerby to do what Serena had done, close the trunk for me. *Excuse me, sir, could you just give me a hand with this? Thanks, that's perfect.*

I slid my hand into my pocket and delicately withdrew Quentin's cell phone, brought it to life. The screen threw off its greenish light, and then the digital display came on. The time was three minutes to nine P.M.

I ran the numbers. We'd left San Francisco a little after three, and if Quentin had driven around eighty miles an hour—he was probably a leadfoot—the timeline worked out. I was inclined to think we'd arrived in Los Angeles.

After perhaps ten minutes of listening and hearing nothing, I pushed the blanket off and edged toward the front of the trunk, my gun still in one hand. My neck was so stiff that I knew when I rolled it, it would crackle like broken glass. This would be a very bad time for Quentin to catch me. After lying still in a cramped space for nearly six hours, I didn't think I could run at all; I'd hardly be able to walk. But I reached out in the dark, found the trunk release, and pulled. There was a dull metal popping sound as the trunk gave way and the interior light came on. Shit. If the car was parked facing the building where Quentin was, and he looked out the window . . . I cupped my free hand over the little clear glass bulb. In the dimness that followed, I saw a sliver of dark blue ambience, the nighttime world outside.

Go on and do this.

I pushed the trunk lid up farther, raised myself up and out, and dropped to the concrete below, crouching so that the body of the car sheltered me.

Quentin's car was parked in the driveway of a one-story house on a quiet residential street. There was a large shade tree overhanging the lawn and a light glowing behind one large window. The other homes on the street were dark, their occupants likely asleep.

I scanned the wider area, getting my bearings. We were in the hills somewhere; I could see their black silhouette above the roofline across the street. While this was clearly a quiet suburban area, there was enough diversity in the sizes and shapes of the houses that I sensed this was an older neighborhood—the homes didn't have the high-end uniformity of a luxury subdivision. There were paved sidewalks along the street, but no streetlights. The air was faintly scented with bougainvillea.

I wanted to go closer to the house, all the way up to the window. Although the shutters behind the glass were closed, at point-blank range there'd be narrow gaps that would provide me a glimpse of the people inside. I was maybe twenty yards away from the woman who'd ruined my name. I wanted pretty badly to see her.

But I couldn't afford it. There were ornamental shrubs in front of every window, and they'd rustle if I pushed them aside to get up close. Under normal circumstances the inhabitants of a house might not be expected to hear it. When most people go into their houses, the world outside becomes a distant abstraction; they're watching TV, talking to family, oblivious to anything else. But if Brittany was inside, with Quentin, both of them were aware of the possibility that I'd show up. That was the whole reason behind Quentin's arrival. They'd be more alert than most people to stray noises.

Would the backyard afford a better view? Possibly. A lot of people kept the windows on their backyard open at night when they closed the blinds in front. But again that meant navigating unknown territory. Was there a dog? More bushes to shove through? Better not to risk it.

I wasn't scared, but I was careful. What was the point of the hours I'd just spent cooped up in Quentin's trunk if I recklessly got myself caught? I needed to confirm that Brittany was here and then tell Ford where she was.

And then what? It wasn't enough for an arrest that I'd seen a woman who could pass for me, associating with the guy who only I knew had stolen my gun. Ford would need more.

Balked, I paced the edge of the property. There was a tall tree in the yard, with wide-spreading branches, and at the boundary line was an oversize oleander bush, or maybe two that had grown together in a shaggy mass. I knew about oleander bushes; they were everywhere in California, famous for being fabulously poisonous but also extremely popular as decorative bushes. When we were kids, CJ and I used to hide ourselves in the mostly hollow center of the oleander on his parents' property, hanging out in the shade and privacy it gave us. This bush, now, might serve a similar purpose, a hiding place where I could watch the people close by.

While I was considering all this, the light in the living-room window went out.

I walked over to the mailbox and opened it. But it was empty. I'd thought if the house's residents hadn't collected their mail, I'd at least have a name to give Ford, maybe one he could link to Brittany's past.

Just then the front yard was bathed in light from the floodlight over the garage door, and I sprinted for the shelter of the oleander bush. I pushed my way in through the dense branches and crouched down, my hand resting on my hol-stered gun.

". . . must've just slid down behind a seat or something," Quentin's voice said. Under his words I heard the clopping of hard-heeled shoes.

He came into view first, moving quickly down the front walk to his parked car. He unlocked the passenger side and stuck his head, then half his body, inside. Languidly, a second figure moved into my narrow field of view. She was shorter than me, maybe five-four, and slighter. Her blond hair, pulled up into a high ponytail, was a brighter, paler shade than mine. I couldn't see her face. She was wearing a silk robe that in the moonlight looked jade green, over pointed-toe cowboy boots. While Quentin poked around for a lost item in his car, she stood at the end of the driveway looking up at the stars.

I leaned forward as much as I dared behind the protec-tive screen of branches. This was her; I wanted to drink in the sight as though I could understand her just by seeing her face.

She had fine bones, eyes more almond-shaped than mine. *Hotter than you,* Quentin had said, and I had to say he was right. But I could see where someone would look from her to my old driver's license photo without saying, *Hey, this isn't you.*

Quentin pulled out and slammed the door.

"Got it?" she said, turning.

She looked so *normal.* I'd expected to see something in her face, a cool vacancy that said sociopath. There was nothing like that.

Quentin was standing with his hands on his hips. "Fuck me," he muttered.

"It wasn't under the seat?" Brittany said. "You think you left it up north?"

"Maybe. Or maybe she's got it."

He was talking about his cell phone, I realized.

"What would she do with it?" Brittany asked him.

He shook his head. "I'm not sure, but she already used it to scam you—"

"That's not my fault! I couldn't have known what was going on! She said she was someone in your boss's office!"

"Calling from my cell?"

"Well . . . I . . . ."

"It's okay, babe," Quentin said. "Maybe I just left it up north." I doubted he really thought so, but he was tired of arguing with Brittany. He changed the subject. "You know what I just thought of? We gotta move this car. She might know what I'm driving. If she sees this parked outside the house, it'll scare her off."

"Good," the girl said.

"No, not good. You know why."

"I don't want—"

"If she doesn't try to approach you, there's no point in me having come here in the first place," Quentin said, putting his hands on her shoulders. "We talked about this."

Then he leaned in and kissed her, and his hand cupped her left breast.

She giggled. "That's kinky, *Cousin* Quentin. Brian wouldn't like it."

His response, against her neck, was unintelligible, but she giggled again and then turned and went back inside.

I wondered how Quentin had explained his developing bruises to her, if he'd admitted I'd given them to him or he'd told her it was unrelated, a bar fight with a guy. A story that didn't compromise his ego.

Quentin went around to the driver's side of the car, got in, and started the engine. I shifted position again, pulling back. I didn't want to be visible if headlights splashed over my hiding place.

It would have been nice if Quentin had called her by name, but there was no doubt in my mind that the young woman in the driveway was Brittany Mercier. It seemed likely that the house belonged to an ex-boyfriend—that was what I'd taken the "Cousin Quentin" remark to mean, that he was posing as family in order to not raise the possessive hackles of their host.

Still, none of this was anything I could adequately support in another call with Ford. *She looks the part,* I'd say, *and she's hanging out with the guy who confessed to selling my ID and gun.*

Actually, that second part—the whole story that Quentin had told me in his apartment—was progress worth reporting to Ford. That was just another reason to get into town. I needed a pay phone.

Quentin returned, his feet tapping soft but fast on the sidewalk. He paused a moment in front of the house, looking around at the shadows, then went inside.

Still under the shelter of the oleander bush, I pulled out Quentin's cell phone. It was time to call Serena, to get a ride into town and regroup. I didn't want to leave Brittany alone for long, but I needed to eat, maybe to get an hour or two of sleep. Serena, if she'd left San Francisco a little before Quentin, should already be home. The timing was perfect for her to come by and pick me up.

First, though, I had to figure out where I was. I got to my feet and emerged from the bush. My legs were unsteady again; it was a surprise that I'd been able to run earlier, when I'd been surprised by the driveway floodlight. Slowly I walked out to the street; it took several minutes of crossing and recrossing the street, checking mailboxes, before I found one with mail in it. I was in Woodland Hills, the western reaches of L.A. County.

I dialed Serena's number. Instead of ringing, her cell went straight into her recorded message: *"It's me, leave a message and I'll call you back."*

She used neither her Christian name nor her street name in her message; some people in her life didn't know the first, while others were ignorant of the second. A terse greeting was the safest kind.

I left her a similarly vague message: "Hey, it's me. I'm safe and watching a house in Woodland Hills. She's here, I saw her. Call me as soon as you can. I'm gonna need help."

I disconnected the call and stood still for a moment, thinking. It wasn't like Serena to have her cell off during waking hours. If she was back in town and had fallen into exhausted sleep, I wouldn't hear from her until well into daylight hours, by which time I'd need to be here, watching the house.

This was more than a logistical problem. Why would Serena turn off her phone? She'd been so worried about me when I'd told her about the trunk-of-the-car plan. Had she, in the past six hours, somehow become cavalier about whether I'd made it to L.A. alive?

Whatever the reason for her silence, just waiting for her to call me back wasn't much of a plan. I didn't merely need stuff brought up from town—though food was becoming urgent—I needed to go *into* town, in order to ride the Aprilia back. Without it I'd be stuck here if Brittany and Quentin decided to move somewhere else tomorrow. It hadn't sounded like they were going to, but you never could tell. Maybe they would even decide to move Brittany someplace more public and visible, in hopes that I'd track her more easily. According to the conversation they'd had, Brittany wasn't keen on being used as bait, but she was allowing it.

If they went somewhere else, I'd have to be ready to tail them, which meant I'd need my bike. Quentin had never seen it, which was good. If I myself had to stay out of his sight, the Aprilia could easily be parked on the street outside a neighbor's place without drawing suspicion.

Now I just needed to get down to where it was.

With long strides I hiked up to the top of the street. The cross street ran along the top of the hill, and it was wide and broad. Turning back, I could see down into the valley and the lights of town and, running through it, the glowing white vein that was the 101. A vague sense of familiarity tickled me, and I went to look at the street sign. I was on Mulholland Drive. *I'll be damned,* I thought. I'd heard of it all my life and never driven it, and now here I was, standing on it, strictly by accident.

My cell phone remained silent. I was tempted to call Serena again, because I had nothing else to do, but it had only been five minutes. Calling so soon was pointless.

Who else was there? I wouldn't drag CJ into this. Nor Tess. Things had gotten too serious.

Resigned, I began to walk toward town. Every time headlights approached, I turned back and stuck out my thumb, hopefully.

•••

Half an hour later, I was at a pay phone outside the glowing windows of an all-night coin-op laundry. No one had picked me up hitchhiking on Mulholland, so I'd walked all the way down into town. Serena still wasn't answering her phone. But when I saw the pay phone, I decided it was time to update Ford on what was going on.

I dialed his cell number. Somehow I never doubted he'd pick up. I imagined him working late at headquarters, his the lone lighted cubicle in an otherwise dim warren of empty desks.

"Ford."

"It's me."

"Hailey," he said. "When do you sleep?"

"I'll sleep when she's in a cell."

"She? The other Hailey?"

"I found her. I've seen her."

"Tell me," he said.

I explained what I'd learned: Brittany's full name, the address where she was staying, and the most salient parts of the story of how she came to kill Greg Stepakoff and V. K. Eastman.

"You got all this from her partner in crime, Corelli?" Ford said.

"Yeah."

"Whom you identified and found how?"

"I had a pretty good idea that it was him who stole the gun," I told him. "After that it was just a matter of getting his current address up north and us having a little meeting of the minds."

"I see. And nothing he said might have been bullshit to get you going the wrong direction?"

"He was pretty inspired to tell the truth."

Long pause after that. I expected Ford to comment, inquire further about my methods, but he didn't.

Finally I said, "How about a little quid pro quo? What's going on behind precinct doors?"

He said, "You don't realize how much quid you've been getting from me already."

Actually, I did, but I couldn't let on that I knew about Joel's fact-finding mission up north. I said, "I just keep hoping that something will come out that tends to exonerate me."

Another pause, this one shorter, and then Ford said, "The SFPD had an interesting piece of information about a city-college newspaper up there."

"The one Brittany enrolled at in order to get a student ID?"

"Did Corelli tell you that?" Ford said. "Then I guess he wasn't jerking you around. The college has a weekly newspaper, and the kids on the staff just came back from spring break and wanted to do a story on this notorious killer being in their student body. They requested her ID photo from the administration offices, and the woman who pulled it for them thought, 'Hey, this doesn't look like the pictures on the news.' "

I felt myself smile, genuinely, for the first time in days.

Ford said, "This hasn't been made public yet. Fortunately the administration staffer called us. Because the student-newspaper kids wouldn't have—it's a freedom-of-information issue for them. A fed went over to their offices and rattled his saber pretty hard for them to sit on the photo, as well as the news about the discrepancy. They didn't like it, but we're hoping they will."

"Because you don't want to spook her."

"Yeah. Hailey, where are you?"

"Close to the finish," I said, and hung up.

21

By midnight I was crossing the L.A. River in a minivan, warm wind lightly battering me from an open rear window. My traveling companions, two of whom were asleep in the cargo area in the back, were UC Santa Cruz students, road-tripping on their spring break. College students are about the only drivers brave enough, or naive enough, to still pick up hitchhikers. If it weren't for them, I would still have been standing at the base of an on-ramp in Woodland Hills. After calling Serena again and getting no answer, I'd stood at the foot of the freeway on-ramp for twenty-five minutes, the breeze from the passing cars tugging at my hair, as one after another drove by without stopping.

Until these kids and their old Toyota Previa. They'd pulled over and rolled open the side door, waved me inside, asked me where I was going, and promised to take me all the way to East Los Angeles: "We're not on a schedule, it's cool."

But about five minutes after we crossed the river, the driver, a guy with pale blond hair and a short beard, looked around at his surroundings, then turned to address me in the backseat, saying politely, "Listen, I think this is getting a little bit out of our way."

I understood immediately what he was saying. He'd recognized what kind of area I was leading them into. He understood it might not be the best place for a van full of white kids after dark.

"That's totally all right," I said. "You can just let me out at the corner, there, where it's well lit."

He slowed and pulled to the curb but then turned to face me, his pale blue eyes concerned. "Are you sure this is where you want to be?"

"Yeah," I said. "I'm very familiar with the area, and I don't have far to go. I promise."

I thanked them all before rolling open the side door and jumping down.

"Good luck!" the girl in the passenger seat called after me.

God knew I'd need that. These were the small hours of a Wednesday morning, which meant the streets were mostly quiet, but any predators who were out tonight were likely to be serious, dedicated ones, and I had no crowd to get lost in, no one else around me to draw their fire. I might as well have been illuminated by a personal spotlight. I did, however, have the Browning concealed at my back.

I stood for a moment outside the darkened windows of a closed mini–grocery store, tempted to check my cell phone for a message from Serena. But I'd had the phone on me this whole time, switched on since I'd called her from Mulholland Drive. I would have heard it ring. *Face it, she hasn't called.*

I began walking, past darkened storefronts, in and out of pools of apricot streetlight. A homeless woman pushed a rattling shopping cart across the street and disappeared down a narrow side lane. The breeze rustled the dried flowers of a sidewalk *descanso,* a memorial for a slain neighborhood teenager, maybe a gangbanger, maybe the random victim of stray gunfire.

I'd covered about half the distance to Thirteenth Street and Diana's building when a police car rounded a corner and turned in my direction, facing me head-on. There was nothing I could have done to protect myself. The sight of it had been blocked by the bulk of a large apartment complex, and it had been moving so slowly that there was barely any engine noise to hear. It was crawling, in that quiet, crocodile-predatory way police do when they're looking for trouble.

I jammed my hands into my pockets protectively but kept walking. To abruptly change direction would have been a sign of guilt that would have immediately piqued their interest. Just ten yards ahead of me was an alley opening. I only had to make that. I walked a little faster, the squad car still crawling toward me. Five yards, three, two . . . I turned sharply right and headed down the alley.

Behind me I heard the siren make a single whoop, the sign that they wanted a pedestrian's attention.

I ducked behind a garbage Dumpster and quickly pulled the gun from under my jacket. This could be an innocent lecture about how dangerous it was for me to be walking here after midnight. But if it wasn't, if they tried to search me, I didn't need to be caught with a gun.

With the safety on, I dropped the Browning to the pavement and kicked it under the Dumpster. From the alley's opening, I heard the slamming of a car door, and cherry-colored lights flickered off the building walls. My hands visible in front of me, I stepped out to face the officer standing at the alley's mouth. He was young, Hispanic, very short-haired, rigid-postured. I raised a hand to above my eyes as though facing a bright light and said, "Is there a problem, sir?"

He lifted his chin, as if about to address me, and stepped forward. Then his dark eyes grew fractionally wider and his hand went to his holster, unsnapping it. He said, "Stay right there. Put your hands up. Do not move."

He'd recognized me. Double zero. Nobody wins.

I turned and bolted for the chain-link fence that cut off the end of the alley.

"I said, *don't move!*"

I hit the fence at a run, hands grabbing for the top rail. My feet were much too big to get a hold in the links of the fencing, so I was mostly hoping to grab-and-vault, using momentum. With my left foot braced on the post, I swung my right leg up to the top.

Behind me the cop fired. Sparks flew off the fence where the slug struck it.

He's actually using deadly force. Holy shit, I have gone platinum in the worst possible way.

I jumped from the fence down into the vacant brown-field beyond it, hearing a second gunshot behind me. I started running. His partner might be out of the car by now and coming around to intercept me, and I had no way of knowing which way he'd go—around the block from the north or the south. Choosing at random, I veered south, toward a line of thin trees at the lot's edge, the best cover available to me. But I didn't stop once I was there. I kept running, across the next street and down a side street after that. Over the sound of my own feet slapping the pavement and my own rapid breathing, I couldn't hear the sound of anyone running behind me, if there was anyone.

I halted and looked around. Parked at the curb was a lunch truck, advertising TACOS BURRITOS HORCHATAS, and I ducked behind it, positioning myself by one of the wheels so even my feet wouldn't show.

Then I heard the purr of an engine, so low it was obviously the engine of a slowly cruising car.

I dropped to the sidewalk and, making myself as small and flat as possible on my stomach, eased over the curb's edge and under the truck, crawling sideways, centering myself so my feet weren't too close to the truck's rear end nor my head to the front.

The squad car inched past, visible to me only by its tires. I lay on my stomach, heels of my hands pressed against the rough pavement, face turned to the side, the smell of axle grease strong in my nostrils. When the cruiser was past, I resisted the urge to stay where I was safe and began inching out from under the truck. There were still about six blocks between me and the safety of Diana's place, and the sooner I got going, the better. Pretty soon those six blocks were going to be so thick with police presence I wasn't going to be able to move at all.

Standing and flipping the hood of my jacket up over my hair, I started out at a quick pace, a walk that was nearly a jog, keeping my face and eyes downcast.

"*Órale*, where you going in this neighborhood?" a female voice purred. "You lost, *turista* girl? You need directions?"

I'd heard rhetorical questions like those before. The helpfulness was insincere. It was the prelude to a jacking.

I also recognized the voice as that of Trippy, Serena's scorned lieutenant.

She stepped out from the shadows and under a streetlight, tall, slim, strong. Her hair was blonder than I remembered—she'd lightened it—and her eyes were gleaming in anticipation of easy prey. When she saw my face, her supercilious expression melted into disbelief. "You've got to be fucking kidding me."

My hand went for the small of my back and skated over empty space where the gun had been until five minutes earlier, when I'd kicked it under the Dumpster. Trippy saw my action and smiled happily. Then she charged forward and knocked me off my feet. My back hit the asphalt, but not hard enough to knock the wind out of me. I tried to reach up and grab her throat, but she had the advantage in position, and she straddled me, pinning my arms with her legs. Whatever her character flaws, Trippy was the veteran of more than a few fights.

"*Bitch*," she spit. She cocked her fist and punched me in the face, hard enough to cause my vision to spark. "I can't believe you're stupid enough to come here. You think you're so tough, like there's no place you can't go." She threw another bomb. "You're in the wrong place, *rubia*. You *been* in the wrong place since you left your trailer park."

Another punch. Blood began trickling from my nose.

She said, "When Warchild's gone, I'm going to run the sucias. I'll own all these streets. You're not going to stop me."

She reached into her shirt and pulled out something that glinted in the streetlight. A butterfly knife, just her style, and she flipped it expertly open.

Pulling the last of my strength together, I wrested my right arm free from under her leg and smashed the heel of my hand into her face. The knife, already coming down, went off course; I heard it scrape the pavement next to my face. She was unbalanced now, and I pulled my other arm free. Capitalizing while she was still surprised, I grabbed her head with both hands and pulled it down while I brought my forehead up, smashing the hardest, least vulnerable part of my skull into her nose. Trippy yelled and fell to the side, cradling her face in her hands. I scrambled to my feet, quickly looking around for police, or anyone else who might have been drawn to the spectacle of our fight.

Sharp pain bloomed in my right foot, and I yelped aloud, then looked down.

Oh, hell no.

In my one moment of distraction, despite her own injury, Trippy had planted the knife in my foot, through the top, as if trying to pin it to the ground.

She wrenched the knife out for a second strike, swaying to her knees, but I grabbed her hair and yanked her off balance. It was a clumsy move, because I was standing on one leg like a flamingo. But she fell back, the knife clattering to the pavement. I kicked it out of her range with my injured foot, then dropped down to straddle her the way she had me, tightening my hands around her throat.

Her face turned red, the part of it that wasn't already masked with blood from her nose. Her golden brown eyes narrowed, even though I wasn't choking her hard enough to really cut off her air supply, just enough to make her pay attention.

"Trippy," I said. Then, "No, *Luisa*. Let's get a couple of things on the record. One, I've never lived in a trailer park. Ever. Two, you're never going to own this neighborhood. Warchild doesn't own it, either. Banks and moneylenders do.

Three, some people have real problems, and tonight I'm one of them. So if you come after me, when I let you go, I'm going to put your own knife in one of your kidneys. Got it?" I eased up on her throat a little.

"*Bitch,*" she said. "I'm going to kill you someday."

"But not today," I said as I drew back my fist and punched her. Not out of anger, just to stun her. I understood now that her hatred didn't allow for reason, that if she were fully conscious, she would have to come after me, even unarmed.

I let go of her, and she fell back to the pavement, her eyes half closed.

I could feel my injured right foot throbbing in time with my heartbeat, and the sock was already damp with blood. But there was no time to check out the extent of the injury.

I picked up Trippy's knife, staggered to my feet, and limped off into the shadows.

22

"**I** can't believe this. I've never seen so many cops in this neighborhood, and that's saying something."

Diana was standing at her kitchen window. I was sitting in a chair I'd pulled away from the kitchen table, with my bloody foot poised over a stainless-steel mixing bowl half full of reddened water. Diana didn't have a first-aid kit, so I was doing the best I could with soap, water, and clean towels.

I'd made it here by dodging from shadow to shadow, running in a kind of uneven lope because of my wounded right foot, changing course and hiding at the sight of police cars, and avoiding even the most harmless-looking civilians. By the time I was standing at the intercom box in the entry cavern of Diana's building, my boot felt as soaked inside as if I'd walked through standing water.

I'd buzzed her apartment and said, "It's Insula. I need to come up."

When I'd reached her place and she let me in, I'd asked first, "Is Warchild here?"

"No."

"Has she been here?"

"No."

Damn. "Okay. I'm going to need a couple of things from you, starting with a first-aid kit."

"I don't think I have one," she'd said. "I have Band-Aids."

"We're a little past that," I'd said. "How about soap and water and clean towels?"

The injury was a puncture wound, potentially more serious than a surface cut that ran horizontally, but it had stopped bleeding, which told me that Trippy had missed the bigger blood vessels. If the knife blade had been clean, infection wasn't a big threat. I dried the top of my foot with another towel, then elevated it onto the seat of the other kitchen chair. Its throbbing had finally abated. Rather, it had shifted to my head, which was starting to ache.

Diana turned from the window. She wore only a T-shirt and pajama bottoms; I'd clearly woken her. "Are all the cops for you?"

"Sure are."

"Damn," she said. Then, "Everyone's been talking about you. They're saying you're making the cops look like *pendejos* because they haven't caught you yet."

Trust the people of Serena's neighborhood to ignore the question of whether I'd killed an old lady and instead focus on the high-stakes hide-and-seek game I was playing with the police.

"Well, they almost did tonight," I said. "If you'll fix me something to eat, I'll tell you about it."

She went to the cupboard and looked over the contents. "What kind of food do you want?"

"Any kind, but a lot of it. I haven't eaten in a while."

While Diana worked, I told her about San Francisco and how I'd ridden down here in the trunk of Quentin Corelli's car—"For real?" she said, amazed—and then how I'd gotten here, including my brush with the cops and the fight with Trippy.

"So what're you going to do?" she said, setting a plate in front of me, laden with warmed tortillas, scrambled eggs, and refried beans. "You can't go back out there, with all those cops looking for you." She reached up into the cupboard again and brought down a tall drinking glass.

"I have to," I said.

"Because of that girl, the one who was pretending to be you?"

"Yeah."

I took a bite of eggs, and suddenly the emptiness in my stomach sharpened to a pitch that was almost painful. The truth was, I'd been hungry for a long time, but the pangs were first suppressed by several shots of raw adrenaline and later overridden by the pain in my injured foot.

Diana opened the refrigerator and reached for a pitcher filled with brightly colored fruit punch. I swallowed quickly in order to say, "No, milk instead."

She glanced at me, eyebrows raised in surprise. Serena's girls lived on sugary drinks, and they largely considered milk undrinkable by itself. The quart in Diana's refrigerator was probably just for Serena's coffee. But I needed protein, ballast for the long day that was coming. I didn't know when I was going to be able to eat again.

She brought the glass to the table. Up close, I could see that her fingernails were painted magenta with a diagonal slash of gold on each, an elaborate treatment that didn't go with her simple T-shirt and pajama bottoms.

Between me and my injured foot, both her kitchen chairs were occupied, and I was too distracted by competing needs—hunger, tiredness, the pain in my foot—to be polite and surrender one. Diana lifted herself up to sit on the kitchen counter, and from there she watched in silence as I ate.

When the worst of the hunger pangs were satisfied, I made myself lean back and slow down. I took the bottle of pills out of my jacket and popped the lid off with my thumbnail, then shook out a pair of Advil and washed them down with milk. My headache hadn't gotten any worse, but it wasn't going anywhere, either. Neither was the ache in my foot.

"So what happens next?" Diana said. "I mean, what do you need from me?"

"Do you know how to ride a motorcycle?"

"Yeah."

"Good. I need you to go get my Aprilia from Chato's shop."

"Aprilia," she repeated. "That's a kind of bike?"

"Yeah."

"It's French?"

"Italian." I tore a long strip off one of the tortillas and began rolling it up. "Do I need to call Chato and tell him you're coming and that he should give the bike to you?"

"No, he'll do it. He knows that anything coming from me is like it's coming from Warchild."

I stopped with the tortilla just short of my mouth. "Really?" I said. "Why is that?" Diana hadn't been around that long and hadn't even been made a sucia yet. Why should she have status in Trece?

There was a moment's pause, and then she said, "Warchild's my *tía*."

"Your aunt?" For a moment the chronology didn't seem to work out, but then, Serena's brothers were all older than her. I tried to remember the name of the oldest and could only come up with his moniker. "Droopy's your father?"

She nodded.

"Serena didn't tell me any of this," I said, perplexed. I remembered clearly Serena's words: *my new girl . . . a lot of potential.* Nothing about the family tie.

"She doesn't want you to think less of her," Diana said.

"For having family?"

"For making me a sucia," she explained. "I want it. I brought it up first. But she feels like you wouldn't approve."

I remembered Serena's irritation when I'd suggested that she steer Diana onto a better path than gang life. "Maybe," I said slowly, "but it's not like her to hide things or act guilty. She's Warchild. There's nobody above her in the sucias. Hell, right now there's no one above her in Trece."

"But this is you," Diana said. "She wants you to think well of her. Hardly anyone's opinion matters to her, but yours does. And maybe she thought that if you knew I was her niece, you wouldn't fight me for my initiation." She looked concerned. "You will, won't you?"

I sighed. "Let's worry about that when the time comes. I've got a lot on my hands right now other than sucia business."

"I'm sorry," she said, her voice full of respectful contrition.

"It's okay," I said. "You're helping me a lot here. I'll remember it."

Outside the window we again heard the rise-and-fall wail of sirens.

I finished my meal, and Diana got up and went into the bedroom to change her clothes. When she returned, she was wearing boot-cut jeans and an Army jacket over a T-shirt, and she was holding a bandanna handkerchief. "Here," she said. "I don't have any gauze, but you can wrap this around your foot. It's clean."

"Thanks." I took it. "I'm not sure it'll fit under my boot, but I can wear it here, while I'm sleeping."

"Sleep?" she said. "Somebody just tried to kill you and the cops are all over looking for you, and you can sleep?"

"Watch me." My stomach felt pleasantly heavy from a full meal, and both my headache and the pain in my foot were rolling out like a tide under the onslaught of ibuprofen. I had no doubt I'd be able to sleep. What I worried about was waking up again. The readout on the microwave oven said it was three minutes to two in the morning. I didn't have long to rest, not if I was to be back up in Woodland Hills around dawn to start a stakeout of the house.

"Don't let me sleep any later than four-thirty, though, okay?" I said. "Don't forget."

I finished tying the handkerchief around my foot and gingerly stood up, anticipating feeling a throb of renewed pain as blood flowed back to the area. I did.

Just before Diana left, I added one last thing. "Listen, I probably don't need to tell you this, but obey all the traffic laws. Don't speed. You're my only ally. I can't afford for you to get arrested."

"I know."

"Plus, I don't want you to get arrested because . . . you know, I don't want you to get arrested." I lifted my shoulders in a self-deprecating shrug. "I know I'm asking a lot of you, but I won't forget all the help you're giving me."

"The sucias are for the sucias," she said. "We represent like the guys." It was one of Serena's old affirmations.

She went out, closing the door behind her. I limped into the bedroom, collapsed on the bed, pulled marijuana-scented covers over my head, and fell into sleep.

23

"Insula? Insula, wake up, it's four-thirty."

No fair. It's only been a minute since I closed my eyes.

Reluctantly I rolled over toward the sound of Diana's voice. She was standing at my bedside, still in jeans and her Army jacket. She looked alert. I felt like I'd been lying in a grave, like the grit in the corners of my eyes could be cemetery dirt.

"I made coffee," she said. "Extra strong."

"Thanks." My voice was a raspy stranger's.

"Do you want milk? I didn't put anything in it."

"No, just sugar. Two spoonfuls."

She sat on the end of the bed while I drank it. She was

right, she'd made it strong. Strong and sweet. I was awake enough now to realize that my head didn't hurt any longer and the pain in my foot was a low-grade, tolerable ache.

"Did you have any trouble getting the bike back here?" I asked. "Did the cops bother you?"

"No, it was fine."

I nodded.

Then she said, "I was listening to the news. They know about your new hair color. That and the bruise."

"I figured as much. That cop in the alley made me so quickly." Had Joel Kelleher reported that? Or was it Pratt, the officer who'd seen me point-blank in King City? "What else are they saying?"

"That you were spotted in this neighborhood, that you should be considered armed and dangerous."

"Armed I'm not, except for Trippy's knife." I frowned. "Serena keeps a weapon here, doesn't she?"

"A couple." Diana pointed toward the tall dresser.

I set down my coffee and reached for my cell phone, flicking it back on. It came to life, but the message-waiting symbol didn't appear on the readout.

"Did Warchild call you?" Diana asked.

"No."

"Is she okay?"

"Warchild can take care of herself," I said, "but this is a strange time for her to go incommunicado."

I swung my legs over the edge of the bed, then gingerly put my weight on my injured foot, checking to see if this would bring on a fresh wave of pain. It didn't. Mostly the bandanna wrapped around it made walking feel awkward, so I bent down to take it off.

I went into the bathroom and surveyed my face in the mirror. Already the caffeine and sugar were beginning to filter into my bloodstream, and I was feeling better, but my face hadn't caught up. The cosmetic bruise was faded and smeared. I set my coffee cup down at the edge of the white porcelain sink, turned on the cold water, and bent to splash my face. The bruise, of no use to me now, began running down my cheek in gray rivulets. I picked up the bar of soap from the soap dish, worked up a lather between my hands, and scrubbed my face until all that remained was a faint outline of thundercloud gray at the edges of my birthmark. The rest of my skin looked clean-scrubbed and fresh. *Better,* I thought.

Serena had two guns in the dresser: the old TEC-9 that she used to keep on the nightstand while she slept, and a Beretta 92F. I chose the latter, checking that it was loaded, and went out.

In the kitchen my motorcycle helmet and keys waited for me on the table, as well as a pair of energy bars—food to go.

Diana was at the stove, fixing herself a cup of instant hot chocolate.

"You don't drink coffee?" I asked.

"Sometimes, if it has a lot of milk."

It was easy to forget that she was only fifteen. She was like her aunt, steady and serious.

She poured the cocoa into a mug, blew on it, and looked at me over the rim. "When you go back up there, to find the girl who was pretending to be you, are you going to kill her?"

"What? No."

"She did kill two people, and she tried to set you up for it."

"I know," I said. "But I think Serena might have built up my reputation for bloodthirstiness to an exaggerated level. I could have killed Trippy last night, and I didn't." I paused, swirling my coffee to make the sugar mix through. "Also, if I kill her, that would make it kind of hard to prove it was her and not me who shot those two people. It's not like she's going to confess from a drawer in the morgue."

"Yeah, that's true."

I drained the last of my coffee and set the mug down in the sink. "Listen, while I'm gone, there are two more things I need from you. First, I left my Browning under a Dumpster when the police were on my tail. I need you to go get it before some kid finds it." Briefly I gave her directions to where it was.

"What's the other thing?"

"Try to get in touch with Serena," I said. "She can take care of herself, I said that already, but I just want to be sure."

"I will, I promise, Insula."

I picked my keys up off the table. "After tonight," I said, "you can call me Hailey."

24

On the drive back up, I was feeling better. I had both caffeine and hope in my system, a Beretta 92F, and Dexedrine in my pharmacy bottle for when my energy started to fail. Maybe that's why, after parking the Aprilia two doors down from where Brittany and Quentin were, I had the strength to scale the big shade tree outside the house instead of hiding in the oleander bush. Grabbing the lowest branch, I put my good left foot against the trunk and hiked myself up. I found a place in the branches, well obscured by leaves, and straightened out my right leg and elevated the right foot on a neighboring branch. Then I settled in to wait. From my perch I could see the whole house and most of the backyard.

Lights bloomed behind the windows of the earliest-rising homes, and the sky lightened as if in competition. Dawn had cracked on the horizon when I saw the shutters of a room in the house open. A man was briefly visible behind them, black-haired, olive-complected.

He seemed to be the first one up; I saw only him moving behind the windows. In time the garage door went up and a black Porsche Boxster eased down the driveway, then into the street.

Before the garage door slid down behind him, I noticed that the Boxster's stablemate was a small silver car, not a make I recognized. An Acura, maybe, or a late-model Honda. It wasn't the Miata that "Hailey Cain" had reportedly been driving. If it was Brittany's, I wondered where she'd acquired it.

As the morning wore on, I came to regret my choice of hiding place. There aren't that many different ways you can shift around when you're sitting on a tree limb that's about seven inches across. Still, I was glad I'd chosen the tree over the oleander bush. It was better cover. People look around more often than they look up.

About midmorning Quentin walked out from under the overhang of the back patio and into my line of sight. He was unshaven, in yesterday's trousers and a white tank undershirt. He strolled casually to the edge of the pool, taking in the yard and its good, manicured landscaping. Then, standing at the pool's edge, he unhooked his belt. I snapped my head away, not wanting to see the man's dick again, but then I did look, just to be sure that he was doing what I thought: urinating in Brian's pool, marking the other man's territory as his own.

A few moments later, Brittany came out as well. She was wearing the same boots I'd seen last night, but with a pair of cutoffs and a baby T that showed a flat line of abdomen. She'd appeared on the scene too late to see what he'd been doing to the pool, and if she'd seen from the window, she didn't care. She went directly to him, and they kissed.

I had very little doubt that if they hadn't already, very soon they would have sex on Brian's bed. More territory marking for Quentin.

He went inside, but she stayed out, sitting at the pool's edge, drinking her Coke apparently for breakfast. She was the picture of leisure. Up in my perch, I watched her and tried to understand her.

I wasn't a noble person; certainly my actions of the past few months attested to that. But since my high-school days, I'd always worked. The kind of academic and athletic efforts required for West Point admission were a job in themselves, and in addition to them I'd had summer and part-time jobs. Even West Point, later, had been employment; cadets at the USMA are paid. Then I'd returned to California, where the work I'd found had been subsistence-level—first merely dangerous, then illegal.

It would never have occurred to me to want what Brittany seemed to: to lie around by a pool or a television set like a college girl on summer vacation. Was that what her crimes, the money she'd gotten from Eastman, had been all about? Not having to work? No ego needs beyond that to be fulfilled, no concern for how the world at large perceived her? No dead parent's memory to live up to, no great failure to live down?

Whatever else you could say about me, I'd felt obligation. I'd felt shame, and I still did to this day, which was why I was up a tree, stiff and uncomfortable, having gotten about three or four hours' sleep in the last day and a half. Because from what I knew about the legal system, I thought it likely that there wouldn't be enough evidence to charge me or, if so, to convict me. But it wasn't enough that I escape charges. If no one was ever caught and convicted, if Brittany went free, there'd always be a question mark over my reputation. It'd linger in the minds of people who'd known me briefly or not well—instructors and cadets at West Point, old classmates and people from Lompoc, which I considered to be my hometown.

So it wasn't enough that this shit not stick to me; it had to stick to somebody else.

Brittany finished her Coke and went back inside. About thirty minutes later, Quentin emerged from the front door, clean-shaven and fully dressed, and headed off down the street, toward the car he'd moved last night. He passed the Aprilia, at the curb, without any sign of interest.

Time passed. I shifted in place, trying to keep my ass from falling asleep. I was getting tired. If I didn't take a

Dexedrine for it, I might nod off, fall out of the tree, and break a few limbs. If I did take one, I'd be twitching with amphetamine needs, the desire to move and to do something. Sitting still would feel like a punishment.

I chose the latter, dry-swallowing the pill with two more ibuprofen to keep the pain of my wounded foot at bay, and ate one of Diana's energy bars so the pills weren't going down on an empty stomach.

Quentin did not return, but when the sun was high in the sky overhead, maybe noon, someone else came along, a young man on foot. He wore a yellow T-shirt, cargo shorts, and hiking boots, and he carried a piece of paper in his hand; he looked like a campaign volunteer going door-to-door for a candidate. His red hair was pulled back once again.

When Joel rang the doorbell, I leaned forward on my branch as though I'd reached the particularly interesting point in a movie, willing Brittany to open the door. And she did.

Although I could clearly hear the noise of a television set from somewhere inside the house, I couldn't make out anything Joel was saying to Brittany. His posture, though, was that of the earnest volunteer he was apparently pretending to be. He held out the piece of paper. Brittany took it and peered closely, the way people do when they're demonstrating that they're paying attention to something you're showing them. Then she shook her head and handed it back.

Joel shrugged and spoke again, clearly something like, *Thank you for your time.*

No, Officer Kelleher, I thought, *thank you.* Because I understood what I'd just seen. Joel had gotten not just an up-close sighting of Brittany but her thumbprint on a piece of paper.

She closed the door, and he headed back down the walk. I held myself very still in my perch. This would be a bad time for Joel to prove extraordinarily observant. But he continued down the sidewalk. I turned my head to watch as he went back to a white sedan, a nondescript, powerful Chevy. He slid behind the wheel. Craning a little to see around a branch, I saw him slide the flyer Brittany had handled into a manila envelope. Then he drove off.

25

The temperature rose steadily, though I was fairly comfortable, sheltered by the same abundant leaves that were hiding me from prying eyes. School broke for the day, apparently, and a pair of boys bicycled down the street and stopped to get off their bikes and circle the Aprilia on foot, admiring it. I watched them a moment, then turned my attention back to the house.

Perhaps another hour passed. I texted Serena: ARE YOU AROUND? WHAT'S GOING ON? I got nothing back.

At maybe eight hours into my stakeout, I was developing a fine tremor in my legs from holding my position, and despite the Dexedrine, I was becoming sleepy again. *Sleepy* didn't quite say it, implying a pleasant somnolence. I felt instead heavy-muscled, heavy-headed, drained. This was bad. If I fell asleep and tumbled out of the damn tree, I'd probably break a limb or two, knock myself out into the bargain. Then Quentin could come along and scoop me up and drag me into the house, and it'd be over. He could set up his grisly suicide-confession scene at his leisure. I didn't want to think—

A scream from inside the house interrupted these thoughts. I lifted my head, newly alert.

It wasn't a piercing, horror-movie scream. It was short and sharp and followed by some unintelligible words, sharp and startled and angry. But loud, loud enough that I was hearing them through the walls, or the sound had carried through an open window on the back of the house. Whatever the situation, Brittany was clearly upset.

Yet alone. *Who are you yelling at? The TV?*

Maybe that was the case. Something tugged at the edges of my mind, something Ford had said about the student newspaper and Brittany's ID photo. *A fed went over to their offices and rattled his saber pretty hard for them to sit on the photo, as well as the news about the discrepancy. They didn't like it, but we're hoping they'll do it.*

What if they hadn't? What if the student newspaper had run a story and released the photo? Maybe Brittany was seeing her own face on the news, linked to the Eastman-Stepakoff murders for the first time. That would be scary enough to merit the kind of response I was hearing. I leaned forward, watching the house intently, but my angle on the front windows wasn't great, and I caught only brief flashes of motion from inside.

Then, a few moments later, the garage door began to roll up.

For the first time that day, I heard Brittany's voice clearly. "No! You said that already, and I'm not . . . I . . . Quentin, I don't *care*!"

She came into view, holding both a suitcase and a half-full pillowcase in one hand, letting them slip to the garage floor as she unlocked the silver car. I had enough time now to see the silver Acura symbol on the trunk.

Brittany threw the passenger door open and flung her suitcase and the pillowcase inside. "It's not just Brian I'm worried about," she said, slamming the door. "There was someone else here. This guy was taking around a flyer about a missing kid who might be in the area." Another interruption on the other end. Then, "What I'm trying to say is that he was part of some fucking missing-kids foundation, an *anticrime* group, and he looked right *at my face*. Not in a crowd, but from just two feet away." She moved back from the car. "Do you understand what that means?"

She disappeared from view, obviously into the house.

Time, Hailey. Stop her now.

Somewhere the fingerprint that Joel had obtained was making its way through the system, undoubtedly expedited, and when it matched prints taken from the Eastman home, everyone would be interested in the pretty young blonde staying in this house. But that would be utterly useless if she wasn't here to be arrested.

So I touched the Beretta in its holster, checking to be sure the safety was on, eased myself to a lower branch, and swung down to hang by my hands. My feet were maybe twenty inches above the ground, and I raised the right one slightly higher, to spare it from the pain of impact. The idea was, I'd drop to the ground and run to the garage to stop Brittany in her escape plans.

Instead I dropped to the ground, hitting first with my left leg, and that knee gave way underneath me like it was made of cardboard. I collapsed onto all fours, the soft springiness of lawn beneath the heels of my hands, and swayed dizzily.

From the garage, Brittany's boot heels were noisy as she walked, quickly now. I raised my face and caught a glimpse of her, back turned to me, putting a large forest green shopping bag with twine handles into the trunk of her car. I struggled to make my stiff, weak legs hold me. *Come on, dammit. Get up.*

There was the sound of a car door slamming, and the Acura's engine came to life. By then I was halfway up and staggering. I willed Brittany to see me and stop the car, exhibit curiosity, get out.

But she didn't. She was so wrapped up in her personal crisis that a UFO could have landed in Brian's front yard and she wouldn't have seen it. She backed fast out of the driveway, made a looping turnaround in reverse, put the Acura in drive, and rocketed away, not up the street toward Mulholland but down, toward town and the 101.

No. This will not happen, she will not disappear again. I forced myself into an awkward lope, across and up the street to where the Aprilia was. My legs were tired, and running woke up the pain in my wounded right foot, but I got there. Then I pulled up short and stared. My helmet was missing.

What else could go wrong? Those goddamn kids, they'd taken the helmet, because that's what bored middle-class kids do when no adults are watching: They steal things.

There was no time to be angry. I swung my leg over the saddle, inserted the key, and pressed the starter. The engine roared to life. I put my sunglasses on and spun the bike around in a hard circle.

Brittany had about a minute on me, and she was moving fast, but there was only one road down. On it I caught sight of the Acura's silver body disappearing around a switchback, and I leaned forward, deeper into my fetal crouch position, and gave chase.

26

It was a steep, sharp descent, the wind playing with my hair. I was going fast enough that an old man doing yard work at the edge of his property looked up and scowled, but I couldn't slow down. If Brittany got to an intersection and I didn't see which way she went, I'd lose her. I shot past lovely homes shaded by oak trees, past kids on bikes and women walking for exercise. Then the street leveled out, and up ahead I saw Brittany's silver car, turning at a traffic light onto the main street. I knew where she was heading: to the 101.

By the time she got there, I was right on her tail. I didn't care if she knew she was being followed; I could drive up her tailpipe if I wanted to. I knew her problem now: She was a coward. She had served Eastman something like tea, spiked with sedatives, and the woman had slipped away into a fog, never aware enough of what was happening to confront Brittany. After the murders she'd fled San Francisco. Now she was running again, not waiting to see if Brian had seen the news or if the young volunteer at her door would remember her face. She never faced opposition straight on. If Brittany could have, she probably would have shot Stepakoff in the back and never let him see her face at all. She felt uncomfortable without her mask—either the mask of my stolen identity or that of the sweet girl who people like Brian seemed to take her for.

So if she looked back and realized that a motorcyclist was following her, she'd probably fear the worst: that I was someone who'd seen the news and knew who she was. In that situation Brittany would stay true to form. She'd panic and try to outrun me, and that wouldn't work. Everyone knows who wins car-versus-motorcycle chases.

We ascended the ramp onto the freeway. I stayed close as we merged. It was only about three-thirty in the afternoon, so the worst of the evening congestion was yet to come; we'd both have room to maneuver, if it came to an outright chase. Brittany didn't seem worried yet, if her speed and the way she was handling the car were any indication. She was going about seventy, which despite the posted limits is considered a sane and civil speed by L.A. motorists, when traffic allows.

We were heading north, away from the city proper, where the congestion would have been thicker. Brittany signaled and eased into the left lane, bumping her speed up to seventy-five. After a second I did the same. As I did, I caught the eye of a man driving a midnight blue Saab; his eyebrows jumped at the sight of me, and I knew why: my bare head. California has a helmet law, and while there'll always be hardcore bikers who flout it, you generally don't see them on the main freeways, courting arrest.

Finding a hole in traffic, the Acura eased over into the farthest-left lane, the passing lane. I followed, bumping my speed up to eighty to match hers, keeping my eyes on her rearview mirror. As I watched, she lifted her eyes to the mirror, and then she knew.

Without signaling, Brittany cut recklessly across four lanes of traffic, toward an exit. I leaned my weight to the right and followed, hearing an angry, shrill horn behind me.

We were moving so fast that I didn't catch the sign for the exit ramp Brittany dived down. The light was green at the foot of the ramp, and she went left, me on her tail. Strip-mall businesses flashed past in the periphery of my vision; it was a shopping district, but I sensed open land ahead. Brittany was looking for a place where she could run. She gunned the Acura's engine, racing for a yellow light. It turned red as we shot under it.

Run, baby, I thought. *Run baby run baby run.* That was just what I wanted. Sooner or later we were going through a speed trap, and boy, were we going to set it off. At last I wasn't hiding from the police anymore. I wanted them to chase me, because I was chasing the Eastman-Stepakoff killer.

In a moment or two, the businesses and gas stations fell away and grassland opened up on the edges of my vision. I lowered my head and watched only the license plate on her car; to me it was the mechanical rabbit at the dog track. Brittany swerved left again, diving at the last minute for a side road in hopes of losing me. I leaned on the left handlebar and followed her, catching only a glimpse of the green-and-white sign on the corner: Something Canyon Road. She'd led us to about where we would have been had she gone uphill from Brian's place onto Mulholland Drive: headed into the open, chaparral-filled wilderness of the Santa Monica Mountains.

The Acura tried to pull away from me, and the needle on my speedometer twitched steadily higher: 95, 100, 105. The wind was no longer just pulling at my hair; it was pulling at my scalp and the skin of my face. Some of my hair had come loose from my ponytail and was fibrillating wildly around the lenses of my sunglasses. My body shook in sympathy with the Aprilia's efforts, like amphetamine tremors. Maybe I was having those, too.

Then I heard a siren behind us.

Brittany didn't stop, so I couldn't, either. In fact, I smiled. This was another chase that individual motorists never win, trying to outrun the cops. *Run, baby,* I thought again. *Because you've got a signed confession at every fingertip, and there's no way you're not getting arrested now, no matter how much you point at me and scream about the crazy girl chasing you.*

When I dared a backward glance, the cop car behind us had multiplied into several, though they had to follow in single file.

The Acura's brake lights flashed briefly as Brittany made another last-minute turn, scaring a red-tailed hawk from a fence post, and I swung after her. The road she'd chosen was old, paved in sun-cracked particulate. Though she quickly picked up speed again, I eased back on the Aprilia's throttle. Roads this old were prone to gravel and loose stones. At high speed, without a helmet, being hit by a stone the Acura threw up would be almost like taking a bullet to the head.

What happened next happened too fast for me to understand right away. I no sooner saw the tumbleweed ahead of Brittany's car than she saw it, her brake lights flashed, and then sparks flew from the Acura's undercarriage as she lost control of the car. I veered left, hard, and then for a minute I didn't think of anything else as I fought for control of the skidding Aprilia, which was in a locked-rear-wheel slide. Unemotionally, I thought, *I'm going down,* and then I felt the bike get its footing under me again.

I braked to a standstill and swung off the saddle. And for the second time that afternoon, my legs betrayed me. I fell to hands and knees, my sunglasses dropping from my face onto the road's edge.

For a moment the silence that replaced the battering of the wind around my head was all I could hear. Then I became aware of a familiar sound: a helicopter hovering overhead, its blades chopping the air. To the right, about fifty yards from me, the Acura sat in a cloud of dust in the center of a field, like a sentient thing in shock. On the shoulder of the road was a large, mangled coil of baling wire—the thing I had taken for an unlikely Southern California tumbleweed, that had thrown up sparks as the Acura dragged it at high speed along the road.

Behind me the police cars had come to a stop.

No one did anything. No doors slammed, no one shouted commands, the helicopter simply hovered. I could see the shape of Brittany's head and shoulders in the car, but it wasn't clear if she was conscious. She couldn't be dead, could she? The car had run off the road at high speed, but it hadn't hit anything. Surely she couldn't be dead. Could she?

Then the driver's-side door opened and Brittany stumbled out and began to run across the field.

I don't know how she could believe that she'd get out of this on foot, but she was trying. Running was just what she did. And chasing her had been my job up until now, so I did. I got to my feet and ran after her, ignoring the pain every time my right foot hit the ground.

She wasn't running very fast. She was wearing cowboy boots and going over rough, uneven soil, and her gait wasn't that of someone used to running. The only hard part was making up the distance she already had on me. Twenty feet, fifteen feet, ten, five . . . I reached out and caught her shoulder. She shrieked and stumbled, then fell on her stomach. I dropped to my knees and then got my weight on her, strad-dling her lower back and keeping her arms pinned. She twisted around but couldn't dislodge me. My heart was pounding from the chase, and the stab wound in my foot was throbbing in time with my heartbeat again.

I leaned down, my mouth close to her ear.

"Brittany, I know what you did in San Francisco," I said. "After the cops fingerprint you, everyone's gonna know. And when you're on death row, I want you to remember one thing: None of these officers here actually ran you to the ground. That was me. Turn around and take a good look at my face."

When she did, when she saw my birthmark and knew who I was, Brittany Mercier began to scream.

27

"*B*oth of you, stay where you are. Do not move. You, on top, place your hands slowly on the back of your neck.*"

The cops had gotten their game plan together and had assembled in a loose ring around us, one of them giving the orders over a bullhorn. They were being careful, but I didn't get a sense of knife-edge tension off them. They didn't know exactly what the situation was, but for now it probably looked like a couple of crazy chicks with a wild hair up their asses.

I laced my hands on the back of my neck, as the guy in charge had said. It didn't seem like they'd seen the outline of the Beretta; the tail of my T-shirt covered it up.

They closed in. I heard footsteps crunching, then a voice behind me, a voice unaided by a megaphone. "You are under arrest. Lower your hands slowly behind your back so I can cuff you. Miss, be quiet." That was to Brittany, who was still shrieking. She gulped and took a breath.

The cop behind me started doing the Miranda thing. He got as far as "to remain silent" before Brittany realized the weapon she had at her disposal and used it.

"She's Hailey Cain!" she yelled. "She killed those people in San Francisco! She killed a cop!"

Holy shit, I heard one of the cops say, and they all stiffened, as though they'd walked up on a rattlesnake in the grass.

"She killed two people! She just told me she did! Get her off me!"

"I didn't kill anyone, but I am Hailey Cain," I said clearly to the ring of raised weapons around me. "I'm not running anymore, and I won't resist arrest."

"She confessed to me! She wants to kill me because I know what she did!"

"Miss, be *quiet,*" the voice behind me said. "I'm going to cuff you now, Miss Cain. You so much as twitch and I will shoot you."

"I'm carrying a piece on my lower back; you'll feel it when you cuff me," I said, still speaking loudly and enunciating clearly to be heard over Brittany's accusations

"Stay very still. You on the ground, *please* be quiet."

I felt his hands on my back, moving, finding the gun and

disarming me. The helicopter was directly over us, and the downdraft was making my hair blow crazily; probably less than half of it was still in its ponytail. Underneath me, Brittany's heartbeat was so forceful I could feel it in my legs.

"Are you carrying any other weapons?"

"No."

I shut my eyes while he searched me to find out. He wasn't gentle. Eyes still closed, I said, "She was the one who killed the cop and Violet Eastman."

"Liar!"

The cop: "You should stay quiet."

"Get her fingerprints and you'll see," I said.

He took one of my wrists in his hand, clicked the steel bracelet of his handcuffs around it, then pulled my other wrist down and did the same. Then he ratcheted them tight. Really, really tight. Then he started the Miranda rights again. "You have the right to remain silent!" he yelled over the helicopter's noise. "If you give up the right to— Will someone get on the blower and call off that damn chopper already!"

"It's not us, it's probably news," said another officer.

The arresting officer decided he needed to preserve his vocal cords more than I needed to hear my last two rights, and he hauled me to my feet, his grip tight on my arm. I saw him for the first time: white guy, short brown hair, neatly trimmed mustache. That guy you see on *Cops* all the time. *Deputy Newton*, his name tag read. He was with the L.A. Sheriff's Office.

As soon as my weight was off Brittany, she jumped to

her feet, surprisingly quick for everything she'd been through. She almost laughed in relief. "Oh, thank God," she said. "I was so scared."

The circle of police officers was all men, a fact not lost on Brittany. She gave them a breathless, tentative smile.

"I'm sorry, miss," another officer said, "but we're going to have to take you in, too. You were operating that vehicle with reckless disregard for—"

"I didn't mean to! She was chasing me!" Brittany interrupted. "I didn't mean to, it wasn't my fault! Oh, please, can't you just—"

One of them moved in, reading Brittany her Miranda rights. She glanced around the circle, as if seeking the most sympathetic pair of eyes. Then she said, "I think I need to go to the hospital."

"—in a court of law," the cop continued.

"I hit my head on the dashboard, really hard, I'm seeing double."

"There's a nurse who can do an assessment at jail intake," he told her, and then took out his handcuffs.

When it sank in that she was really going to jail, Brittany began to cry.

28

Deputy Newton took both of us to a prisoner-transport van and shackled us to opposite benches, out of reach of each other. He said, "I'll be right back. You girls just stay there and don't move a muscle," and jumped down to the ground.

When we were alone, no cops in earshot, no audience to play to, Brittany looked at me and said, "Why are you doing this to me?"

At that moment I gave up on ever truly trying to understand her. Because on some level she considered that to be a legitimate question. Somewhere in her mind, she was the victim; I'd made this happen.

Then movement outside the van caught my eye, a little bit of commotion, a raised voice. I looked over to see Joel Kelleher approaching. He had changed out of his college-volunteer clothes and was recognizably a cop again in a dark blue LAPD T-shirt, black jeans, and boots, a badge on a chain around his neck. His wasn't the raised voice. That was my friend Deputy Newton. "—without a compelling reason. Hey, are you listening?" he was saying, trailing behind with a reddening, frustrated face. He couldn't keep up, and Joel wasn't slowing down for him any. He vaulted up easily into the back of the van. Brittany stared at him, her mouth slightly open, recognizing the "volunteer" who'd rung her doorbell earlier and understanding the extent to which she'd been fooled. "You *bastard*," she said, and started to cry again.

Joel looked at me without any sign that we'd ever met. "Hailey Cain, I'm Officer Joel Kelleher with the Los Angeles Police Department. I'm here to take you into custody."

"You can't *do* this," Newton said, still outside the van.

"Actually, I can," Joel said. "They gave me the authority to transport prisoners when they swore me in."

Newton said, "You know what I'm saying. We've arrested her, we've Mirandized her—"

"Not completely," I said helpfully.

"—and we've arranged for transport to the jail. There's absolutely no reason for this."

"None except that I'm the only officer here I know for sure won't have her fall down a flight of stairs in handcuffs as soon as she's out of sight of reporters," Joel said.

"That's offensive."

"And painful, which is why I want to keep it from happening," Joel said. "Look, if you have any more questions, talk to Magnus Ford, under whose authority I'm doing this. You have heard of Ford, I assume?"

Newton closed his mouth, and his eyes narrowed slightly. Joel knelt down by my side.

Newton found his voice. "No matter whose authority, I'm reporting you for this."

"For taking a prisoner to custody?" Joel said. "That'll excite IAD. Listen, I'm not stealing your collar. I'm only taking her in." He nudged his chin at me. "That woman"—looking over his shoulder at Brittany—"is the one you really want to be photographed perp-walking into central lockup. That's the AP photo you'll show your grandkids. When all this shakes out, you'll thank me."

Though the big game was finished, the turnstiles kept rolling over: More official-looking vehicles had arrived, and there were several knots of uniformed and plainclothes officers around, plus a few in suits who could have been pretty high up the command chain. Joel walked me through a gauntlet of hostile gazes to the unmarked white sedan I'd seen him driving earlier.

Once I was in the backseat, still handcuffed, and he was behind the wheel, he said, "You're not going to central lockup. I'm taking you to a sheriff's substation until all this settles down. I know the guy in charge. He's a good man. No one's going to mess with you."

"Okay," I'd said. "Thank you" wasn't right here. He wasn't doing it as a favor for me personally. It was just a practical concern.

Then I said, "Do you always talk like that to other officers, like you did to Newton? In the Army someone with your kind of mouth would constantly be losing privileges and working chickenshit details."

"He wasn't my superior." Joel glanced at me in the rearview. "I have a hard time remembering you were at West Point. It just doesn't seem very you."

"Things were a lot different then. *I* was different."

Joel didn't pursue that. He was looking out the window at the ongoing mop-up of the scene and said, "I'd better get us out of here."

He turned the key in the ignition, and the engine rumbled to life. Then, rather than make a U-turn, Joel cocked his chin over his shoulder and reversed all the way to the road under the malevolent eyes of his peers.

29

Dry east-county landscape rolled past outside the windows of Joel's car, and I watched it with a placid feeling, as if it were something on film, a peaceful interlude in an otherwise chaotic movie. I didn't know where we were headed and didn't care.

I leaned forward. "Joel?"

"Mmm?"

"Are you allowed to talk about the case at all?"

"What do you want to know?"

"Was Brittany's student-ID picture on the news? Is that what made her run?"

"The photo was on the news, yeah," he said. "Whether

that was the reason she ran, I don't know. You'd know better than me—you were obviously watching the house. Where were you, by the way? I didn't have any sense you were around."

"I was up the tree in the front yard."

"Jesus." I saw his head move slightly, as if he were about to turn and look at me, but then he didn't. He said, "That's crazy. You were fifteen feet from the front door, maybe less? That's a dangerous place to survey from."

I didn't say anything.

"You saw me, then?"

"Yeah."

"I was going to come back after I took the flyer to the lab. I was supposed to stake out the house, not just to watch her but to look out for you," he said. "When I heard on the radio about a couple of women in a high-speed chase, I didn't automatically think of you, until they were running footage on KTLA. I remembered the motorcycle parked on Brittany's street. Plus, it looked like you, with the new brown hair." Then he changed the subject. "It wasn't too smart for Brittany to have that picture taken and her real face linked with your name."

"You have to look at it from her point of view. She expected to bilk Eastman and disappear. She never planned to commit two murders and get her stolen identity onto the front page of newspapers. There wasn't supposed to be anything near that level of scrutiny."

"I guess not," Joel said.

His cell phone buzzed, and he picked it up. "Kelleher." He listened briefly. "Yeah, we're about five minutes or so out from the substation, everything's fine."

Ford, obviously.

"That might not be the last phone call you get," Joel said. "I made some friends today." He slowed for an isolated intersection where the signal light hung from a cable over the road. Then he said, "Interesting. Can I tell her? . . . No, I'm not. . . . Okay. See you soon."

When he'd disconnected, I said, "Tell me what?"

"The thumbprint off the flyer, it got a hit," he said. "It was in several places in the Eastman home. That's not in itself enough to exculpate you. We can't just let you walk." He paused. "The good thing is, Magnus thinks we can hold you on the charges related to the chase—the speed violation and reckless endangerment—and not anything connected to Stepakoff and Eastman. San Francisco hasn't charged you yet."

"Really?"

"Prosecutors work a little slower than cops. You were the only suspect, yeah, and everyone was hung up on finding you, but the lawyers were still preparing their case. Anyway, it's useful to have the other charges against you—I know it doesn't seem like a good thing to you, probably, but it's better than being charged with two homicides, which someone might've had to do if we didn't have anything else to hold you on."

"Mmm," I said, noncommittal. He was right, I wasn't

exactly feeling grateful about that. I moved on to something else. "So am I ever going to meet Ford?"

"That's hard to say. The man does keep to himself."

"What is it with this guy? Is he just a brain floating in a vat of preservative fluids, with some kind of voice-simulator box?"

Joel laughed. "No, he's a real guy."

"Is he horribly disfigured?"

"Nope, not disfigured. If you passed him on the street, he wouldn't really stand out." Then he said, "I never heard of him until my lieutenant told me I was being taken off my regular detail, in Special Weapons and Tactics, to work with the guy, at his request. When I found out the work was a lot of covert investigative organized-crime stuff, I asked him, 'What made you want to pull someone off the adrenaline-cowboy squad to do this?' He says, 'You don't think you're up for it? I can get someone else.' I never talked myself down in front of him again."

"Harsh."

"Straightforward," Joel corrected. "Anyway, I don't ask Magnus a lot of questions about himself. He asked me about my background and all, but he's not the kind of guy who makes you feel like it's a two-way street."

The sheriff's substation was a one-story building of pinkish gray stucco with a Joshua tree out front. I could hear the firecracker-like pops of a firing range somewhere beyond the building. Joel parked and killed the engine. At that moment his cell rang again.

"Ford's a demanding boss," I commented.

He was looking at the screen. "It's not Magnus, it's my girlfriend."

"Girlfriend?"

"Fiancée, actually," Joel said. "I'll call her back later. Come on, let's get you processed in, so I can get going."

"Sorry," I said, "I'm making you late for supper, is that it?"

"Yup," he said, "and two cold bottles of Stella Artois."

He put his hand on the door handle, but I leaned forward. "Wait a minute," I said. "I've been wanting to tell you something."

"If this is something about Eastman and Stepakoff, it should wait until—"

"No," I said. "It's not that."

"Yeah?" He waited.

I'd figured out what it was I should have told him about fear, back in the Eastman house, and this was maybe my last chance to say it. I wanted to say that fear isn't a barrier to courage, it's a source material. The brave people I knew— and I couldn't include myself among them, not honestly— created their courage out of fear.

"Hailey?" Joel prompted.

"Yeah, sorry," I said. "I wanted to say, you remember in San Francisco, when you told me about how you had to repress a lot of fear to do your job?"

He said, "No."

That stopped me short. The question hadn't really been

a question, just a reminder. I tried again. "In the Eastman house," I prompted him. "You were going under from the Ambien, and you said you had to swallow a lot of fear to do what you do, and no one else on the job talked about that kind of thing. Remember?"

He shook his head and studied me with his hazel-green eyes. "Sorry, no," he said. "It must have been the drug talking. That just doesn't sound like me. I really don't have a problem in that area."

After a moment I said, "Sorry. I must have misunderstood."

30

When the life and times of Brittany Mercier began to come out, what surprised a lot of people was how much it *didn't* amount to. The first thing: There was no abuse. Sure, she had poor beginnings in a small Washington State town, Dad drank a little too much, her parents divorced when she was young. But nothing about her past suggested the kind of toxic psychological cauldron that would produce a murderer.

What Brittany had appeared to be, from early on, was a girl with an endless appetite for pretty and expensive things and an aversion to work. Elementary-school teachers remembered a bright and lovely child who had a troubling penchant for telling lies, often for no apparent reason. Friends from the same time remembered a girl whom everyone tried to befriend but who repaid that friendship by stealing things she coveted from the homes she was invited into. Confronted, she would deny it and cry, and more than a few schoolmates convinced themselves that the fault was theirs for making the accusation.

In Los Angeles, when she was eighteen, her looks opened the very first doors in the entertainment business. She found an agent and landed a few commercials. But Brittany quickly tired of the grind of auditions and lost interest in acting lessons. She didn't, though, fill the lack of acting jobs with other work, instead living off the indulgence of roommates and the generosity of boyfriends.

By the age of twenty-one, Brittany had used up the goodwill she had in Los Angeles. The agent had tired of her, as had a number of ex-friends and ex-roommates, all of them owed back rent or cash loans they realized would never be repaid. Brittany went to San Francisco. There she tried out her first "short cons." A favorite trick was putting a broken vase in the twine-handled bag of an expensive shop and walking around retail centers until she could find a distracted person to run into her, causing her to drop and "break" her new purchase. Foreign tourists, uncertain in their English, afraid of giving offense, and unfamiliar with the value of American banknotes, were a favorite mark; invariably, Brittany's distress occasioned the waving of generous amounts of American dollars.

At some point she met a young man named Quentin Corelli.

Of course, all this didn't come out right away. But once Brittany was in custody, the evidence began to pile up. Items taken from the trunk of her car matched those bought by "Hailey Cain" in San Francisco with V. K. Eastman's credit cards. And if there had been any doubt about the thumbprint that Joel had gotten, the full set of prints killed it; they were all matches for ones left in the San Francisco house, just as her DNA matched a hair in Eastman's living room.

But Brittany was mentally nimble, if nothing else. Perhaps her deftest stroke was telling her interrogators that she'd befriended Violet Eastman in San Francisco and was a frequent guest in her house, hence the fingerprint and DNA evidence gleaned there.

Maybe Cain had even seen her there, Brittany suggested, and noticed the similarities in their age and coloring and thus had chosen her as the target for a deadly setup. Because she certainly *had* been set up, Brittany said. The student-ID photo of her must have been stolen and planted in the city college's files. The credit-card purchases in the trunk? Also planted. She'd done nothing wrong.

Asked for corroborating details—even just her address in the city—or to take a polygraph, Brittany turned tearfully sullen and uncooperative.

Despite all this, interest in me died slowly. I probably got interviewed nearly as much as Brittany did, by major-case detectives from San Francisco and FBI agents who worked on the task force. They wanted to understand my role in the story, how my ID and gun had fallen into Brittany's hands, why I hadn't gone immediately to the police with my story of identity theft, and how I ended up racing after Brittany on the highway.

I didn't feel like revealing the whole messy story of Nidia Hernandez and Tony Skouras, and I didn't. I simply told them that I'd lost my passport, my driver's license, and my gun in a highway robbery in Mexico. It was a story that conflated my two encounters with Skouras's guys; I didn't actually lose the SIG until later. But they didn't need to know how long I'd tangled with Skouras, or how much it had cost me.

Life at the sheriff's substation was okay. The deputy in charge, the one Joel had vouched for, was Deputy Cory Wellman, around fifty, tanned, nearly bald, quiet. He was decent, as Joel had said. My second day there, he brought in a doctor to look at the stab wound on my foot, who said it was uninfected and would continue healing on its own.

Cory also let me wear my street clothes in my cell, as if I were just a town drunk brought in to sober up, and he delivered me several paperback novels from the library. The other two holding cells were often empty. Country music drifted under the sound of the police radio. The food wasn't very good, but it's not supposed to be.

As Joel had predicted, no one gave me trouble. But people came to *look* at me; that was the weirdest thing. I'd thought that tradition had gone out with Jesse James, you know, "going to the jailhouse to look at the famous outlaw." Reporters came, too, of course. I didn't speak to any of them.

On day four I had a visitor who was neither sightseer

nor journalist; he was an Asian man of middle years in a white lab coat.

"Hailey," Cory said, unlocking the cell door, "this is Dr. Tanaka. He needs to take a quick look at you."

"Pleased to meet you," I said. "Are you here to look at my foot? I thought it was okay."

"Not your foot," Tanaka said. "May I look at your left hand?"

Mystified, I raised my hand and let him take it. He looked closely at hardened tissue where my left pinkie had once been, tilting my hand up toward the light. I felt like an animal at the vet.

"How long ago did this happen?" he asked.

"Nearly five months. Late December," I said.

His eyebrows lowered in concentration. "I see a little bit of more recent damage—"

I was immediately embarrassed. "From a burn?" I said. "Yeah, I know. I did it with a cigarette. The nerve endings haven't grown back properly. I was impressing a guy."

Cory poked his tongue into his cheek as if he were trying not to laugh. Tanaka said, "Maybe you shouldn't do that anymore."

"Yes, Doc," I said.

He returned his attention to the scar tissue. "This was a very clean cut. What did it?"

"Tin snips."

"This was deliberate?"

"Yeah." This time I didn't look over at Cory. I didn't mind his private amusement, but I didn't want to see his pity.

Dr. Tanaka said, "I hope the police caught up with the man who did that."

Quentin had probably split L.A. as soon as he'd heard about Brittany's arrest. I wondered if she would eventually implicate him in her crimes and, if so, how much he would pay for them. If the law even caught up with him.

It was believed to be Quentin, incidentally, who gave Brittany the silver Acura she drove to Los Angeles, instead of the far-too-hot-to-drive Miata. This was a detail that did not capture the public imagination, but I'd been wondering about it since seeing the Acura in the garage.

Cory and Dr. Tanaka left without explaining the doctor's odd errand, and I didn't inquire. I took it as a matter of pride not to ask questions that weren't going to be answered. There was no point in pretending that I was in control.

31

The next day, a little after lunch, Cory asked me if I was up for another ride into the city. It wasn't a question, though—another interview awaited. *What more can these guys need to ask me?* I'd been interviewed by everyone but Parks and Recreation.

All my previous interviews had taken place at the FBI field office on Wilshire, the FBI apparently having taken point on the Eastman-Stepakoff murders. This time the travelogue was different. Cory drove us across the mostly dry L.A. River and across Alameda Street, and then I saw the buildings of the Civic Center rising before us: the County Courthouse, the Hall of Justice, and all its satellite buildings.

Cory's Crown Vic descended into a deep subterranean parking garage, and then we rode the elevators up into a warren of hallways and plate glass. I was still following my policy of not asking questions that wouldn't be answered. The last clock that I passed on the way into yet another interrogation room read 2:35 P.M. I'd learned to catch a glimpse of the time whenever possible, then try to gauge how long I was left waiting in the interrogation room. It was never a short time.

Cory apologized for handcuffing me to the D-ring of the table; he felt sheepish about it because I'd never offered him any resistance. Then the door closed behind him and the wait began. Bored and resentful, I distracted myself by trying to remember some of the Latin passages I'd memorized years ago as a student, Virgil and Terence and others.

I was on the creation story as translated by Jerome—*"In principio creavit Deus caelum et terram"*—when the door opened and someone came in. Don't ask me how I knew: I just knew, even before he gave me a voice to recognize. If you passed him on the street, he wouldn't really stand out, Joel had said. I wasn't sure I agreed.

Magnus Ford was quite big, well over six feet, with ash-blond hair cropped almost to his scalp, maybe two days' growth of beard, eyes of an indeterminate color. He was strong-looking in a stocky way but moved lightly, with an air of stillness, even in motion.

"Mr. Ford," I said.

"Hailey." He pulled out the interviewer's chair from its place up against the table and sat down.

He wore mostly standard detective wear: shirt and tie, creased trousers, loafers. Instead of a blazer, he wore a dark leather coat that came to midthigh. It was the only touch of flash in his wardrobe, and made it hard to tell what of his bulky upper body was muscle and what was fat. And even the coat was standard department-store stuff, nothing custom that suggested a cop on the take.

He said, "The first thing is, you've been exonerated, whether or not the charges stick to Brittany Mercier."

"How?" I said.

"There's bank video of her cashing one of the checks she forged on Eastman's account. She's wearing a cap and keeping her face away from the camera, but you can see that she has all ten fingers. She didn't know enough about you to hide that."

"That's why they sent the doc yesterday, to gauge how old my injury was."

"Yes."

"And Brittany's been charged with the murders."

"Yes. You should know, there's an outside chance that she won't be convicted. A good defense lawyer is going to exploit all the maybes, and the psychologist who's been in the observation room during several of the interrogations is saying that he thinks Brittany might never recant her story of being set up. She's a pathological liar, and the strength of those people is that on some level they convince themselves of what they're saying. She's young, very convincing in her own defense, very hurt and confused that nobody believes her. A hung jury is a possibility here. I'm telling you this because I know that having someone else found guilty was important to you, that you saw it as necessary to clearing your name."

"I did what I could."

"You did. And it's possible that the jury won't hang. We'll wait and see."

"But I'm free to go."

"Not exactly," he said. "There's still the matter of a couple of truck hijackings out in the desert, Insula."

Insula.

I made sure my face stayed carefully neutral. It was possible he could just be fishing. The least I could do was make him put all his cards on the table.

"You've seen my tattoo," I said mildly. "It's Latin for 'island.' That's how I feel sometimes. Solitary."

"Actually, it was Joel who saw your tattoo," he said. "The second time you came over to talk to him in the park, it was a hot day, and you were wearing a thin tank shirt. He read the tattoo through it. A little later, even though you'd never mentioned your friend in that neighborhood by name, Joel dropped a casual reference to 'your friend Serena' into the conversation, and you didn't even blink. That's when he knew." Ford smiled a little. "Did you know that up until that moment we thought you were some kind of urban legend? 'Insula, the white sucia.' We'd seen pictures of Warchild, knew she was some kind of fine-looking. For her to have a blond female lieutenant, that was about two steps away from being some *cholo*'s letter to *Penthouse Forum*."

I didn't feel like laughing.

"Joel came in real excited, told me what he'd found. After you gave him your cell number, we were brainstorming ways to best use that, and then the APB on you came in from San Francisco. Joel brought it to me and said, 'You're not going to believe this, but you remember how I told you that Insula told me her name was Hailey? That's her, Hailey Cain. I know it sounds crazy, but it's true.'

"It's funny, but one of the early things that worked in your favor, as far as convincing me you didn't kill Eastman and Stepakoff, was the truck hijackings. We knew right away it was you and Warchild. Two females who spoke a mix of English, Spanish, and Latin? That narrowed the suspect list considerably."

I hoped the irritation I felt at myself didn't show on my face; the code Serena and I had used hadn't been such a smart idea after all.

"So the timeline didn't work out. The idea that you were cleaning up a murder scene in San Francisco at five or six P.M. and jacking a truck outside Los Angeles at midnight . . . it just didn't scan. Then your fingerprints came across the wire from the military database, and Joel said, 'This isn't right, either. She's only got nine fingers.'

"Now, *that* was interesting, because it seemed to be a detail no one else knew, not even people in San Francisco. That was when I got curious enough to call you.'

And the rest was history.

Ford said, "You shouldn't make too much of the fact that

I helped you with the San Francisco murders, Hailey. I'm a cop. The evidence against you didn't add up, so it just made sense to look into things further. But I also have a lot of sympathy for a pair of pharmaceutical-company truck drivers who were made to lie down in a ditch with a gun at their backs."

I didn't respond to that. A defense of my behavior was also an admission.

"In the legal system, drug- and gang-related crimes are among the least sympathized with. Judges and prosecutors are anxious to look tough on them. If I can convince just one prosecutor that you were in on the truck robberies, do you realize how many charges he can make out of that? Hijacking, armed robbery, assault, kidnapping, possession with intent to distribute, possession of an unregistered firearm . . . That's a long time in prison you're looking at."

"And you'll make it stick how? Gonna get the truck drivers in here for a voice lineup, make me say some Latin words for them?"

"Tell me, where'd you get your law degree?" he said, amused. Then, "Where were you around nine P.M. on Tuesday?"

It took me a moment to adjust to the shift in direction, but I thought back. "I'd only just gotten to Brian's place, in Woodland Hills. You remember, I called you not long after."

"Maybe an hour after," he said. "Are you sure you weren't, at any point, at a rented storage unit off Olympic?"

He knew about the place where Serena stored boxes of pharmaceuticals, her cache of weapons, and her money. "No," I said. "Why?"

"Your good friend Warchild Delgadillo has established quite a successful sideline in marijuana-infused oils. It's apparently been quite a moneymaker for her and a select group of her girls." He raised a pale eyebrow. "How long did you think a lucrative operation like that was going to go unnoticed by higher-ups in the gang underworld?"

"That's your rhetorical way of telling me it didn't?"

"It's a sucker's game, trying to keep a sideline like that unnoticed," he said. "Either you have to stay so small it's not worth the effort, or you come to someone's attention and pay the penalty for not cutting the right people in."

I didn't like where this was going.

"On Tuesday night Warchild went to her garage unit and caught someone breaking in. Maybe she thought he was some random street thief. He wasn't. He was a foot soldier for one of the *sureño* bosses around here, who sent him to impound everything she had. I guess between back payments and punitive damages, the bosses decided Warchild was in the hundred-percent tax bracket. They wanted everything."

He left unsaid something I was sure he also understood: that Serena, in particular, had to be taught a lesson because she was female.

"What happened?" I said.

"She and this gunny shot at each other."

"Was she hit?"

"No. He was. Warchild fled the scene, but we caught her a few miles away. She's in custody."

Good, I thought. Well, it wasn't good, but at least I knew she was safe.

But then Ford said, "She's facing a homicide charge. The guy she shot died in intensive care."

God, Serena. Last year, when we were in the thick of our troubles with Skouras, I'd asked her if she'd ever killed anyone, back when she was running with the guys of Trece. She'd evaded the question in a teasing way, and I'd hoped she was being coy. Now I didn't have to hope. Couldn't hope. That line had been crossed.

"It's good she's in custody," Ford said. "La Eme put out a fifty-thousand-dollar hit on her, in retaliation for the foot soldier's life."

"They can't do that," I objected. "She's *familia.* She's made her bones."

"Of course they can. Who's she going to appeal to, the *sureño* HR department?" He let that settle. Then he said, "This isn't really about Serena Delgadillo, though. She's not the person I have sitting in front of me. You are."

Before I could adjust to the shift in focus, Ford got to his feet and walked to the interrogation-room mirror. He pressed his face against the glass to see through.

"Who's in there?"

"No one. I didn't think there was, but sometimes cops get bored, just hang out in there for no good reason, watch the show. I wanted to be sure."

Interesting. Magnus Ford was about to say something that he didn't want his colleagues to hear.

He turned away from the mirror and said, "I'm retiring soon."

"Congratulations?" I offered blankly.

He came back to stand over the table, pulling his billfold out of his jacket. He opened it and laid a business card on the table between us. I picked it up and read it. THE FORD GROUP, it read, in a spare, clean font.

He said, "I'm going into a private line of work. Personal security, surveillance, property recovery, negotiation, ransoms. A kind of private police work that wouldn't have to abide by jurisdictional lines."

"Wow. That must be a generous pension you're getting, to be able to do all that."

There was an answering flash of wry humor in his eyes. "I have financial resources beyond this job. Which I'll be using to hire and to adequately compensate the right people. People with special talents."

He stopped there, went around to the other side of the table, and sat down again. "This is the deal, Hailey: You agree to come work for me and you'll walk out of here. What I know about your crimes as 'Insula,' that retires with me. I won't take it to a prosecutor, and you won't get charged. In addition, I'll make the homicide rap against Warchild go away."

"You can *do* that?"

"I'm not your average patrolman. I've made some friends in my time in government work."

Not police work, but government work. That was interesting. I filed it away for the future.

He went on, "In addition, I'll get Delgadillo a plane ticket out of state. She won't be safe here, even if she went up to Northern California. There are *sureño* guys who'd follow her there, for a fifty-thousand-dollar payday."

That was true. I said, "I'm not necessarily saying yes, but why me? I don't have any special talents."

He merely tilted his head.

"Oh, God," I said. "You know about the brain tumor. That's not a talent. And it won't stay asymptomatic forever. That makes me a relatively short-term investment. I don't see how I could be all that valuable to you."

Ford reached into his coat pocket and took out a Hershey bar, unwrapped it. "Sweet tooth," he said, as if apologizing. "You want some?"

I shook my head.

He broke off a rectangle of chocolate and put it in his mouth, sucked gently for a moment, and swallowed. "In a way you make a good point," he said. "Your lack of fear could be a liability as much as an asset, if it makes you behave in unnecessarily reckless ways. As for your other assets, you're a good fighter and shooter, but a lot of people have military training. And then you're trilingual, but one of those languages is useless to me. French or German would be far more useful than Latin."

My high-school guidance counselor had argued much

the same thing, pushing me to enroll in French courses rather than leave campus and sit in on Latin classes at the community college. If only she were here. Vindication at last.

"You have potential," Ford continued, "but that potential remains raw, and it'll take time and work to develop. You are, as you said, an investment."

He'd been *thinking* about this.

"How long would I be in the service of the"—I glanced at the business card again—"the Ford Group?"

"Well," he said, "given the generous offer I'm making you here, your freedom and Warchild's, plus the resources I'm going to put into your training, to fill in the gaps left by West Point and the streets . . . I'd say it's fair to call your term of service 'indefinite.' Put another way, as long as you can realistically commit."

"Realistically commit?" I repeated. "You're talking about the tumor again. Are you saying I'm coming to work with you for the rest of my life?"

"It was you who called yourself a short-term investment. That wasn't me."

"Can I just stop here and congratulate you on your tact? You're really putting on a clinic in sensitivity."

He sighed and lifted a shoulder. "Be that as it may, I'm going to need an answer from you. The prosecutor's office closes in"—he checked the readout on his cell phone—"forty minutes."

I said nothing.

He added, "I should also have mentioned, in addition to

the legal considerations you'd get from me for joining up, of course you'd be paid. You might be pleasantly surprised."

He really was offering a lot. But it couldn't exactly be called a choice, and I was pretty tired of being manipulated and boxed into corners.

He was watching me, waiting for me to get uncomfortable and fill the silence. He was very, very still: I'd rarely met anyone who made so few little, incidental movements.

Finally I cleared my throat.

"If I come work for you," I said, "there's one other thing I need, as part of my recruitment package."

His eyebrows rose again, skeptically. "The package I've already offered isn't generous enough for you?"

"This is important. It's something I can't leave unfinished."

"I'll consider it, then. Tell me."

"There's a girl in Serena's neighborhood named Luisa Ramos. She goes by Trippy, though she might have a new moniker now. She used to be a sucia, but now she runs with Tenth Street. She's a figure who's probably beneath your notice, at least for now."

He nodded but said nothing.

"I need your guys in gang intelligence to focus their attention on her and get her off the streets. They won't have to manufacture any charges. If they watch her, she'll give them reason. I think she's a blossoming psychopath."

It wasn't just her attack on me I was thinking of. When she'd had me pinned, Trippy had said, *When Warchild's gone, I'm going to run the sucias.* Not *someday if,* but *when.* It sounded like she'd known that Serena was going away.

The missing detail in Ford's story, about the gunfight at the storage unit, was this: There were many ways the *sureño* bosses could have found out about Serena's oil-of-chronic trade, but how did the foot soldier know exactly which storage facility, and which unit, was hers? Serena was cagey, and the only person who knew the location of her biggest stash was her lieutenant. That was me, and I hadn't told anyone.

But before me it was Trippy. I felt fairly certain she'd betrayed Serena to La Eme.

Ford tapped the ends of his fingertips together. "You're leaving that world behind you, though. You'll be safe from this girl. So getting her arrested and imprisoned, is that just retaliation for past wrongs?"

I shook my head. "There are other people she could still hurt."

"I see," he said. "And if I do that, you'll come work for me?"

"Yes." Such a small word.

"Done," he said, then he stood up and unlocked me from the D-ring.

I stood up, too, stretching my limbs after such a long time of sitting. "What happens now?"

Ford reached into his coat again and set a pager on the table. "That's yours, as my employee. Don't give the number to anyone else. It's just for me to contact you. It won't be this week, or next week, but when I'm ready, I'll page you." He put his handcuff key back in his pocket. "I'm putting a lot of trust in you, here, that you won't be on the first Greyhound out of town once the charges against Warchild are dropped. So I'd like you to stay in Los Angeles. I'm not saying that I'll be checking up on you, but you might find it wise to remember that I know where you live. In fact, I thought I might give you a ride home, unless there's someone else you'd like to call."

"No," I said. "There isn't."

"All right," he said. "If you're ready, I'll take you to say good-bye to your friend."

EPILOGUE

1

Once I was proved innocent, I became the subject of a small media-feeding frenzy. My other life as "Insula" never came out, since only Ford and Joel Kelleher knew that particular detail, and neither of them spoke to the media. Given that, there was nothing to take the luster off my story, which became uncomplicatedly heroic. The *Dateline* and *20/20* types acted accordingly, immediately revising their take on me to stress my West Point accomplishments (whereas before they stressed my stigmatizing failure to graduate). They drew attention to the "mystery" of my "lost" years, the way I "dropped off the grid" after leaving West Point, then "came virtually out of nowhere" to "run Brittany Mercier literally to the ground on national television." And then, they said dramatically, I walked out of a sheriff's substation a free woman "and, once again, simply disappeared."

Not true, of course. I hadn't gone very far at all, just back to Crenshaw. I cleaned my apartment in anticipation of leaving it for good, scrubbing the corners of the kitchen linoleum, chasing dust kitties from under the couch. I ran for miles to stay in shape and did push-ups and sit-ups in my living room, but I stayed away from the Slaughterhouse.

Which isn't to say I didn't fight at all.

It was an unusually warm evening in Los Angeles, almost humid. The sun had set, but the streetlights weren't yet on as I guided the Aprilia through waning traffic. Ford didn't want me to leave the city, but he hadn't said anything about staying out of Trece territory.

I parked my bike and dismounted in front of a stuccoed-over, one-story Craftsman house with bars on the windows. I didn't bother with the front door, because there was noise from the backyard, a surf of female voices in mixed Spanish and English. The sucias were gathered.

I reached over the top of the gate, felt for the gravity latch, and pulled it up. The yard was a scene that looked like casual weeknight partying: some beers and cigarettes going, easy chatter. The sharp tang of lighter fluid rode on the breeze, and I saw a gunmetal-colored kettle grill, not yet lit. A picnic-style table with attached benches was pushed to the edge of the yard, and it was there that I saw Diana, not drinking, not smoking, wearing long, baggy shorts and a tight black tank shirt and hard work boots.

"Hey," I said. Conversation stilled as everyone looked at me.

Diana stood up, and we inventoried each other. It was the first time I'd seen her wear any makeup: black eyeliner that made her gaze hard.

"I'm ready," she said.

"Come on, then," I said.

Her booted foot flashed out. I dodged it. *Oh, faster than that,* I thought.

She planted the foot that had missed and readied to come at me again, but behind her raised hands her eyes were a little less hard and sure than they'd been a second before. I raised my hands, too, and twitched my left as though about to jab but struck with my leg instead, launching my shin into the side of her knee at a forty-five-degree angle. She wasn't ready—I hadn't even glanced downward toward her legs— and her knee gave way, and she fell.

For just a second, she looked up at me from the ground as if to say, *Why are you doing this to me?*

You know why, I thought. She scrambled to her feet.

And we fought.

She had heart, and clearly some experience, but not technique, and, worse, she telegraphed everything by looking first where she intended to strike. I blocked everything she threw at me and bloodied her nose though I didn't mean to do it. Her eyes were narrowed with determination, but she was breathing hard, and in another minute she'd tire, and her hands would begin to drop, and her blows wouldn't be convincingly strong to those watching.

Now. I let my left hand waver downward, like I might in a moment of carelessness, and she saw it and capitalized.

I'd been hit harder, but even so, one of those bright neurological camera flashes went off in the periphery of my vision. *Good girl.*

I came back with a hard flurry, as if angered. Actually, I was backing her up to a slender strip of grass, off the concrete. When I had her there, I closed in, swept her right leg with my foot, grabbed her shoulders and wrenched them to the right. Then her center of gravity was over the place where her leg should have been but wasn't, and she fell.

When she was pinned, her face turned to the side against the turf, I put my elbow against her jaw and said, loud enough for those watching to hear, "Give it up. Tap out."

"No," she said.

I leaned forward to get a little more weight on her. "Give it up."

"Bullshit."

I lowered my face and whispered. "Do you think you could really be Warchild's equal?"

Her eyes were squeezed closed in discomfort. "*Not hers, maybe. But yours.*"

It was a sign of the defiance she was supposed to demonstrate and, more than that, of family pride. I took my weight off her, got to my feet, and extended a hand. She looked up at it with uncertainty. "It's okay. You did good," I said, and she let me pull her up. She fell against me in a rough, bloody hug, whispering. "Thank you," she said. "Thank you, Hailey."

I patted her shoulder and then pulled back to speak to the assembled girls. "I'm not going to be around from now on. Neither is Warchild." I put my hand on Diana's shoulder. "This is Gladia. She's in charge. Anyone has a problem with that, say something now. To me. Don't sneak around talking shit later."

I let my gaze roam over them, looking for resistance. There were sucias here who were older than Diana, and nearly all had put in more work than she had. But no one said anything.

"Okay, then," I said.

"Serena wanted this," I said, into Diana's ear. "She told me so."

It was also for Diana's sake that I'd asked Ford to take Trippy out of commission. With a power vacuum in the sucias—and however strong and smart Diana was, Trippy would consider her leadership a vacuum—she'd come back to take by force what she considered her rightful place, and Diana—who I'd known even before speaking to Serena was the best choice to fill the leadership role—would be directly in her crosshairs.

"She also chose your new name," I told her. "It's from the Latin *gladius*. You should look it up."

More beers were brought out from an ice chest, and a cold, wet can was thrust into my hands. Diana pressed hers against the back of her neck, a home remedy to stop the last seepage of blood from her injured nose.

Someone lit the charcoal grill, and when the flames died down, one of the other girls laid a slab of ribs marinated in honey-jalapeño barbecue sauce on the grate. It was tradition to party after a jumping-in, even in hard times.

No one asked me why I was leaving. I was nearly twenty-five, an eternity in gang years, an age where those who had escaped a violent death or imprisonment counted their blessings and stopped banging, even if they were, technically, down for life. And I was white. I'd always been an anomaly, someone who shouldn't have been in their world in the first place.

What the girls of Trece did ask me was what I knew about Serena. I told them as much as I could: that she'd gotten into an unfortunate clash with a guy who was breaking into her storage unit, that she'd shot him and had faced a murder rap, but that it had been dismissed, and now she'd left town. When they asked me where she'd gone, I lied and said I didn't know.

"You caught that girl. I knew you would, prima."

"Yeah, I did. How are you, Serena?"

"*What's to say? I finally found out what the limit of my fate is. Chicago. That's where the Shadow Man is sending me. Can you believe it? Me in Illinois, in the fucking snow? You know what they call the two big gang nations out there? The People and the Folks. The first time somebody told me that, I was like, are you playing with me?*"

"*I don't think the Folks Nation is going to have much room for a homegirl from East L.A. Maybe it's time to go legit. You dodged a real bullet today.*"

"*Yeah, a murder rap. That was your doing, right? What'd you give the Shadow Man in trade?*"

"*Nothing I can't afford. I'll be fine.*"

I'd known that Serena had served time, but I'd never seen her that way before, in loose county blues, makeup-less, eyes shadowed from lack of sleep. She'd laughed and slipped back into the speech patterns of the adolescent *chola* she'd once been, something she did when she was nervous or upset.

I understood why. The most frightening thing ahead of her wasn't the cold weather of Chicago, or loneliness, or going legit. It was the memory of the man she'd shot and killed. No matter how bad a guy he'd been, he'd been a person, and she'd pointed her gun at him and pulled the trigger and taken away his everything. He was going to visit her in her dreams. Trey Marsellus still sometimes visited me, and his death had been solely accidental.

I wanted to ask her if he'd drawn on her first and if the

shooting had at least been self-defense. But either it had been or it hadn't, and Serena already knew. It wouldn't change anything for me to have that information.

Then I'd asked if there were messages she wanted me to carry back to the people she knew, and she nodded and beckoned me closer to the bars, telling me her succession plan for the sucias, and I'd promised her that I'd fight Diana and make sure the other girls knew that it was Serena's will that she be the new leader. Then we'd said our good-byes, as Magnus Ford waited, out of earshot, by the gate at the end of the cell block.

2

Back at my apartment building, after Diana's initiation, I was slowing the Aprilia to park when I saw him across the street: a tall, lanky young man with curling reddish blond hair, leaning against a late-model Porsche, his eyes hidden behind aviator shades despite the fading light. My heart skipped a beat with anticipation.

But as I was pulling off my helmet, I realized that something was off. CJ seemed out of proportion to his car. It was as if he were too *short*.

Then he took off his sunglasses, and I understood.

"Virgil?" I said.

It was really the midnight blue Porsche that had thrown me off. It was nothing that Virgil Mooney should have been able to afford. Beyond that, CJ and Virgil had always looked very much alike, and if Virgil's West L.A. style was very like his older brother's . . . well, it wasn't like a lot of the guys under thirty in Southern California weren't wearing the same thing.

But Virgil, at five-eleven, was well shy of CJ's height, and beyond that, there was a kind of spark that was missing in him. I'd always felt that the gods had touched CJ in a way they hadn't his older and younger brothers. But Virgil had a sunny simplicity that made him straightforwardly easy to love, compared to his sometimes maddening older brother.

I loped across the street to him. "Virgil?" I said, as if still not sure of his identity. I hadn't seen him in years.

"Hi, Cousin Hailey," he said.

"Hi," I said. "How did you find me?"

"You mailed your address to CJ," he said. "I have his house key, so I can check in once in a while, and I saw the postcard."

He smiled at me, but I didn't miss the serious cast of his eyes.

"Is everything okay?" I said, meaning, *Is CJ okay?*

"It's Dad," he said, and brushed a stray hank of hair away from his face. "He had a little heart attack, then a bigger one in the hospital, and then they think he's got blood clots in his carotid. It's a lot at once. He's going to have surgery, early tomorrow. They said they could put it off a little while, for his kids to get into town." He swallowed. "You know what that means."

I did know. Porter's doctors wanted him to have a chance to say his good-byes. Just in case.

Virgil went on, "He asked to see you. He considers you one of his kids, he and Mom both."

How long had it been since I'd spoken to either of them, Porter or Angeline? Virgil was absolutely right: They'd treated me as one of their own children, given me the kind of non-judgmental guidance and approval my mother had been by nature incapable of and my father had not lived to provide.

"I should've kept in touch with them better," I told Virgil.

And though I would have a hard time explaining it to Virgil, there was going to be a problem in rectifying that now, if it meant going to Nevada, across state lines. Ford had been very clear on that point. He didn't even want me to leave Los Angeles. He'd also been clear on having powerful friends, from his time in "government work." I wouldn't have been surprised to learn that my name was on some kind of list: if not the actual Homeland Security no-fly list, then something that would assure that Ford would be contacted as soon as my name turned up on a passenger manifest.

I sighed. "This is hard to explain, but I don't think I can fly."

Virgil didn't do the obvious, which would have been to ask why not. Instead he smiled slyly and held up his car keys. "Oh, we can *fly*," he said.

The car, it turned out, was a repair job Virgil was doing. "I called the owner and said there was an emergency in the family and I'd be delayed in getting it back to him," Virgil told me. "I didn't promise that the car was going to be locked in my garage that whole time."

"Is this thing going to break down somewhere in the desert?"

Virgil shook his head. "It's minor stuff. The heater/AC fan is broken, and the passenger-door gasket is warped so that it leaks in the rain. Nothing that'll keep us from getting up to Nevada in time."

So I'd napped in the passenger seat while Virgil, as he'd promised, flew us across black and empty highway, unpatrolled secondary roads where he could drive as fast as he liked, under a blanket of night sky broken by icy stars.

Porter was at the main hospital in Reno, and it was there that I greeted my family, each in turn. Angeline wore her hair shorter now than she had most of her life, but still long enough to wrap in a short knot on her neck, and her face was only gently lined—laugh lines around the eyes and such. Then Moira, with whom I had briefly shared a room during my first days in California. By an accident of genetics, she looked more like my mother than I did, with Julianne McNair's dark hair and good bones. She was quieter than her brothers, but underneath it kind and nonjudgmental like her parents, and I leaned in for a feminine wishbone hug, shoulders and chest touching but hips separate.

Constantine was nearly as tall as CJ but kept his red-gold hair short, and his nails were clipped but still stained faintly with grease from his mechanic's job; he thumped me on the back like he might have a guy.

"Is CJ on his way?" I asked when the greetings were finished.

Moira said, "We've left him two messages, but we're not sure exactly where he is right now," and Angeline added, "I never knew his job required him to travel so much. It didn't used to. Seemed like he was always in L.A. when his daddy or I needed to talk to him."

I didn't see a need to add anything to that, though I could have enlightened them on CJ's desire not to be in Los Angeles.

Angeline said, "Why don't you go on in and see your uncle? We've all already been, and he was asking specifically if you were coming."

Porter looked frail and wan, but who didn't, in pajamas and a hospital bed? His eyes were bright and sharp, though, as I came in. "There's my youngest daughter," he said, and a smile creased his work-worn face.

"Hi, Uncle Porter." I kissed his forehead. "How are you feeling? Didn't you tell them you're a Mooney, that there's never anything wrong with you a Goody's Headache Powder won't fix?"

He lifted a hand from the bedsheet and waved it. "I used to think that. It's all vanity, like the man says. Sit down, kid."

I did as he said.

"I'd ask if you were keeping out of trouble, like I used to, but . . . well, I've seen the news."

"Yeah," I said. "Things got a little crazy for a while."

"But now they know"—he gestured at the TV, indicating the mass media and the police beyond—"that you didn't hurt anybody."

"Yes," I reassured him. "They do."

"That's good," he said. "We need you, you know."

"Me?" I gave him a "that's crazy" look. "You guys don't need me."

"I do," he said. "Listen, this is a good hospital, and I'm getting good care, but . . . Hailey, promise me you'll watch out for your cousin." He didn't have to specify which one.

"CJ doesn't need looking after," I said. "Are you worried that he'll get addicted to something?"

It was the only thing I could imagine Porter or Angeline lying awake at night about; they'd known about his marijuana use in high school, and they were smart enough to know that anything else he wanted was readily available to him now, in the circles he moved in.

I said, "Trust me, I've never seen any sign that he's using anything to excess. He doesn't even drink very much."

"I know," Porter said. "That's not what I'm worried about."

"Then what? CJ's smart, you know that, and he's got more money than most of us will earn in five lifetimes. He's handling success fine."

"He is right now," Porter said. "You make sure it stays that way. Don't let him find a guru and move to an ashram."

I laughed in spite of myself.

Porter didn't. "You may not think so, Hailey, but of all my kids, Cletus has the hardest row to hoe as he gets older, and I think you're the only one tough enough to put a boot up his ass if the day comes that he really needs it. If I'm not around then, you tell him I told you to do it."

"Yes, sir," I said, and was surprised to find my vision blurring with tears.

"Don't do that, kid," he said gently.

"He's on his way here," I said, knowing it'd be true soon enough; CJ never neglected his voice mail very long. "I'll do what you're asking, but when he gets here, give him the guru-and-ashram speech yourself. It'll have more weight coming from you."

"Are you kidding me?" he said. "That boy adores you."

Those words almost prickled on my skin, like an unexpected caress. "I love you, Uncle Porter," I said, standing up, "and I don't think he'll need it, but I'll look out for CJ."

The afternoon wore on; Moira and I went to the hotel down the street where the rest of the family was staying and found they had no more rooms left, but Moira told me I could stay in her room, which had two beds. I left my overnight bag in the room, and we went out looking for food. When we returned to the hospital with containers of Chinese takeout, Constantine told us that CJ had called.

"He was in Haiti," he said. "Now he's in Atlanta, but there's severe thunderstorms in the area and they've grounded the planes. He's trying to get onto a standby list for the first flight out here, because of the family emergency. But you know how that goes. Cletus didn't say as much, but half the people in that airport are probably claiming that Western civilization will fall if they don't get to their destination on time."

"He'll get through," I said. It wouldn't be because of his semifamous name, either. It would be partly because of the medical emergency in the family and partly because CJ would use his good Southern manners and give the ticketing agent the look that made women from all walks of life lose their train of thought, and somehow he'd get on that plane ahead of all the blustering petty tyrants who had crucial business waiting.

"Well, he sounded bent out of shape about being stuck there," Constantine said. He took off his ball cap and ran a hand through his hair.

"Bent out of shape" probably didn't do justice to how CJ felt right now, I knew. The Mooneys were a close-knit clan. But I didn't worry about it. I had always said that CJ had a blessed life. The universe seemed to repay his essential decency with favors large and small, and I felt certain that a hole would open in the storm system and CJ would get here well before Porter's scheduled nine A.M. surgery.

Except that around ten-thirty that evening, maybe two hours after CJ texted us to say he was in Denver trying to get a connecting flight, some kind of alarm went off on Porter's monitoring equipment. The doctor on call came into the room, and then Porter's doctor was paged to come in from home. She came out and said something about a clot shifting, being dangerously unstable, and by half past eleven Porter was in surgery.

Fuck, I thought, and took Virgil's hand.

"Hailey. Hey, Hailey."

I woke with the hard plastic of waiting-room chairs pressing into my flesh. For a minute, I was disoriented, thinking of Serena saying, *They're still getting the baby out,* and that Nidia Hernandez was dead.

No, that wasn't right. I realized it was Virgil sitting on his heels in front of me. He was smiling.

"What's going on?" I said.

"Dad's out of surgery. He's fine," Virgil said. "He's in recovery."

"Oh, that's wonderful," I said.

"Mom went to the hotel to get a couple hours of sleep before he comes around," Virgil said. "But us kids are having a kind of family reunion up on the roof. You're invited, of course."

"The roof?" I said.

"We stole a couple blankets to spread out. And it's really warm out. Nearly a full moon, too. Oh, and there's a bottle."

"You're too young to drink, you delinquent," I said.

"There's no such thing."

I knew I should leave. The sooner I went back to L.A., the less likelihood that Magnus Ford would even know I was gone. Besides, when CJ got in, he probably wouldn't care about seeing me. He'd want to see his dad; that was the important thing.

Then I said, "Okay, let me just wash my face and brush my teeth, and I'll be right up."

I did those things, then climbed the stairwell to the roof access, as Virgil had directed.

He'd been right. It was a beautiful night out, the American flag snapping in the warm wind, the lights of central Reno in the distance. My cousins were sitting in a rough circle on two blankets that eased the bite of the pebbly rooftop.

Then I realized that we were not a reunion of four. We were five.

As if it were a formal event, like a treaty signing, CJ got to his feet while his siblings remained seated, and he crossed the rooftop alone to meet me. I stayed where I was, near the door. When he reached me, we did not touch. He was wearing a white dress shirt, dark trousers, good shoes; obviously he'd dressed for the possibility that the only open seating on flights west would be in first class.

"Hey," I said.

"Hey."

"I'm glad your father's all right."

"Me, too."

There was a moment's silence. Then he said, "On the

phone I didn't ask if you'd come up to the hospital. On the plane I kept wishing I had asked. I kept thinking that if something went wrong in surgery and Dad didn't make it out, above all people I would want you with me."

To take care of him. Like Porter had said.

I wanted to say, *You know I'll always be there,* but it wasn't a promise I could keep. Instead I raised myself on my toes and put my arms around him.

"I'm here."

"I missed you," he said.

"I did, too," I said. "I'm sorry."

He lowered his face into my hair, and I sighed. But then, by some unspoken agreement, we both stood back, both feeling the eyes on us and our display of affection.

"Come on," CJ said, and led me to the rest of our family.

". . . so okay, it's Christmas morning, and suddenly Mom's got this idea to hunt up the home video of their first Christmas with Constantine," CJ was saying. "So Dad goes to the closet where they keep all that stuff, and before he can find that tape, there's a video just labeled 'Ball Game.' Nothing else. Dad perks up, pulls it out, and says, 'Hey, want to watch the ball game?' No idea what ball game or anything. So that's what we do. Watch the Braves play the Giants in a regular-season game from 1996. On Christmas Day 2001."

"That's so Dad," Moira said.

They were telling stories about their father. It was like a

wake. Better, though: one with no bereavement, and a very fine scotch whisky.

"Where did you get this?" Virgil demanded, holding the bottle of Laphroaig.

"Duty-free shop in Atlanta," CJ said.

"How could you buy something in a duty-free shop? You were taking a domestic flight." That was Constantine.

"I was extremely nice to the clerk."

General laughter. Virgil said, "How nice, exactly? Did you have to get your hand wet? Did she—"

"Virgil!" Moira said. "That's enough."

Unperturbed, CJ said, "How do you know the clerk was a she?"

The laughter that followed was both scandalized and delighted. We were all pretty well lit up. CJ was stretched out, resting his head in my lap in the casually entitled way I remembered. He didn't have a sexist bone in his body, but he'd grown up being loved on by a mother and an older sister, and as a result he was like a Labrador who feels it's always a good time for you to scratch his ears. For my part, I was resisting the urge to stroke his hair.

"Well," Moira said with one of those sighs that's half a farewell, "it's getting late."

"Getting early," CJ corrected. It had to be nearly four in the morning.

"I'm glad none of us has to drive. Particularly this kid." Constantine rubbed Virgil's head with his knuckles. "Virg, you hold your liquor worse than any Mooney I know. Hailey here could drink you under the table, and she's two-thirds your weight and not even a Mooney."

"Yes she is," CJ corrected.

"By DNA. You know what I mean."

They began getting up, stretching, Constantine picking up the empty bottle of Laphroaig. Only CJ stayed where he was.

"Hey," I said. "Are you getting up?"

"No."

"I can't leave without my lap," I pointed out.

"I don't think it's a good idea for me to try those stairs in my condition."

Constantine gave him a surprised look. "You kidding? I've seen you drink twice that amount and not be impaired."

CJ sighed irritably. "I just want to stay out here a minute and sober up and enjoy the night. Is that a problem?"

But Virgil said, "He wants to be alone with Haaaaileeeeeey," drawing my name out in a schoolyard tease. "Aren't you guys getting old for the kissing-cousins act?"

"Virgil, you're drunk." That was Moira again. "Leave your brother alone. We're going."

Chastised, Virgil said, "I didn't mean anything by it." He looked at the two of us, hangdog.

"S'okay," CJ said.

"Is it, Hailey?" Virgil pursued, like a child.

"Yes," I said, "we're good. We'll see you tomorrow."

But as they disappeared through the stairwell door, I wondered if I would stay that long, or when I'd see my cousins again. Ford had flickered on the edge of my consciousness like heat lightning all night.

"That feels good," CJ said, his eyes closed.

I realized I was stroking his hair, like I'd been wanting to, grooming it gently. That hadn't taken long. His siblings had been gone all of a minute.

I said, "You're not really drunk, are you?"

"Not so's you'd notice," CJ said.

Virgil had been right: CJ had stayed because he wanted us to be alone. We hadn't been able to talk, not really, in front of his siblings. Except now we were alone, and I couldn't think of a start. Maybe nothing needed saying. Maybe "I missed you" and "I'm sorry" had covered it.

CJ said, "This last week I was in Haiti, visiting a friend of mine who went down there to volunteer."

"Yeah?"

"We were hanging out with some international aid workers in the country. They listened to BBC Radio on the shortwave, and that was about it. Not a lot of American news. So I didn't know anything about you getting accused of murder," he said. "The first I heard about it was today, trying to get home. At Hartsfield I was in the Delta lounge, watching their TV. The news was replaying the aerial footage of you running that woman to the ground, and I watched it and thought, 'When did I stop knowing what Hailey's life was about? Or did I just never know?' "

"You know me better than anyone," I reassured him. "You know the real me. That person on TV, she's just some crazy chick who grew up from the wreckage when I got kicked out of West Point."

"That was really hard on you, getting sent home."

"Sure."

"I never really got that, I guess," he said. "You came back and said you were okay. You moved out of my place after just a couple of weeks and found your own apartment. You acted like West Point was behind you. I should have known better."

"It's okay."

"There were some heavy things that happened last year, weren't there, though?" he persisted. "You've never really talked about what happened down in Mexico."

It didn't sound like a question, but it was. I was silent a moment. I'd tried so hard to keep my messy life from spilling over onto CJ's clean, golden one, but maybe I'd been trying too hard. Maybe I didn't need to see myself as having a double life, but rather one big, expansive one, with CJ part of it.

"Listen," I said. "Whatever you want to know about my life, just ask me, but do it tomorrow. Tonight you're tired."

"I'm okay."

"No you're not. Come on. The hotel's right across the—" I stopped.

"Street?" CJ supplied. "I know."

"It's not that," I said. "I just remembered that they're booked up. Never mind. I'm sleeping in Moira's room. You can probably crash with one of your brothers. Unless they're sharing a room already. That might be a little too crowded."

"Doesn't matter," CJ said. "I'll get a cab into town. There are other hotels. With Dad out of the woods, it's not like I need to be right across the way."

"Okay."

"Come with me?"

"What?"

"You walk in on Moira now, you'll wake her up. Come with me. You can sleep in my room."

"CJ, I think—"

"We've done it before. Nothing ever happens." Then, "I don't want to sleep alone."

"Are you still worried about your dad? I thought the doctors said he was going to be fine."

"I know. That's not what I meant. I just don't like sleeping alone. It's lonely."

"You mean you don't do it very often." I hated the jealousy that immediately rose up inside me.

CJ sat up and faced me, sensing the new seriousness in the conversation. "I do it a lot more than I'd like." He looked down at our interlaced fingers. "You?"

"Almost all the time."

He seemed sure that nothing would happen, as it never had before. I wasn't sure he was right. I didn't want to be having the thoughts I was having: about being in a dim hotel room with him, the unaccustomed feel of the crisp material of a dress shirt against my cheek. I'd had only a few guys in the past half year, and none of them, to say the least, had been junior-executive types. I was thinking of how it would feel to help CJ take off those formal clothes and touch the smooth, warm skin underneath.

I said, "CJ, I'm not sure how long I can stay up here. And even back in L.A. . . . my life there is unsettled, to say the least."

"Look," he said, "all I want is to sleep about ten hours with you somewhere near me. Doesn't have to be in the bed, maybe just the next bed over. Then I want a long, hot shower. Then, probably, a blueberry waffle. Maybe two. That's as far ahead as I'm thinking."

I played with a strand of hair. "That sounds . . ."

"What?"

"Like heaven."

We took the stairs down one flight and the elevator the rest of the way. I emerged into the lobby slightly in front of CJ, holding his hand, and stopped so abruptly he stepped on my heel.

Magnus Ford stood to greet us. He'd probably been down here awhile. My cousins had walked right past him, unaware.

What had been about to happen between CJ and me in the hotel room was going to stay a matter of conjecture, as was my stupid fantasy of a bigger, more whole life with CJ an integrated part of it.

"It was a family emergency," I said to Ford. "I was coming right back."

"Hailey?" CJ said, meaning, *Who's this guy?*

"You thought I wouldn't let you come?" Ford addressed

me, ignoring CJ. "You should have talked to me first. I would let you come."

CJ said, "What's going on?"

"He's a cop," I said.

"Oh, I'm a little more than *that*," Ford said dryly. "Time to go, Hailey."

When Ford stepped forward, CJ put his arms around me from behind and stared him down. He still didn't understand the situation; it was simply a hardwired response to a challenge from another male.

"I have to go with him," I said. "I'm sorry."

CJ didn't move. "Where's your arrest warrant?"

"Don't need one," Ford said. "I'm not arresting your cousin. But we had an agreement, which she violated the terms of by coming here."

CJ said, "If she's not under arrest—"

"It's complicated, but I have to do this," I said. "Don't worry. I'll be fine." I rose up on my toes and kissed his cheek. "You know I'm bulletproof, right?"

What I'd wanted to say was, *I love you,* but I couldn't say it in front of Ford.

"I know," CJ said softly.

And then he gave me to Magnus Ford.

Ten minutes later Ford and I were sitting outside a mini-mart in his powerful but nondescript black SUV. There were two cups of hot coffee in the cup holders. He'd drunk a little of his. I hadn't touched mine. I was crying. Not with any energy, just a steady drip of tears that, maddeningly, I couldn't stem.

"Come on, Hailey," he said. "You know better. You *know* better. You think what's back at that hospital is for you?" His voice was soft, gentle, gravelly. "Does he know about the brain tumor?"

I shook my head.

"When were you planning on telling him?"

I was silent.

"You think that's what he deserves, to stand next to your grave at twenty-eight, twenty-nine years old?" He let that sink in. "Some guys, they'd bounce back fast from burying a wife, be remarried in a year. Not a guy like that. You know how long he'd be waking up at night and reaching over to your side of the bed?"

I just don't like sleeping alone. CJ had said it himself.

"Hailey," Ford said, "we got off to a bad start last week. That's my fault. I've learned to be a tough negotiator. Sometimes I can't throttle back when I should."

He picked up my cup of coffee, pried off the lid. "You want some sugar in this?"

I nodded. At least my tears had dried up. For good, I hoped, wiping under my eyes with the caution of someone checking a wound for signs of bleeding.

He tore open a sugar packet, poured it in, and stirred it with a red plastic stick. Then he handed it to me, directly, instead of returning it to the cup holder.

"I don't think I gave you a clear picture of what it is I

was offering you in the interrogation room, other than freedom from prosecution for you and your friend," he went on.

"Which is?"

"What you were seeking at West Point," he said. "The development of your gifts to their fullest and an opportunity to be of some value to the world. You need that. It's not really optional for someone like you."

"Tell me," I said. "Where'd you get your psychology degree?"

"Harvard."

It was on the tip of my tongue to say, *Are you kidding?* but his face was completely serious. He wasn't kidding. I was speechless.

"I can make you do this, Hailey," Ford said. "But if you go into this with the attitude of a child forced to serve an after-school detention, you will be of limited use to me. It's better if you want it. Do you? Want it?"

The thing was, everything Magnus Ford had said was true. About what CJ deserved out of life and about why I'd gone to West Point. More than that, the man sitting next to me was interesting. Here was a man whose career in government work I probably hadn't heard the half of, who had a personal fortune yet wore generic cop clothes, and who held an Ivy League degree he didn't feel the need to tell people about unless asked point-blank. This had the potential to be interesting.

"Yes," I said. "I want it."

"Good," Ford said. He switched on the ignition. "Let's go."

about the author

JODI COMPTON is a graduate of UC Berkeley and has lived in various parts of California, as well as Minneapolis, Minnesota. She currently makes her home outside San Luis Obispo, California.

Read on for the opening chapters of
Jodi Compton's first Hailey Cain novel,
the thrilling

Hailey's War

prologue

The moon rises over the mountains of central Mexico, a nearly full moon in a sky the deep blue of an hour past sunset.

Get up.

I'm lying on a slope just down from a rural highway, lying in a mix of slate and grass and dirt that is damp with blood. There is dirt in my eyelashes and blood in what little of my hair I can see. There isn't much pain, but I'm very, very tired.

Get up or you'll die here.

My memories of what happened are inexact. I remember driving on a narrow highway through the mountains and into a dim tunnel with rough stone walls. Then this, looking up at the mountain ridge and the sky. I don't know how I got from the tunnel to here. It seems impossible, but I think I was shot.

I search my memories for some explanation. A rough voice: *You're one of our most promising cadets. I hate like hell to see this happen to you.*

No, that was too long ago.

A younger voice: *Pack up just what you need, I'm getting you out of L.A.*

That's not it, either.

I'm so tired, I just want to close my eyes. Except for that moon. It's getting brighter and higher, like God lifting his lamp, looking for his lost sheep.

I think the highway is up the slope, above me. If I were nearer to it, someone might see me. It might make a difference.

I get to my hands and knees, swaying, and put the waxing moon in my sights.

On your feet, soldier. You can do this. You're made outta this.

Then I stand up.

one

"Do you ever think about Jonah?"

"Jesus, is that my Bible? I haven't opened that thing in years. So you're talking about the guy that was swallowed by a whale?"

"Yeah."

"No, I'd have to say I don't think about him. I wouldn't think you would, either. I didn't take you for particularly religious."

"I'm not. That's my point, though. When you're not raised religious, you think of Jonah as the swallowed-by-a-whale guy, like Noah is the ark guy. But when you actually read the Book of Jonah, it's not what you expect."

"You read the whole book?"

"It's three pages long."

Morning in San Francisco. Jack Foreman, tall and thin, in his early forties, with a premature streak of gray in his light brown hair, was across the room, already dressed at quarter to eight, already having cleared away last night's Ketel One bottle and two glasses, showered, dressed, and fixed and consumed breakfast and an espresso. He was now scanning the headlines of both the *San Francisco Chronicle* and the *Los Angeles Times,* and at the same time keeping an eye on CNN with the sound off. I was still in his bed, naked, with my hair half raveled in the braids I forgot to take out last night, reading his Bible for no particular reason other than that it had caught my eye while Jack was still in the shower.

"The thing that's strange about the story is, Jonah doesn't seem to be scared of anything, even when he should be."

"No?"

"No. The story goes that God tells Jonah to go to the city of Nineveh to preach, and Jonah doesn't want to, so he gets on a ship for Spain. God sends a violent storm, and the ship's crew is scared. But when they go down to the hold to find Jonah, he's sleeping."

"Yeah?"

"*Sleeping.* Through a storm that has veteran sailors scared. So they wake him up and tell him, 'We're pretty sure we haven't done anything to anger our gods, might you have done something to anger yours?' And Jonah suggests that if they think this is the case, maybe they should throw him overboard."

"Huh."

"They're way out at sea. Jonah's effectively asking to be *drowned*. The crew says no at first, but later they decide he's right, and they throw him over, and then comes the whale part that everyone knows about. That's what it takes for him to finally decide that maybe he's in trouble. He prays to God—it's kind of a pretty poem, by the way—and God intervenes, so the whale spits him up onto dry land. And then he does go to Nineveh, and everyone in Nineveh really gets with the program, from the king on down. They repent in a big way. And Jonah isn't happy about it. He gets mad. He goes out in the desert and argues with God about destroying Nineveh."

"He wants Nineveh destroyed?"

"Yeah, but the bigger point is, he's arguing with the God of the Old Testament, the all-powerful white-beard guy who used to strike people dead. Doesn't that seem a little insane? Shouldn't Jonah be a little more afraid?"

"You think Jonah was suicidal."

"No. I mean, not necessarily."

"Then what's your theory? You sound like you've been putting a lot of thought into this. You must have one."

"No, sorry. I'm just a bike messenger. I don't get paid enough to theorize."

"Hailey . . ." he said, his tone a change of subject in itself.

"I know. You're ready for work. I've got to get up and dressed and out. I'll hurry." I was already sliding his Bible back onto the book-shelf.

Jack was a newsman for the Associated Press, a Midwestern trans-plant to California by way of, apparently, everywhere. Photographs on the far wall of his studio, Jack's own amateur work, attested to the width and breadth of his reporting career. Fellow reporters, editors, photographers, and other acquaintances looked out from pictures taken in the world's capitals and war zones, places Jack had been a correspondent.

He and I had crossed paths several times at the courthouse, where he covered motions and trials and I, a bike courier, dropped off and picked up legal papers. But we didn't get to know each other until the Friday night I'd literally backed into him in a tiny, crowded Asian grocery. When, after a few minutes of conversation, he asked me if I wanted company for dinner, I surprised myself by saying yes. Maybe it had been so long since I'd seen a guy who was neither a metrosex-ual nor a pierced and dreadlocked bike messenger that he had been exotic to me.

He was the first guy I ever slept with who wore boxer shorts. I didn't tell him that, our first night together. Guys have lost erections over less.

Now, as I was pulling on my long-sleeved thermal shirt and cargo pants, Jack said, "Are you hungry? There's bagels."

I shook my head. "I'll eat later." It was my day off, and a small plan for the morning was forming.

I sat on the floor to put on my boots. When I looked up, Jack was watching me.

He said, "Every time I see you lacing up those boots, I think I'm sleeping with an undercover DEA agent."

Bates Enforcers, heavy-soled black lace-ups with a side zip, draw a lot of attention.

"They're comfortable, is all."

Jack had never seen the gun. It was a .38 caliber Smith & Wesson Airweight, easy to conceal. Just five shots, but the kind of trouble I was likely to get into was the up-close-and-personal kind, and if

I couldn't get out of it with five rounds, I wasn't getting out of it at all.

I stood and gathered up my single-strap messenger bag, putting it over my shoulder, when the newspapers on the counter caught my attention.

"Are you done with this?" I asked, indicating the *Los Angeles Times* Calendar section, its front page dominated by a profile of a young white hip-hop producer. "Can I have it?"

"Sure," Jack said.

I slid the section of the paper into my bag, then walked ahead of Jack into the entryway, where my bicycle—it was my private transportation as well as my livelihood—leaned against the wall.

We emerged into the cool gray of June in San Francisco, me wheeling the bike and Jack holding the keys to his old Saab. He stopped for a moment, tapping a cigarette out of a pack, his first of the day. While he lit up, I looked downhill, toward the rest of the city. Jack's studio was at the edge of Parnassus Heights, and the view was fantastic.

It's hard to find anyone who doesn't find San Francisco beautiful, and I couldn't argue. I had been in San Francisco nearly a year. I had ridden every inch of its neighborhoods, the storied ones like Chinatown and North Beach, the quiet ones like the Sunset and Presidio Heights. Late at night, I had watched the lights of great containerships as they ghosted into the port of Oakland, across the water. I had seen this city in the rain, the sun, the fog, the moonlight, on moonless evenings illuminated by its own city lights. San Francisco seemed to pose for you endlessly, proving it could look beautiful under any conditions. People came from all over the country and paid exorbitant prices to own or rent a tiny part of San Francisco.

Only a philistine could stand on a hill, look out at San Francisco, and wish she were seeing the overheated sprawl of L.A. instead. But I did.

Jack had gotten his cigarette going; I could smell the fragrant-acrid smoke from behind me. I turned back to him and was just about to say, *I'll call you sometime this week*, when he spoke first. "Hailey?"

"What?"

"When you say you're going to get something to eat later, you mean later this morning, right? Not late this afternoon?"

"Yeah," I said, baffled. "Why?"

"We had a lot to drink last night, but I didn't see you eat anything. You're getting thin."

"Jack, my job burns, like, eight thousand calories an hour. I couldn't do it if I wasn't eating enough," I pointed out.

He was not appeased. I said, "Something else on your mind?"

He said, "You treat yourself with a certain amount of disregard, Hailey. I've known you for six months, and how often in that time have you been injured on the job? First those stitches in your eyebrow, then that thing with your wrist—"

"That was an old break. The bone was weak," I argued. "Look, I'm a bike messenger. I've been the top-earning rider for my service nearly every month since I hired on. I couldn't do that without taking some risks. There's a lot of competition."

Jack closed his eyes briefly, then said, "You don't want to be the most reckless bike messenger in San Francisco, Hailey. That's like being the town drunk in New Orleans."

"I didn't know you cared."

"You ever think about school?"

"I thought I mentioned that before," I said. "I did a little school back east. It didn't work out."

"And you can never go back?"

"What's with you today?" I asked him. "The thing I like most about you is that you're free of all the middle-class rhetoric, and now suddenly you're doing a guidance-counselor thing."

Jack sighed. "I'm not trying to make you angry."

"I'm not," I said, relenting.

"Really?" He threw down the cigarette and stepped on it.

"Really. I'll call you tomorrow. We'll get together, I'll eat a whole pile of food. You can watch."

Besides, I hadn't been lying when I said I was planning on having breakfast. Just not right away.

I didn't own a car, which wasn't supposed to be a problem in San Francisco. It's said to be one of the world's great walking cities—fairly compact, with temperate weather and beautiful neighborhoods. All true, but even so: forty-nine square miles. In my first weeks here, I'd chronically underjudged the time it was going to take me to walk places. Now, of course, I had my bike—an old silver Motobecane, very fast, with drop handlebars and paint rubbed off the top tube where someone had probably kept a chain wrapped around it.

I'd been a messenger for eight months, long enough to develop the cyclist's long, flat ellipse of muscle in my calf—I didn't have that even back east in school, when I'd thought I was in the best shape of my life. Now a short, easy ride brought me to my destination, the Golden Gate Bridge. Ever since I'd come out to San Francisco, it had become something of a habit of mine to come up here when I didn't have any big plan for my day.

If you've driven in California and visited the Bay Area, the bridge you most likely drove on was the Bay Bridge. It connects San Francisco to the East Bay. It is heavily trafficked, double-decked, beautiful in an industrial way. But it isn't an icon. The Golden Gate Bridge is, largely due to its location: It serves as a kind of borderline between the enclosed waters of the Bay and the open water of the Pacific, between the American continent and the rest of the world. It is open to cyclists and to pedestrians, many of whom are dazzled tourists. In its most mundane sense, it is the bridge between the city and the Marin headlands. But to twenty or more people a year, it is the bridge to eternity.

The Golden Gate Bridge is America's foremost suicide destination. The first suicide off the bridge was a WWI veteran who appeared to be out for a stroll until he told a passerby, "This is as far as I go." That was three months after the bridge was opened; it was still in its infancy. Sometimes I wondered: If that man had stayed home and stuck his head in an oven instead, would it have changed the bridge's destiny? Without his precedent, would the next person and the next have reconsidered, until it was understood that jumping off the Golden Gate just wasn't done? There are other bridges in America that are as accessible and potentially fatal but have virtually no history of suicides, apparently because it just didn't become a tradition.

Psychologists know there is a contagious aspect to suicide—not merely the destructive impulse itself, but also the where and the how of it. In Japan, they've had to close public attractions because they've become magnets for suicides. One person jumps into a volcano and more people get the idea. In other countries, the authorities intervene. In America, land of the individual destiny, not so much.

Cops who try to prevent suicides up here will tell you that they'll see a pedestrian with that end-it-all look and ask them if they're thinking of jumping. The pedestrian denies it and the cop has to take their word for it and move on. Then they'll look back and the guy is just gone. It's that quick. You don't even hear anything. I know, I've seen it, too.

I asked a patrolman once how he recognized someone with the suicide look. He told me, "You'll know it when you see it." And I do. It's in what they're *not* looking at. Unlike the tourists, they're not looking at the city skyline or the Marin headlands. They're looking at the water. Or at nothing, because all their attention is directed inside, replaying the past and seeing the bleak endless nothing of the future.

That's the thing I don't understand: How exactly do they choose their spot? What says to them, *This far but no farther*? I've never asked a potential jumper how they choose their spot. It's too flippant, and when I'm up here, I'm very, very careful. It's probably the most careful I ever am.

There was a man standing by the railing ten feet ahead of me. He wasn't even a particularly hard guess. He was pretty obviously homeless, skin leathery from sun and wind and maybe drug use. He wasn't looking at anything in particular, and he was too caught up in his internal weather to notice me approach.

The men were usually easier than the women. They could usually be softened by a young woman taking interest in them. The women were sometimes hostile. They told me that *someone like you* couldn't understand their problems. It was never quite clear what they meant by *someone like you*.

"Hey," I said quietly.

He was a big man, maybe six-foot-six, with shaggy hair and a shaggy beard. I could imagine him, at a happier point in his life, dressing as a pirate for Halloween, scaring little kids and then making them laugh.

"Are you hungry?" I said.

He looked at me flatly. "No," he said.

So much for the easy way, getting him off the bridge first, under a pretext. I said, "I thought you might want to get something to eat." I paused. "You know, instead of jumping."

He blinked, startled.

"I'm sorry to be so blunt," I said, "but that's the plan, isn't it? Jumping?"

"So what?" he said, and it wasn't hostile. He was probably too depressed to get really angry anymore. At least I hoped so. He was big enough that even if he wasn't in shape anymore, he could still pick me up and throw me off the bridge without much effort. I thought of the edged ripples of iron-colored water below, of Jonah's prayer: *You cast me into the deep, and all the flood surrounded me.*

I said: "I'm not here to tell you I understand all your problems or that everything's going to be okay. But I'm hungry, and I've got enough money to buy two breakfasts. If you're hungry, too."

And then, at the worst time, my cell phone began to ring. I really should shut it off when I'm up here. I knew who it was: work. Someone had called in sick, or just hadn't shown up. I was needed. And normally I'd have answered, except that right now the guy in front of me was about to make a life-or-death decision and I couldn't just say, *Hold that thought, I have to take this.*

The man in front of me was curious: "Don't you want to answer that?"

"Not really," I said, and it stopped ringing, going into voice mail. I persisted: "What do you say? Breakfast? And you leave the bridge alone at least one more day?"

He nodded slowly. "Yeah," he said. "Yeah, okay."

I'd like to tell you that Todd's story—that was his name—was original and fascinating. It wasn't. I'd heard it before: A good and happy life in an average way, until the onset of a chronic illness, exacerbated by drink. He went on disability until the money ran out. His marriage failed. He was unable to pay child support, so his wife saw no reason for him to know where she'd moved with their two kids. He'd stayed with a buddy until the buddy's wife wouldn't have it anymore. That left no one to care that he was standing on the bridge, ready to jump.

Todd and I made a plan for him that involved having only one drink and going to the VA to look up the brother he hadn't seen in twenty years, but who just might take him in. To level the playing field a bit, I told Todd part of my story—the part about going east to school and why I came back. Without that, the potential jumpers usually looked at me like some idealist who'd read a few too many inspirational books. Like if I weren't doing this, I'd be at the mission feeding the homeless, or in Africa doing medical work.

In someone else, what I did on the bridge would be philanthropy. For me it wasn't. A shrink would probably have a field day with it, trying to put the pieces together, how it fit with the reason I came back from the East Coast, and the reason I had to leave L.A. Those are two different stories, by the way. I'm getting to that.

I hadn't left Todd behind at the diner for more than three minutes when my cell rang again, and with a stab of guilt, remembering the call I'd ignored on the bridge, I immediately brought the Motobecane to a stop.

"It's me." Shay Clements was the owner of Aries Courier. "Fabian just radioed in. His crank's busted, he's stranded on Market Street. Can you go meet him, pick up his packages, and make his drops?"

"Yeah."

"Like, right now?"

Shay wasn't being pushy. A courier service stood or failed on its on-time performance, and that in itself gave me a twinge of confusion: The hour that had passed between the phone call on the bridge and this one was far too much time for Shay to wait. But there wasn't time to wonder about that. "I'm on it right now," I said. "I'm literally standing over my bike."

"Thanks," Shay said after giving me the intersection where I was to meet Fabian.

"It's no problem," I said.

And it wasn't. This was my work now, and I did it with the great humility life has taught me since I washed out of the United States Military Academy at West Point, just two months before I would have graduated and become a second lieutenant in the United States Army.

two

My name is Hailey Cain. I'm twenty-three and have one of the most popular first names for girls of my generation. Every year in school there were half a dozen Hailies or Haleys or Haileys in my class.

I'm Californian in a way that a lot of people are Californian: I was born somewhere else. My father was Texan, my mother from West Virginia. I was born in an off-base hospital near Fort Hood, Texas, where Staff Sgt. Henry Cain was stationed at the time. I missed being born on the Fourth of July by one day; my birthday was the fifth. Maybe I was born to be a failed patriot.

I take after my father in looks; I have his straw-blond hair and open face, except that mine is marked by a port-wine birthmark high on my right cheekbone. In my one photo of him, he's a big guy, shouldery, and I have a similar mesomorphic build at five-foot-seven. My only really good feature is my full lips. In high school, reading beauty-magazine articles about the power of a sultry movie-star gaze, I'd wished I could trade my good lips for thick double-fringed eyelashes. My cousin CJ had waved that off, saying, *Guys don't fantasize about how* eyelashes *will feel wrapped around the johnson.* CJ could get away with saying outrageous shit like that because he had never fully lost his Southern accent, and it gave everything he said a good-old-boy innocence.

After Texas, my father was posted in Hawaii and Kentucky and then Illinois, where he died in an accident, a truck rollover on the base. I was eleven at the time. The Army's death benefit wasn't going to keep my mother and me solvent very long; Julianne had never been what you'd call a career woman. So we went to California, where her sister Angeline had already moved with her husband, Porter Mooney, and their four kids.

Porter was a guard at the federal prison in Lompoc, and the Mooneys had a big falling-down house outside of town that re-created the way they'd lived in West Virginia. There were always half a dozen cars in the yard—Porter and his oldest son, Constantine, were mechanics par excellence. They didn't just fix up cars and trucks; they worked on farm equipment, too, when people brought it to them. Behind the house was a half-acre of kitchen garden, and a dozen chickens roamed the yard. Angeline sold the eggs they didn't need at the farmers' market, along with sunflowers from the garden, and she gave piano lessons to local kids. There were always people who would sneer at how the West Virginia Mooneys lived, but the fact that six people got by comfortably on just one full-time salary and a few sidelines shamed the debt culture that most of middle-class California was mired in.

When Julianne and I arrived from Illinois, bereaved and nearly broke, theirs became an eight-person household. Porter and Angeline's two oldest kids were almost finished with high school, and I never got too close to them. And the baby of the family, Virgil, was only starting first grade. But the middle son, my cousin CJ, he was a different story.

CJ and I were the same age, almost literally. We'd been born ten days and a thousand miles apart, and never met until I came to California. We were in the same grade and same class in school, and if it hadn't been for that, I would have been friendless pretty much until high school. I was skinny and unprepossessing, self-conscious about my birthmark, shell-shocked over my father's death, culture-shocked over my arrival in California.

I was used to moving—all Army kids are—but Santa Barbara County was different. People hear the words *Santa Barbara* and they think of wealth, and that was certainly true of the city itself, with its gleaming white Mission-style architecture and streets generously lined with bougainvillea. But where the Mooneys lived, east of Vandenberg Air Force Base, was mostly rural, and yet more racially and economically diverse than an outsider would have thought. In the halls of my new school quite a few of the white students, and some black, were the children of Air Force personnel or staff at the federal prison. Many others were Latino, the sons and daughters of agricultural workers, some of them undocumented. In this working-class mix moved the well-dressed children of winemaker families, new money that had recently gravitated to what was becoming a hotbed of viticulture. Old California was here, too, in the kids with Chumash blood, the Indians who originally settled the area. Our high-school salutatorian was a Japanese boy whose family had farmed its acreage for generations—all except for those years spent in an internment camp during World War II.

Put another way: There's a certain kind of white person I like to tell about my first real kiss. It was with a classmate in the seventh grade who was black. *Awww, isn't that great,* I can almost see the listener thinking. Then I tell the rest of it. The next day, three girls cornered me out behind one of the portable classrooms at the edge of the school grounds. They were black. Their leader was a girl who'd been the boy's best friend since childhood and felt that she should have been first in line to get that kiss. Her two friends had held my arms while she gave me a pretty good beatdown.

And that's all I say. Usually, it's clear that the listener wants there to be more: some throat-clearing rhetoric about how I understand the social tensions that led to et cetera cetera cetera, or maybe that the girl and I had become friends later in high school. When I don't say anything like that, sometimes people look uncomfortable, like I've said something racist, though they can't identify exactly what it is.

The truth is that the girl and I didn't become friends, but by a year later, if either of us thought about the incident at all, we remembered it as just girls fighting over a boy. It could have happened between two black girls or two white girls, but it hadn't. The difference between the way middle-class educated people thought about race and the way people like me lived it was like the difference between what was in surgical textbooks and what happened in an Army field hospital.

When I say that the only thing that made those early years bearable was my cousin CJ, though, I don't mean that he knew everybody at school and introduced me around, easing my way into social success. The Mooneys had arrived in California only a year before Julianne and me, and though CJ would later become Californian in a big way, it hadn't happened by the time I got there. In sixth grade, CJ was already six feet tall, but too skinny, with rawboned hands. The other kids found his Appalachian accent incomprehensible and his first name laughably Southern. I never used it; I always called him CJ, which he liked.

CJ had one advantage over me, though: The other kids learned pretty quickly that he could fight, and they left him alone. I served my fistfight apprenticeship a lot more slowly and painfully. To his credit, CJ never jumped in and fought my battles for me. He understood, the way an adult wouldn't have, that I had to earn my respect myself.

If nothing else, though, CJ's friendship soothed the pains of early adolescence. At school, we ate lunch together when the longtime Californians and the Air Force kids were branched off in their cliques. After school, we halved the time it took us to do homework by splitting the assignments and copying each other's answers. It was probably that joint arrangement that kept CJ's grades up in junior high. It's not that he wasn't bright—he was—but his studies had never interested him much.

What interested him was music. CJ's mother had started teaching him the piano when he wasn't yet old enough to read, and though he was good at it, by junior high he rarely played, considering the piano to be a feminine, Victorian instrument. But he did love music, black music in particular—blues, gospel, and jazz. Even at thirteen, if he owned a CD by a white artist, I didn't know what it was. He was forever slipping his headphones over my ears so I could appreciate something about Miles Davis or John Lee Hooker.

In the insecurity of youth, I'd felt I deserved my outsider status, but often I wondered why the other kids didn't see the CJ I knew. He was kind and funny; he was smart. And he was an excellent kisser. That part, of course, I would rather have died than let the other girls know that I knew.

Yes, I've heard all the jokes about the South and kissing cousins. But most people I know have at least one I-didn't-know-any-better incident in their early sexual history. CJ and I had just been experimenting. It wasn't like we'd had anyone else to practice on.

I'd started things, one night when we were outside on a sleeping bag after dark, waiting to watch a rocket launch from Vandenberg. Offhandedly I told CJ that I'd never kissed with an open mouth, and I wanted to learn. CJ said that I'd get a chance soon enough and to be patient. Patience had not been my strong suit, so finally he relented and showed me. And kept showing me. Those satellite launches got delayed a lot. It wasn't like there'd been anything else for us to do.

For about a year after that, making out was just something we did when we had time and privacy. It was mostly kissing, except that when I started getting my breasts, I let CJ cup them in his gentle, long-fingered hands. And the summer before we started high school—I admit there was a bottle of Jack Daniel's involved in this— he let me touch him down low. He was hard, and when I wrapped my hand around him, I was amazed at how it felt, so powerful and yet vulnerable, all at once.

Then CJ rolled away from me, breathing hard, and said, "We probably ought to knock this shit off."

And I said, "Yeah, I know."

So we stopped. We were going to be in high school next year; it was time to put away childish things. No big deal.

In high school, we drifted apart a little. This was partly because Julianne scraped together the money to move us out of the Mooney home and into a rented house in town. But what really set CJ and me on different paths was something that happened to me in a bookstore, a few months before I finished eighth grade.

I was looking for a present for Julianne's birthday. I knew she didn't want a book as a gift, but I was mad at her for moving us out of the Mooney house, where I'd felt comfortable. In theory, Julianne and I had moved "so Hailey can have her own room." In reality, it was so she could have privacy to entertain the Air Force guys she liked. I hated the house—it was cramped and Helen Keller could have done a more tasteful job on the color scheme—and disliked most of the men she dated. I missed the Mooney house with its warmth and life. So there I was, browsing, when I passed a display of educational books and a thick volume caught my attention.

It was *Wheelock's Latin*. I wasn't interested in foreign languages, but even so I picked it up and ran my finger along the words inside— difficult, opaque, more than merely foreign, almost alien—and somehow they dazzled me. This, I thought, was the language of ancient soldiers and empire builders, of discipline and honor. And it seemed to me that it was somehow my birthright, because of my father, who had been in my eyes a warrior. By the time I left the store, I'd not only bought my mother's birthday gift but also the *Wheelock's*, and it wasn't long after that I understood that I would someday apply to West Point.

That's a pretty big leap in logic, I know. The ideas that you have at thirteen rarely stand up to the test of time. But they're very powerful in the moment; you feel things at that age with an intensity that few people can still access in adulthood.

Those feelings also run pretty hot and cold. I studied the Latin text voraciously for about five days before casting it aside in frustration. But I started up again when I began high school in the fall, and worked at it more slowly and patiently. When it was time for my appointment with the guidance counselor, and she asked me what I thought I might like to do for a living, I told her about West Point. Her eyebrows inched toward her hairline, and I couldn't blame her: Nothing in my life that far suggested any latent achieverhood. To give her credit, she didn't voice her skepticism. Instead, she asked me if I'd thought about the Air Force Academy in Colorado—remember, we were in Air Force territory. I told her to fuck off the way fourteen-year-olds tell adults to fuck off—"I'll think about it"—and she nodded and then did something to my file that switched me from graduation track to college preparatory.

She explained the drill: four years of math, four years of English, three years of science, two years of foreign language. I asked her if there was any way I could get credit for studying Latin instead of the Spanish, French, or German our school offered. Her eyebrows made that same ascent and she said she didn't see how that would work, and besides, for a military officer who might be stationed overseas, French would be a much more useful language.

I spited her by enrolling in Spanish instead, and on my own time I studied Latin. By the time I was a junior, the principal was sufficiently impressed with my resolve that he signed off on the deal that let me out of study hall twice a week to bus over to the community college to take Latin classes there.

It's hard for me to explain what Latin means to me. My guidance counselor had been right: It wasn't at all useful to a military career. But to be fair, I think Latin got me into West Point, because studying it was how I learned I could do difficult things. Hard things had happened to me—my father's death, most of all—but Latin was the first burden I picked up of my own choice.

It has to be said that I wasn't squeaky clean in high school. I got in some fights, and I got in some backseats. I can't say I don't know what a meth high feels like. You have to grow up in a small town to understand. On Friday and Saturday nights, things go on in farmhouses that would shock the ghetto. But I was always in homeroom with my schoolwork done on Monday morning, so the adults around me never knew. That's something that all smart kids figure out pretty early on: As long as your grades are good and you don't smoke or wear heavy eyeliner, the authority figures around you generally don't look any deeper than that.

Don't get me wrong, I wasn't a delinquent. I didn't start fights, but I didn't back down from them either, so I had some pretty good scraps with girls I wasn't even sure how I'd offended. Some of it was about my plans for the future, I guess, my grades and West Point ambitions. Some people will tear you down for no reason other than that you're trying to build yourself up.

And the sex? I never actually went all the way, not back then. Like many girls, I protected my reputation by making the distinction between giving head and giving it up. If my generation didn't invent the idea of "oral sex isn't sex," we'd popularized it, and I wasn't reluctant to show a guy I liked him in that way.

And maybe on some level I was competing with CJ, who was going through my female classmates at a truly amazing rate. Because while I was becoming somebody different, my cousin was, too.

All the Mooney kids adapted to California—their accents softened, and they called the freeway "the 246," not just "246," and so forth. But it was CJ who went native in a big way. In his freshman year he'd started going to the ocean with friends who had driver's licenses, and the sun and salt water brought out gold lights in his reddish-blond hair, which he let grow out to his shoulders, smoothing out the tightness of its curls. He traded in his checked flannel shirts and dark-blue jeans for T-shirts and faded, ripped Levi's and casually unlaced basketball shoes. Though I could always spot him in the halls because of his height, sometimes I barely recognized the skinny country cousin I'd first met.

In our second year of high school, CJ got his driver's license, and not long after he bought a twenty-year-old silver BMW that he'd seen advertised "for parts" and rebuilt it from the ground up. He also won a starting spot on the baseball team, where he vexed opposing batters with the deep sinker and nasty screwball that Porter had taught him.

I don't know if my cousin ever had the kind of life-changing moment that I did in the bookstore, but he told me a story about the time when, as far as he could tell, school turned around for him. It was in the middle of that sophomore year. CJ was getting books from his locker when a pretty black girl, a new transfer from Oxnard, took in his height—he was six-three then, on his way to six-five—and said teasingly, "Do you hang off the end of your bed?"

CJ had winked at her and said, "Only recreationally," and not only had she laughed, the kids around her had, too.

By the end of that week, CJ and the girl from Oxnard were going out, and suddenly the entire female population of our school discovered, seemingly all at once, the aphrodisiac qualities of a Southern accent. CJ, of course, was happy to help them enjoy that discovery.

By our junior year I saw very little of him on weekends, not just because he was out with girlfriends—though he often was—but because once he got his car running, he could go to Los Angeles without waiting to ride along with friends. CJ wasn't antisocial, but his interest in L.A. wasn't the same as that of his friends. They went to surf and drink around campfires on the beach. CJ went to sweet-talk his way into L.A.'s music venues, the eighteen-and-over or twenty-one-only clubs where the new hip-hop acts debuted. All the money he earned repairing cars for his father went either to gas money or to two-drink minimums. He kept his grades up just high enough to stay on the baseball team, but that was all.

Teachers sighed and shook their heads about CJ Mooney, but there was no animus in it. The guidance counselor, she of the mobile eyebrows, saw that he'd inherited the Mooney gift with cars, put him on the graduation track, and loaded his schedule with shop classes.

They didn't see what he was. Back then, none of us did.

Sure, it was obvious that he loved music. But in high school, what kid doesn't? Even the fact that he was a white boy in love with black music didn't raise any eyebrows; that was a story older than Elvis Presley.

Then, after our junior year, he dropped out of high school and moved to Los Angeles to try to find work in the music business.

Even in poor and rural areas, that doesn't happen so much anymore. It caused a stir. At school, the teachers were shocked, the baseball coach cursed the loss of his best pitching arm, and the girls went into mourning. But his parents took it hardest. Several Mooneys of their generation had dropped out, but they'd made damn sure none of CJ's had. They were convinced he was on the road to ruin: just seventeen, talented but with no marketable skills, in a town that ate gifted youth for breakfast and sent them home broke and failed. Both Porter and Angeline called me, asking me to talk to him. I said I couldn't; it was his life. Secretly I believed what everyone else did—that in a year or two CJ would get disillusioned and come home—but I couldn't be disloyal enough to say it aloud.

After that, CJ's parents regularly asked me for news about their son. It wasn't that he didn't call them, but they thought I was getting the true, uncensored news of his life in L.A. "Really, how's he doing down there? Is he working?" they'd ask. And I'd say he was getting by, because I didn't want them to know the truth: Unable to get even the lowest-level job in the music business, CJ was supporting himself by dealing pot.

On the night before I left for West Point, I slept on the floor of his flophouse room, just like he'd done in my bedroom so many times before. He tried strenuously to give me the bed, but I said no, tomorrow I was going to be in Beast Barracks, and if I couldn't tolerate sleeping on the floor, then the outlook was pretty bleak. CJ gave up, but joined me about halfway through the night, dragging a blanket down with him to nestle companionably behind me. I shouldn't have let him, but I was secretly glad for his nearness, because it was the only thing that kept me from spending the night wondering what the hell made me think I could cut it at the United States Military Academy and deciding that it wasn't too late for me to stay in California and go to community college.

The next morning, CJ drove me to LAX. Standing in the departures drop-off zone, he'd joked, "Look at you, baby, you're the pride of the Mooneys, and you're a Cain. That hardly seems fair." Then he'd turned serious, pulled me close, and said, "I am so very proud of you, baby."

I wanted to tell him that I was proud of him, too, the way he lived life on his own terms. But I couldn't, because it would have sounded condescending. He was right: I was the standard-bearer of our family, making my place in the world, and he was the black-sheep under-achiever, going nowhere. In that moment, our paths in life seemed set in stone.

Funny how four years can change everything.

Four years later, I was getting off a Greyhound at the downtown L.A. depot, with no commission in the Army, no college degree, less than two hundred dollars to my name, and no place to live. It took the last of my pride to do it, but I called CJ at his office. By which I mean I tried to. I left several messages with a cool-voiced receptionist ("Yeah . . . his cousin Hailey . . . he'll know who you mean") and stood for two hours in the Southern California sun by a pay phone, tired and out of sorts, itching with impatience when passersby stopped to use the phone and tied it up. The next day I'd have a pretty bad sunburn.

Finally the phone rang. I only had to say, "Hello?" and, to my vast relief, I heard that familiar half-Appalachian, half-Californian drawl: "Where are you? I'll come get you."

His first words to me in person, as he was jumping out of the same old silver BMW, were, "Shoot, I am so sorry, baby. My people didn't know who you were."

"I know," I said against his cheek, already enfolded in his long arms.

That was the month that CJ was in *Vanity Fair*'s music issue. In the photo essay of that year's most influential figures, he was labeled "The Prodigy" and was photographed standing on a gritty hotel rooftop, the sun behind him sinking into layers of L.A. atmosphere, the camera angle low enough to make him look seven feet tall. He's turned away from the camera, an abstracted visionary.

At just twenty-two, he had become one of L.A.'s most sought-after producers. No one doubted the depth of his understanding of hip-hop or his respect for it. Some people who saw him in deep concentration, listening to something only he could hear over headphones, said they'd looked at his eyes and thought at first that he was blind.

He had also taken back his name, in the liner notes of the two CDs he'd produced and on the Grammy he'd won. The name Cletus Mooney now commanded respect throughout the music industry.

Practically the first thing I asked him, that day in L.A., was which name he wanted me to use.

He said, "Whatever you want to call me is fine." He checked the traffic before pulling out onto the street. As he did so, he said, "What's wrong with your arm?" He'd noticed the cast on my wrist.

"Broken bone," I said. "I fell. It's no big deal."

"You're not out here on some kind of medical leave, are you?"

"No," I said. "I . . . CJ, I'm not going back."

I could see his confusion, and in a moment he articulated it. "You mean, you graduated early?"

He knew that wasn't it, but denial is like that. Often there's a short detour on the way to the unhappy truth.

"No," I said. "I'm not going to finish."

"Are you serious? Baby, what happened?"

"A lot of people wash out," I said tiredly. "I warned you about that before I went. Do we have to talk about it?"

"No."

"I'm okay. I'll be okay."

"I know you will," he said finally. "Sure you will."

I'm not sure what I was expecting from the place that CJ, with his newfound wealth, would call home. Maybe a retro-Rat-Pack condo with a wet bar, or a beach house in Malibu.

Instead, he drove us up into the hills outside the city, an ascent so steep and fast it reminded me of taking off in a plane, to an area of no particular repute, where acres of land separated the houses and amateur spray paint on the road warned: SLOW! CHILDREN AND

ANIMALS. On the way, his cell phone rang so incessantly that he finally shut it off.

His driveway wasn't even paved, and as we pulled up in a cloud of dust, I looked curiously at the home he'd chosen. It wasn't big, but somehow rambling, built of weathered wood, with old sash windows with little scrapes on them from many cleanings. A live oak tree bent toward the roof as though it wanted to enfold the whole house. There was a deck with a hot tub in it, but no landscaping. The grass that surrounded the house was natural. A Volkswagen Corrado, clearly in mid-repair, stood at a small distance. I observed all this with a growing sense of familiarity.

For as shy as he'd been about bringing people to the Mooney home of his adolescence, CJ had chosen to re-create it here. It wasn't until I'd known the adult CJ awhile that I understood. He had to live a certain kind of life down in the city: the velvet-rope-and-VIP-room life, riding in Navigators with the talent and their entourages, getting drive-thru from In-N-Out Burger after midnight and washing it down with Cristal. But when he was ready to buy a home, CJ chose a place where he could be who he really was: someone who listened to baseball games on the radio while working on cars with his hands.

"Nice," I said. It was inadequate.

"I took just about the first thing the agent showed me," he said. "I just wanted someplace quiet." He watched a red-tailed hawk wheel overhead a moment, then went on. "Look, I'd like to stay here tonight while you get settled in, but I have dinner plans, and actresses can be touchy about things like broken dates."

"My, an *actress*. Aren't you something?"

"Hey," he said, "I'm gonna ask you to think twice about how you talk to someone who walked away from a meeting with two very big record label executives to drive across town to the Greyhound station to collect your stranded ass."

"I know," I said, chastened.

He smiled at me in the old way I remembered, eyes crinkling. "I'm glad you're here," he said. "It's going to be good, having you around."

"Thanks," I said, "but it's only for a while, until I get on my feet."

"No hurry," CJ said.

"No, I understand that you bought this place so you could have some privacy," I said.

He looked at me as if I'd said something incomprehensible, and said, "Not from *you*."

I lived with CJ a month, long enough to find three part-time jobs—none of them particularly interesting or challenging, but the checks cashed fine. When I'd saved enough, I put down money on a tiny studio in town. CJ tried to talk me out of leaving, and I was reluctant, too, but I couldn't have a life that was just an offshoot of his. And I wasn't going far, just down into the city. So he yielded and helped me move.

I wouldn't realize until later—when I had to leave—how much Los Angeles had gotten under my skin. Mostly I'd sat out the long-standing Love L.A./Hate L.A. debate. When I'd chosen to go there after leaving West Point, my decision had been fairly arbitrary. I didn't have roots in Lompoc anymore. Julianne had moved away during my plebe year at West Point, and even the Mooneys, CJ's parents, had done something quintessentially Californian: They'd sold their real estate at a profit and bought a bigger, cheaper place out of state, in Nevada's Washoe Valley. But L.A. was the nearest big city to where I'd grown up. My feeling had been, *I suppose if I'm from anywhere, I'm from here.*

Later, if you'd asked me why I liked it there, I'd have given you everyone's general paean to L.A.: the open streets and the palm trees and the laid-back vibe, et cetera cetera cetera. The truth was simpler: L.A. just felt like a place for people like me, young people raised on high-fructose corn syrup, long on energy and short on a sense of history.

I doubt I would have approved if I'd moved straight there after high school. I'd gone to West Point to test myself against hardship and privation, to see how little comfort and pleasure I could get by on. But I came home in a very different frame of mind. Then, I wanted what I called *omnia gaudia vitae,* all the pleasures of life, and L.A. was the place for that. Vietnamese iced coffee, British Columbian marijuana, Colombian cocaine, French film noir, Israeli krav maga training—you could get it all here, and if it was all imported, like the water supply and the workforce and even the iconic palm trees, who cared?

I told CJ when I moved into town that we'd still see each other all the time, and we did. He opened the doors to the West Hollywood clubs he was always waved into, and I spent many nights drinking and dancing, sometimes in his immediate company, other times only knowing that he was somewhere in the same vast and densely packed venue. I wasn't ever lonely. CJ's circle of friends, friendly acquaintances, and hangers-on was enormous, and they were always willing to share space at their tables, their drugs, even their bodies. I left footprints on the windows of a few Navigators and Escalades owned by guys I didn't know very well.

Some mornings I dreamed of the clean citadel of West Point and woke up first disoriented, then unhappy. I chased that feeling away with strong coffee or a joint, or sometimes a hard workout.

I attained something of a reputation in CJ's crowd as that mostly quiet girl with the birthmark and the occasional hair-trigger temper. From time to time CJ had to drag me away from a vending machine I was trying to bust up for taking my money or a bouncer twice my size I felt provoked by. Sometimes CJ had to wrap his arms around me from behind and negotiate over my shoulder, telling people that I was on mood-altering meds or just getting over a bad breakup.

Later, when I apologized to him, he always said, pleasantly, not to worry about it. Some of that was CJ being CJ, so mellow that one friend of his joked that his adrenal glands secreted some kind of cannabinoid substance instead of adrenaline. But I think CJ chalked most of it up to my washing out of West Point. It's amazing the shit people will let you get away with if they think it's coming from a place of anger and low self-respect.

Nonetheless, I always told him I was sorry—often too abjectly, because I was usually still drunk or high or stoned and therefore able to access my feelings in a way I couldn't when sober. "I love you," I'd tell him. "I'd kill anyone who'd try to hurt you."

"Those are lovely sentiments; go sleep them off," he'd say.

But underneath the fevered language, I meant it. The way I thought of it was, I had been born an only child, but in time, the gods took pity and gave me a brother and a sister.

three

The sister was Serena Delgadillo.

Technically, Serena and I went back to the seventh grade together. We'd both been chosen for an academic-achievement program called ReachUP, which singled out promising students in rural or disadvantaged schools in hopes of helping them compete with middle-class students at college admissions time. We'd also both played on the girls' soccer team that year, alongside each other as forwards. No question, she was better than me. The daughter of migrant workers, she had learned soccer on the hard brown fields of California's inland valleys from her four older brothers and other immigrant kids, all *futbol* fanatics.

We weren't friends, but we were friendly. That had been a big step for both of us at the time. Like me, Serena was skinny then, with Kmart clothes and hair her mother cut in harsh black bangs directly across Serena's forehead. It made her self-conscious except on the soccer field, where she lost her inhibitions, becoming speedy and fluid and exuberant.

Then, in eighth grade, something changed. Serena dropped out of ReachUP and grew distant. She began styling her hair in the high, lofty wall of bangs that hadn't quite gone out of style among Latina girls back then, and I only saw her with other Mexicans in the hallways. We sat next to each other in study hall, but she only spoke to me once, to poke me in the shoulder and say, "What's that?" She'd been looking at the Latin flashcards I was reviewing instead of doing my schoolwork.

"It's Latin," I'd said.

She'd flipped through a few cards. "Weird," she'd said, shrugging, and had gone back to her homework.

The next year, Serena was gone. That was a common thing. Farmworker families are nomadic; the population of our school was always in flux.

I forgot her pretty quickly.

In my early days in L.A., after moving down from CJ's place, I was broke. The one luxury I allowed myself was food from cheap ethnic places. That month, I'd discovered pho, the Vietnamese noodle soup made with oxtail and rare beef. Late one Saturday afternoon, I was waiting in line to get my fix, when I saw that I was being watched by a tall young Latina.

She was good-looking and slender, her cargo pants hanging off sharp hip bones, braless under a strappy tank shirt, her hoop earrings so large you could have worn them as bracelets. She had straight hair, not quite black, pulled back off her face, and almond-shaped eyes. When I caught her looking at me, she didn't smile or say "Sorry" like a lot of people would have.

"I think I know you," she said thoughtfully.

"Okay," I said. She wasn't familiar to me, but I've learned not to argue with people about that. When you've got a birthmark on your face, people can recognize you long after they've changed beyond identifiability for you.

"We played soccer together in junior high," she said. "Remember?"

"Holy shit," I said. "Serena?"

"Yeah," she said, laughing. Then: "You're at the front of the line."

I bought my pho; she bought hers, and we moved off to the side to talk. She remembered that I used to hang out with "that Southern boy," and that I'd been studying Latin. I asked her where her family had gone after eighth grade. She explained that her father had hurt his back and couldn't do farm work anymore, so their family had come to L.A. looking for industrial work for her mother and aunt.

Then she said, "Did you ever get to West Point?"

I'd felt my mouth drop open slightly and couldn't answer right away. First, because she must have heard that secondhand; I knew I hadn't told her about what had been, back then, an unlikely dream. Second, because it brought up the fresh pain of saying, *Yes, I was there; no, I didn't finish.*

"Yeah," I said. "I was at West Point for a while."

She said, "So what happened?"

"Didn't make it all four years," I said. "That's a story for another time."

Sometime after midnight we were in her car, or what I thought was her car. I was driving and she was in the passenger seat, leaning forward laughing, a bottle of Jack Daniel's wedged between her thighs. I forget what story I'd been telling or she'd been telling, just that we were both laughing and laughing and then she'd said, "Slow down, okay, *esa*? You're speeding. We can't afford to get pulled over."

And I'd joked, "Why, is this car stolen?"

And she'd said, "Yeah, it is."

That was when I sobered up and really looked at her, and I realized that what I'd been registering as a birthmark high on her cheekbone wasn't; it was three tiny dots, the tattoo that symbolized *la vida loca,* the gang life.

At that point I had a choice: I could have drawn on the battered last of my West Point ideals, said, *This isn't cool,* and then found a place to pull over and walk away.

Instead, I said, "For how long?"

Serena knew I meant how long had she been in the life. She said, "Since I was fourteen."

I said: "I'll slow down."

That was how I learned what happened to her in the eighth grade.

Gang life is popularly associated with the cities, but it's been in the rural areas a long time. In our small school, Serena had drawn the attention of Lita, a leader in a girls' gang. She recruited Serena, who'd said no, she couldn't, her parents wouldn't understand.

The next day, Serena heard that Lita had called her out. Serena's refusal to join had been a loss of face for Lita, a slur on her pride. From now until Serena gave in and let herself be initiated, no day would pass without the prospect of a fight with Lita or one of Lita's girls.

Serena wasn't stupid. She chose to have sisters instead of enemies.

"Looking back," Serena told me, "it was the best thing that could have happened. I wouldn't have wanted to come to L.A. a total virgin. When I got here, I knew the life. Well, sort of. Nothing can prepare you for what it's like in L.A."

What most people don't realize about urban gangs is how small their individual territories actually are. Many people have the vague idea that Gang A is on the East Side and Gang B on the West Side. In truth, the part of L.A. that Serena and her family moved to was like a checkerboard: Various Latino gangs—or rather, small splinters of the gangs, called sets or cliques—were spread out in small pockets throughout. A gang member could walk for only a few blocks, be in enemy territory, then a few more blocks and be safe again. Bitter, fatal rivals lived right on top of each other. It was impossible to ever feel truly secure.

It also made the question of gang allegiance an open one. Regardless of who controlled your particular stretch of your particular street, there was always a chance you could claim a different clique or an entirely different gang.

But virtually every young person claimed. Everyone needed protection, *familia*. Those who had no gang affiliation were in the worst of all worlds: considered untrustworthy by everyone, always at risk of being attacked, with no one backing them up.

Serena's older brothers immediately claimed the 13th Street clique, or El Trece. Serena wasn't unwilling to follow in their path, but this time her qualms were different from the ones she'd cited to Lita. She looked at the neighborhood girls who had affiliations to Trece and didn't like what she saw.

"They weren't really down," she told me. "They were just hoochies who slept with the guys. They didn't even get jumped in. They said they didn't have to, they were 'already down,' whatever that means." Her voice had filled with scorn.

It wasn't anything you could have made a high-school counselor see, but Serena Delgadillo was an overachiever. One short year after she tried to refuse Lita's initiation, Serena shaved her head, borrowed her older brother's flannel shirt and chinos, and went to Payaso, the leader of El Trece, and asked to be jumped in. Her brothers vouched for her toughness, and Serena, bloody and bruised, became a member of the gang.

Serena had to prove herself over and over again, backing up her guys, stealing cars, driving getaway, lying to the cops, and doing a six-month stretch in the California Youth Authority camp. It was the ironically familiar refrain of a woman in a man's job: She had to do twice as much as the guys to get equal standing with them. Through it all, she kept her head shaved and her clothes masculine. Sometimes the cops mistook her for a boy.

"I have a picture," she told me that night, "but it's at my house." She looked up at me, slyly. "Unless you're afraid to come to the hood to see it."

"Let's go," I'd said.

She lived in a one-story house of pale yellow stucco, with an orange tree in the yard and bars on the windows. A motion-sensor light flashed on as we walked up the driveway. Not surprisingly, the dead bolt on the front door was probably the newest and most expensive thing about Serena's home.

It wasn't dark inside, though it was dim. We came into the kitchen, and Serena peered over a cracked Formica counter into her living room and then raised a finger to her lips. I followed her gaze and saw a rumpled sleeping bag. It rustled, and a girl stuck her tousled head out and looked at us.

"Quien es la rubia?" she said. *Who's the blond girl?*

"Nadie," said Serena. *No one.*

The girl withdrew back into her nest.

"Thanks a lot," I said.

"You know what I mean," Serena said mildly. "Are you hungry?"

We didn't talk much while she cooked, out of consideration for the girl sleeping in the dining room. As she heated water to boiling and poured in some short-grain white rice from a ten-pound sack, I looked around the kitchen. There were photographs on the refrigerator, and the subjects were all male—some school pictures, others obviously taken to establish gang cred, as the boys posed with guns and cars. All, though, were bordered with colored paper. On the margins were roses and *virgenes* and the initials *q.d.e.p.*

"What's q.d.e.p?" I asked Serena.

"Que descansa en paz," she said quietly.

"These guys are all . . ."

"Dead," she confirmed.

"No girls?"

She said, "I've got the roll call for my *hermanas* on my leg."

"Your leg?" I echoed, not understanding.

She hiked her right foot onto the counter and pulled up the cuff of her pants so I could easily see the tattooed letters *qdep* high on her calf, and underneath that, two names: Tania and Dreamer.

I asked, "How did you decide whether to use the given name or their gang name?"

"Well, Tania didn't have a moniker," she said. "She wasn't in the life, she was just kicking it with some homeboys who were on their porch and got blasted in a walk-up shooting." She put her leg down.

Noting the way the names would descend to her ankle, I said, "What happens when you run out of room?"

She said, "Maybe I'll get out of the life."

. . .

When she was done cooking, Serena and I carried our late-night meal into her bedroom. Just before I followed her in, though, I heard the sleeping bag in the dining room stir, looked back, and did a slight double take.

Serena switched on a lamp and shut the bedroom door.

I said, "Either the girl out there has three legs, or there were two girls under that sleeping bag."

"Yeah, there were."

"Are you that low on blankets and sleeping space?"

"Well, the spare bedroom's taken, and so is the living-room couch," she said. "But the girls just like to be close. They're not gay, it's just that they like to feel . . ." She trailed off. "It's safety in numbers. It's just something you have to understand."

"Sure," I said. "I didn't mean anything by it."

We sat on her bed and ate, and then Serena reached under the bed for an old wooden box. She rummaged inside and found a Polaroid of a group of teenage boys, all with heads shaved, in voluminous shirts buttoned only at the top, and creased khakis. Serena tapped her finger on one of them, sitting on "his" heels in front. "That's me," she said, "at sixteen, when I was banging hardest."

I held the photo by the edges and marveled at it, half in amazement that I would never have recognized her, but also because the picture reminded me strongly of something else.

I had a photo from my West Point days that looked remarkably similar. It was me in full camo, posing with my Sandhurst team. Sandhurst is the war-games competition West Point holds every year against the British and the Canadians. All of West Point's companies field teams, who compete against one another as well as the foreigners. Every team has one female member, and I was chosen from my company.

Of course, the Brits kicked our asses—they do almost every year—but our company had a pretty good showing, and that day I was glowing with the pleasure of just being part of it. And then we'd posed for the photo in which I, like Serena, had to point out to people which cadet among the guys was me.

When I told Serena this, she looked at me in shared fascination. That was probably the main reason we didn't hug each other around the neck at the end of the night and go our separate ways. The outside world would have said we were nothing alike, but we were. Those parallels cemented our friendship, and that friendship would set a lot of other things in motion.

In time, Serena told me about her dreams of Vietnam.

They had started in early childhood, around five or six. They weren't frequent, but they were vivid and remarkably consistent. Serena dreamed of explosions and bloody chaos in the jungle. She dreamed of white and black men in olive drab. She dreamed of snake-silver rivers and huge machines that hovered in the air, the wind they generated beating the grass flat.

"It was Vietnam," she told me. "I know what you're thinking, that it's Mexico, right? But I've never been to Mexico, and even if I had, my parents are from the north; it's dry as Arizona. There's no jungle there."

Serena believed that not only had she served in Vietnam as an American GI, but that she had died there.

I must have looked skeptical, because she'd gone on. "I saw white men and black men in my dreams back when I'd only ever been around Mexicans," she said. "Come on, where would I see a helicopter at that age? Five years old?"

"There are helicopters all over California," I pointed out. "They're in the sky all the time."

"*Way* up in the sky," she corrected me. "Not down low where the sound of the blades feels like your own heart beating." She placed her fist on her sternum. "I swear, Hailey. The first time I saw a helicopter up close, on TV, I *knew* that sound. I had this feeling like someone walked over the place my grave is going to be."

The dreams had stopped around the age of fifteen, when she'd been jumped into El Trece. "When *mi guerra nueva* started, I stopped dreaming about the old one," was how she put it.

I don't think Serena told many people this story. At least she said she didn't. But she wore a pair of dog tags as jewelry, dangling low under her shirt. And somehow her gang brothers had sensed something of her beliefs, because among the cheery, innocuous gang monikers they gave one another—Droopy and Smiley and Shorty—they'd given Serena the name Warchild.

Two years after her juvenile conviction, Serena did a second stretch, this time in jail. It was there that she finally began to let her hair grow. Jail was a clarifying time for her. She was eighteen now. By middle-class America's standards, that was barely out of childhood, but gangbangers aged differently. For them, twenty was virtually middle-aged. Serena, having survived to eighteen, was a *veterana*. She had some thinking to do about the future.

The movies spread an old, common misperception about gang life: the "blood in, blood out" thing. It was a saying that meant that your gang jumped you in with a bloody beating and you stayed in until you were cut down in a bloody premature death . . . or, if you tried to leave the life, that your own gang assassinated you.

The less exciting truth was that gang members left the life all the time, especially girls. It was *por vida* in name, but age and motherhood often slowed girls down, sidelined them from the life. Others went straight after doing jail time. A few were even "jumped out," meaning they failed to be tough enough or ruthless enough for gang life, and were beaten by their gang as a contemptuous dismissal.

Serena was not married, nor was she tied down to a baby. And modesty aside, she was more than *veterana*, she was *leyenda*, a legend, because of her exploits with El Trece. There were plenty of Serena stories in the neighborhood, not all of them true. Serena had jacked a pharmacy not just for prescription drugs, but carried away boxes and boxes of contraceptives that she'd distributed for free among the girls of her neighborhood. Serena had gone into Crip territory, Grape Street, and robbed a crack dealer there. In the sexy clothes of an aspiring actress, Serena had trolled Westwood and Burbank, stealing Mercedeses and Jaguars right from under the noses of the Beautiful People.

A reputation is capital, and in jail, Serena began to think about how she wanted to spend that capital.

She realized that she wanted to lead a girls' clique, a satellite to Trece, the kind she hadn't found when she moved to the neighborhood. And when it came time to name her *cliqua,* Serena knew one thing: It wasn't going to be the "Lady" anythings, an innocent naming convention some gangs borrowed from high-school athletics.

Serena named her girls the Trece Sucias. It didn't translate directly to English. To call them the 13th Street Dirty Girls just didn't say it. The name *sucias* could evoke different things, the nasty girls or the sexy girls, but it also suggested dirty hands, with blood and guilt on them.

For all the fearsomeness of the name, though, Serena had higher standards for her sucias than a lot of leaders would have set. She wouldn't take girls under fifteen, the *quinceanera* year being symbolic of womanhood in Hispanic culture. That might sound painfully young to the rest of America, but in gang life, it was a high standard—it wasn't uncommon for children to start banging at ten or eleven years old. And the two crimes that the Trece Sucias specialized in—car theft and pharmacy burglaries—were both nonviolent, if done with enough caution.

And Serena was careful. Her crew only knocked over a few pharmacies a year, at quiet suburban locations Serena carefully scouted, and while she and a trusted second raided the back for lucrative prescription drugs that Serena resold around her neighborhood, younger girls swept the shelves of Pampers, baby food, cough syrup, and OTC meds—all things desperately needed among the young mothers of the barrio.

It would be nice to imagine Serena as a kind of urban feminist Robin Hood, but I knew better than to indulge in that kind of fantasy. Violence was inextricable from gang life: grudges and retaliations, attacks and counterattacks, beatings and shootings. I heard the stories Serena's girls told, thinking I didn't know enough Spanish to understand. And they routinely went around strapped, meaning carrying a gun.

But this lifestyle of retaliation and revenge was the price of having *familia*. In its perverse way, it was a virtue, the dark side of loyalty. Serena encouraged the same kind of loyalty among them that the guys had for one another. Unlike male gang members, though, girls affiliated with the same clique often fought viciously with one another, sometimes over gossip, more often over a boy. Serena said she'd never let her clique be divided over a man: "The sucias are for the sucias," she told them. "We represent like the guys."

I didn't learn all of this at once, of course. But after that first night, Serena was surprisingly open with me, given that we'd hardly known each other back in school, and that I'd once been the straightest of straight arrows, Cadet Hailey Cain.

I think that Serena had been waiting for someone she could talk to. She had to front around the guys, with whom sharing her feelings would have been a liability. And she cared for her sucias, but they were little more than children, with short attention spans and narrow worldviews. There wasn't anyone else like Serena in Serena's world. The person who came closest, skin color notwithstanding, was me.

Maybe she understood, too, that I'd honored her when, in time, I told her the full truth about why I had to leave West Point.

I'd like to say that I was wracked with guilt over telling her something I hadn't even shared with CJ, but it wasn't true. I didn't tell CJ because I knew he'd lie awake at night thinking about it. Serena wouldn't. She understood about bad luck.

The day after I told her, we went to the Beverly Center, L.A.'s cathedral of capitalism, and did something the rest of the world wouldn't understand but that made sense to us.

Perhaps it was inevitable that Serena started to kid me about getting initiated into her clique. She said I could become her second. I took it as gentle condescension. But she kept on it, asking me when I was going to take my beating, get jumped in for real. Slowly I began to realize that she wasn't entirely kidding, and I began to understand. The things that set me apart from her sucias were, in fact, assets—chief among them my white skin and blond hair. Those alone would make me the ideal driver on a pharmacy job. I was the anti-profile; any LAPD officer would think twice before pulling me over.

"Look at the way you live now," she said one evening, watching me gingerly put makeup on a bruise I'd gotten in a bar fight. "Getting beat on, partying, sleeping until noon, no plans for the future—how is that any different from *la vida*?" She'd put an arm around me and looked at us in the mirror. "Come and be *mi gladia*."

"*Gladius meus*," I said. *My sword*. Serena had learned all the words that went with her warlike life—*milites, hostes, bellum, mors*—but she tended to hybridize them with Spanish. "And no thanks. I've seen the beatings that your girls give each other jumping them in, and those are bad enough. I don't want to go through the beatdown they'd give a white girl to make her prove herself."

"Scared?" she said.

"You know better. But what's the point? I'd never be one of you. What would my street name be? Blondie?"

"The girls will accept you if they see I accept you. And they can learn from you. Nobody ever taught them anything about fighting, about protecting themselves."

"Think about what you're asking me. To teach young gangbangers to be better shots, better at beating someone up? I really need *that* on my conscience."

"You can teach them honor. Teach them when *not* to throw down, when to walk away."

"Honor?" I'd said. "Been there, done that, didn't get the gold bars. Listen, Serena, I don't make moral judgments about what you're doing. I'm happy you've got something that means something to you. But it's not for me."

She'd shrugged. "You'll come around," she said. That was how we left things. The last time Serena came by my place, I was waiting for my ride up to San Francisco, my old Army duffel at my feet. Serena had pressed the five-shot Airweight into my hands, told me to watch out for myself, and then kissed me on both cheeks, like an old-style gangster.

We hadn't kept in contact. Ours wasn't the kind of friendship that would survive long-distance. Which is why it surprised me to learn that she was trying to get in touch with me.

four

My living situation in San Francisco was pretty simple: I rented a room over the base of Aries Courier, in Japantown.

To get to my room, as I did when I came back from what had become a day's worth of pickups and drops, I had to walk through Aries's ground-floor space, which resembled a garage more than an office: bike frames and parts, freestanding filing cabinets, posters advertising bike races and rallies, a big, circa-1950s refrigerator full of Red Bull and Tupperware containers it was best not to open. When I came in, Motobecane over my shoulder, the owner, Shay Clements, was on the phone with his back to me.

Shay was a hard guy to figure out. Rather, he was the sort of person whom people assumed they understood immediately upon meeting him: bike messenger turned slightly bohemian entrepreneur. He was about thirty-five, six-foot-four with a straight, ice-blond ponytail and blue eyes and good facial bones. He still had the build of a cyclist. He wasn't married, and I didn't think he ever had been, but he would never lack for dates as long as there were coffeehouses and the kind of women who frequented them, looking for guys who were sexy in a left-wing way. You just looked at Shay and thought, *pesco-pollo-vegetarian, knows some yoga asanas, votes Democrat.*

In truth, like all blue-state small-business owners, Shay was remarkably Republican when it came to his own bottom line, full of complaints about regulations and taxes, and nearly as resentful of his own employees. Aries was all-1099, as riders put it, meaning everyone was an independent contractor, without job security or health insurance. This didn't do much to foster loyalty. Riders regularly quit Aries without notice. This led Shay to look on his riders as irresponsible flakes. It was a vicious circle.

My relationship with him was a little better than that, largely because I was reliable. I didn't kiss his ass, but I didn't have to. As I'd told Jack, I was usually his top-earning rider. I got hurt sometimes, true, but I also rode hurt, so it didn't cost Shay any downtime. Beyond that, if Shay wasn't the warmest guy in the world, well, he probably thought the same about me.

Seeing me out of the corner of his eye, Shay waved me over, not interrupting his conversation on the phone. I came over without speaking, and he handed off a pink slip of paper, a phone message. *Please call Serena Delgadillo.*

Only then did I remember the call I hadn't answered on the bridge. I took out my cell and brought up the call log, and sure enough, there they were, Serena's familiar digits. I raised my eyebrows, but Shay had already turned back to what he was doing and didn't notice my surprise. I slipped the message into my bag, lifted my bike to my shoulders, and went up the stairs.

Once in my room, I hung the Motobecane on its hooks on the wall, then went over to my little half-height refrigerator. I took out a pint bottle of vodka, drank, then kicked off my shoes and lay down with my bare feet up on the wall.

I'd lived over Aries for nearly as long as I'd been in San Francisco— not quite a year—and I still didn't have enough possessions even to make this small room look lived in. There was the bed and a dresser and a mirror. The bathroom was down the hall, and the kitchen was the little refrigerator and a single-coil burner, with my few cooking supplies on a pair of high, plain shelves.

Had I been religious, a cross on the wall or a Buddhist altar would have given the room's bareness a kind of monastic sense. But I wasn't. Nor could I bring myself to care about personalizing the place. The things that made me who I was weren't on display, but under the bed, out of sight: My *Wheelock's Latin,* with my birth certificate and my only photo of my father tucked inside. A scarlet dress, never worn and still in the box. My class ring, set with real West Point granite, and my cadet sword.

Feeling the vodka filtering into my bloodstream, feeling relaxed, I dialed Serena's number.

"Hailecita," she said. "It's been a while, eh?"

"Yeah."

"How's life up there?"

"It's all right," I said. "Kind of dull."

"I figured," she said, and the conversation lagged.

I tipped the bottle again, drinking. "This isn't just a call to catch up, is it?" I said. "You want something."

"Yeah," she said. "It's not a big thing, honest."

"What?"

"There's a girl up in your part of California who needs to go back to Mexico, to the village where her mother grew up and her grandmother still lives. The *abuela*'s sick, and this girl, Nidia, is going to take care of her."

"Okay," I said, meaning, *Go on.*

"This girl needs a, what do you call it, an escort. There's no one who can take her, and I thought of you."

"Me?" I said, surprised. "What, on my bicycle? I don't even have a car. And what do you mean, there's no one who can take her? I don't want to be racial here, but don't Mexicans do everything together? Go places eight to a car, sleep four to a bed?"

Serena laughed, unoffended. "Her family is undocumented, and so are a lot of the people they know. They're scared to cross the border and try to come back."

"They can't put her on a bus?"

"She's not just crossing the border into Tijuana," Serena said. "*Abuelita* lives up in the mountains of Chihuahua state, the northern end of the Sierra Madre. It's a long way, and off the main roads. And the family doesn't want this girl to have to travel alone. She's not a tough Americanized girl who knows what time it is. She's different."

"Oh, yeah? How'd that happen?"

"She's really religious," Serena said. "She used to want to be a nun, until she was thirteen years old."

"Let me guess," I said. "Then she discovered boys."

"She discovered a boy," Serena said. "Johnny Cedillo, his name was. He was Dominican and part black, and her parents were kinda worked up about that until they saw how serious he was about her. He was talking about marrying her from high school on, gave her a ring, like, what do they call it? Not a real engagement ring, but—"

"A promise ring." Some of the more sincere kids in my high-school class had done that.

"Yeah, a promise ring. They were real serious about each other. Nobody doubted they were really gonna get married and have beautiful little kids."

"So what went wrong?" I said. "Where's Johnny now? Did he go to Vegas, get a little on the side, and Nidia found out about it?"

"No," she said. "He was totally into her, and since she was making him wait for their wedding night, as far as anyone knows, Johnny Cedillo died a virgin."

"He's dead?"

"Johnny didn't go to Vegas. He went to Iraq."

"Ah, shit."

We were quiet a second, then Serena said, "The other problem with her traveling alone is that apparently this girl's beautiful, a real knockout. In her neighborhood, even after Johnny went away to war, no one bothered her. It got around that she was saving herself for her wedding night with him, and even the *vatos* respected that. But strange men, on a cross-country trip? They'd hassle this girl no end."

"Wait, back up," I interrupted. "You're talking about this girl like you know her, but you said 'apparently' she's beautiful. What's up?"

"I don't know her personally," she said. "But you remember Teaser?"

"Sure." Teaser was Serena's lieutenant, her most trusted among the sucias.

"She's dead," Serena said.

"Sorry," I said. I didn't have to ask how. Another name for Serena's roll call in tattoo ink.

She went on: "Teaser was her cousin. They didn't live in my neighborhood, Nidia and Johnny, so I never met either of them," Serena explained. "But I guess they were pretty well known around their neighborhood. People looked up to Johnny; he was an athlete in high school and never got ganged-up, but he was a stand-up guy with his friends, not a squeaky-clean teacher's pet type. That whole trip. Teaser would ask me why guys like that don't go for girls like us, and I'd tell her, Because we're girls like us, that's why. She also said that people liked Nidia a little more because of him."

"Liked her more than what?"

"Well, she's pretty religious, didn't go out or party. Not the sort of girl you'd expect people like us to like," Serena said.

Then she realized she was getting off point. "Anyway, I got a phone call from Teaser's sister, Lara Cortez, about Nidia needing to get to Mexico and asked if I could help. So I called Nidia's family to talk about it, and I mentioned you. I told them that you could handle yourself and look out for Nidia."

"You can handle yourself, too," I pointed out, "and you're someone they'd trust, a Mexican. Why not you?"

"I don't have a passport," Serena said. "They changed the rules about the border, remember? It takes weeks to get one, and the family doesn't want to wait that long." Then, in a lighter tone, she said, "Besides, you know what *la vida* is like. I gotta TCB"—take care of business, she meant—"here, in my neighborhood."

"Yeah," I agreed, "those cars won't steal themselves."

"I don't do that small-time shit anymore, you know that," she said.

"Yeah, I know," I said.

"And, I should've said right up front, you'd get paid. Her family's sending some money to cover the expenses, but if it's not enough, I'll make up the rest. And I'll match whatever you'd make per day up there."

"You don't know what you're offering," I said. "A good bike messenger pulls down a lot of money."

It was a little-known truth about the job: If you were committed to it—steady and reliable in reporting for work but fast and heedless on the street—you could outearn some of the young suits you sped past on the street.

I stood up and walked over to the window, looking down at the traffic. "You're doing all this for Teaser's memory?"

"Yeah," she said. "I know it may not seem like there's much of a connection to you, but *la raza* can be a small community. And Teaser was one of mine. The sucias are for the sucias. You know how it works."

"I know," I said.

"No you don't, not really," Serena said. "You ought to get you some *familia,* someone who'll never not back you up."

I'd never told her about CJ. The two of them had been the bright and dark of my old life. They didn't mix.

"But don't worry about the money," she said. "Times are good right now."

I didn't believe her. I'd seen the truth of Serena's glamorous gangster life in the faded brown shag rug of her rented house and the twenty-year-old sedan under her carport.

But then she added, "You know, your pay wouldn't have to be all in cash. I could open up the drugstore for you."

Her gang brothers in Trece dealt coke; Serena had her pharmacy heists. Cocaine meant speed for the street, and Xanax and Ambien were peace for the evenings, when memories of West Point and Wilshire Boulevard troubled me most. Serena was smart. She once told me that drugs were money in places money couldn't go. Clearly she hadn't forgotten that. I hadn't used since I'd left L.A., but now the prospect was tempting to me where mere cash wouldn't have been.

I ran my hand through my hair. "I'm not saying yes right away, but let me think about it," I said. "I'll have to look at a map and figure out how many days this'll take, then I'll give you an estimate on what it'll cost. I'd want to be sure the expenses were really covered."

"They will be," she said. "Whatever you need."

"I just mean this trip is going to take the time it takes," I said. "I'm not going to drive way over the speed limit, or push myself until I could get tired and make an error in judgment. I can't be reckless on the road. You know why."

"Yeah," Serena said. "I know."

What we were both remembering was the reason I left L.A.

five

If you keep up with the entertainment news at all, you've probably heard of a man named Lucius "Luke" Marsellus. He ran maybe the second-biggest gangsta rap label in America. Or, if you were an LAPD cop doing gang suppression in South Central about fifteen years ago, you knew him for different reasons. I could say that people who knew Marsellus when he was a teenager knew him "before he was famous," but that wasn't quite accurate. He just had a different kind of notoriety back then. There are different words for it—*made guy, OG, veterano*—but most gang members reach that status young. When you're liable to be dead by twenty-one, you have to. Luke Marsellus was ganged-up by the time he was ten and a hood celebrity by fifteen.

At that age, Marsellus had become the right-hand man to a dealer named J. G. Deauville, a man who'd climbed the distribution chain from street-corner dealer to having two dozen guys working for him. And Marsellus was constantly by his side, his protection and enforcer. His shadow: tall, silent, feared. The extent of his crimes in Deauville's service still isn't known: The gang unit never made anything stick to him.

His boss wasn't so fortunate. Deauville taught Marsellus a lot, but perhaps the most important lesson was this: Luck always runs out. He taught his lieutenant that the hard way: After years of luck, in which the DEA and the LAPD failed to touch him, the IRS nailed Deauville, like Al Capone before him, on tax evasion, and he went to prison.

Marsellus was the obvious heir to Deauville's enterprise, but he didn't do the expected thing. To the eyes of those who'd long been watching him—the police, the feds, gang rivals—he seemed to drop off the radar. Several smaller, warring gang sets carved up Deauville's territory, and life went on.

Maybe a year after Deauville's arrest, Marsellus resurfaced in an entirely new role. Using money he'd apparently saved from his gangland years, and completely unknown talent from the streets, Marsellus founded a rap label. He was twenty-two years old.

But he quickly proved to have a natural business acumen rivaling that of his old boss. Marsellus signed the coldest and angriest of the gangsta rappers; their live-fast-die-young words were echoed by white kids in the leafiest of suburbs. The usual suspects boycotted his music—parents' groups, law enforcement—but that only sold more CDs.

So Marsellus became a legit businessman, but it'd be going too far to say that he'd entirely left his old ways of doing things behind. He made no apologies for the fact that his private security men were all ganged-up. And while nothing stuck to him, disturbing incidents followed the Marsellus name. A troublesome ex-girlfriend, reportedly about to sign a contract for a tell-all book, was beaten so severely she lost the hearing in one ear. A young white talent agent who'd lured several artists away from the Marsellus fold found a new line of work after a gunman put two rounds through the window of his house. Federal agents subpoenaed boxes and boxes of documents from Marsellus's downtown L.A. offices, but no charges ever followed. The local cops hadn't been able to nail Marsellus on anything in his dealing days, and in his newer, bigger life, the feds couldn't, either.

This was how Marsellus ultimately defied them: He became respectable. When a South Central African Baptist church was burned down in what was assumed to be a hate crime, Marsellus paid to have it rebuilt from the ground up, not as the humble shag-carpeted refuge it had been before, but as a graceful edifice with high clerestory windows and slate floors. He bought a home in Beverly Hills. He was generous with his siblings, and threw storied birthday parties for his nieces and nephews. And when he married, the ceremony was attended by not only his large extended family and his music-industry peers but by a former congressman, and several well-known actors and pro athletes.

And about seven years after their marriage, Luke Marsellus and his wife became parents. They'd been trying in vain for some time to conceive, so when their son was born, it was cause for greater celebration than their marriage. In a ceremony even better attended than the Marsellus wedding, the infant Trey was baptized at the church his father had had rebuilt, wearing a christening gown from Neiman Marcus.

I learned everything I knew about Marsellus in my last days in Los Angeles. Before that, I wouldn't even have recognized his face. Even CJ didn't know him, not beyond shaking his hand at a fund-raiser.

I did remember liking some of the music Marsellus's artists put out. Angry, unapologetic, fatalistic, unafraid—the music had fit with my life-after-West-Point frame of mind. In those days I hadn't thought any further ahead than sundown. Those had been my *omnia gaudia vitae* days, and to be honest, I'd been partying a lot, whether it was beer and grass with Serena, or kaffir lime vodka shots in the Westside clubs I went to with CJ.

But on what I consider my last real day in L.A., I was sober. It was important to me that people knew that, or it would have been if I ever told anyone this story, which I didn't. But I was sober and driving the speed limit that day on Wilshire Boulevard; it's just that the late-afternoon sun was in my eyes, and when six-year-old Trey Marsellus ran out in front of my car, I hit and killed him.

six

I never saw Marsellus, not once. Trey hadn't been with his father, nor any of his family. He'd been out with his young Haitian au pair. It had been her shrill screams that made me realize I hadn't hit a large dog, which was what I'd thought at first.

The family, once notified, went directly to the hospital. I was taken to the precinct "while we straighten this out," in the words of the traffic-division sergeant. Once there, I called CJ, but he didn't answer.

I was at the precinct for several hours. The police hadn't been sure at first what really happened. They couldn't get anything out of the grief-stricken nanny. I kept saying that Trey had run right out in front of me—which was true, though what else would you have expected someone who'd hit a child to say?

Fortunately, there had been pedestrians who'd seen the accident—not the usual "I heard squealing brakes and shattering glass and turned to look," but people who'd actually seen Trey Marsellus run from his nanny and dart from between two parallel-parked cars.

As the traffic sergeant said to me, "We're not going to hold you, but don't leave town, okay? Not until we've closed the official investigation."

I agreed, walked stiffly out the front door, and went to the hospital. I had an immediate and all-consuming need to apologize to the family.

I hadn't succeeded. Two very large young black men, with tattoos and exquisitely tailored suits, blocked my way. "The family's not seeing anyone right now," one of them said.

At the time, the question *Who are these guys?* didn't occur to me. I was mentally numb, except for being fixated on making this right. "I need to talk to them," I said. "I'm the one who—"

"The family's not seeing anyone," he said again, and I broke off, finally realizing they were serious.

CJ, who'd gone to the precinct too late, found me as I was walking back to visitor parking. He was pale and shaken, almost as if he'd been the one to hit a child, but he was immediately supportive. He took me back to his place, where I paced, angry and guilty, saying over and over that the kid had run right in front of me, that the sun was in my eyes, that I couldn't have stopped.

"I know, baby," CJ said. Then he asked me to repeat the boy's name.

"Trey Marsellus," I said.

"Mmm," he said.

"What?"

"Nothing." ·

"What?" I persisted.

"I think you might've hit Luke Marsellus's kid," he said, pensive.

"Who?" I'd said.

An hour later it was on the news: Rap mogul's son killed in Wilshire Boulevard accident. I still didn't get it. The news reports cast him only as a respected music-world figure, not as Marsellus the South Central OG.

I should have known something was really wrong when CJ picked up a pack of cigarettes a friend had left on the coffee table and tapped one out. CJ almost never smoked, so this meant he needed something to do with his hands, which meant he was nervous. Which was bad, because CJ was almost never nervous.

"Are you okay?" I asked. Stupid question, considering.

"Yeah," he said. He lit the cigarette, exhaled smoke, and said, "Listen, give the family a couple of days, all right? Marsellus is . . ."

"Is what?"

"He's kind of heavy."

"I can't turn my back on this," I said.

"I know," he said, "but I need to think about how best you should approach him."

As it turned out, CJ never did hit on the right way for me to talk to Marsellus. Something else happened first that changed everything.

Two days later, I was awakened by my phone ringing at ten-fifteen in the morning. I picked up the receiver and found myself talking to the traffic sergeant who'd taken my statement and then kicked me loose. His question was direct and to the point: Had Miss Beauvais, Trey's au pair, been in touch with me?

No, I said, why would she have been?

I'm just checking in with you, he'd said.

Not seeing any significance, I tried to go back to sleep—I hadn't been sleeping well at night—but an hour later, CJ was pounding on my door.

"Take it easy, would you," I said, pushing hair out of my eyes and letting him in.

"Pack up your things," he said as soon as I'd closed the door behind him. "Not everything, just what you really want."

"What?" I thought it was a joke, though he seemed genuinely on edge.

"Trey's nanny is missing. The cops are looking for her. Nobody's seen her. Pack up just what you need, I'm getting you out of L.A."

I pulled back. "What are you trying to say?"

CJ ran his hands through his hair. "Just listen to me, Hailey. I didn't want to scare you the other night, but as soon as you told me Trey Marsellus's name, I was thinking of something like this. I hoped I was overreacting."

"Something like what?"

"This happened in New York," he said. "A mobster's son was hit by a car, by accident, and not long after that, the neighbor who did it just disappeared."

I said, "You of all people know that 'gangsta' is just a figure of speech. Marsellus isn't really a gangster."

"Yes, he is, Hailey." He paused. "I hear things, and maybe I don't know for sure what's rumor and what's fact, but I meant what I said the other day, when I called Marsellus 'heavy.' He's not a 'no harm, no foul' kind of guy. And he and his wife tried for years to conceive before finally having Trey. She hasn't been pregnant again since. What does that tell you?" He answered his own question: "You took from him the one thing that can't be replaced."

My face felt hot. "Don't you think I feel bad enough—"

"You're not *listening,*" he said. I'd never heard CJ sound so frustrated. "Goddammit, what's it going to take to get through to you? You can feel as bad as humanly possible; it won't help. You killed this guy's only son. 'Sorry' isn't going to fix it."

I said, "But if he's really the kind of man you say, I think not apologizing and then running away is only going to make it worse."

"There isn't a way to make it better."

"But—"

"No," he said, taking both my hands in his. "I know what you're thinking of, all that honor-and-duty bullshit you never really left behind, but that doesn't apply out here, and it's going to get you killed. West Point is over, and now L.A. is over for you, too. Pack your things."

What convinced me that he was right was this: His hands were very slightly shaking. It had been a long time since I'd felt those kind of nerves, so his anxiety served as a kind of external gauge for me, of what I should be feeling but wasn't.

"Are you sure about this?" I'd said.

"I don't like it, either, baby," he'd said quietly. "But this is how it's gotta be."

To this day I don't know if there were any ramifications, criminally, for my leaving town before the traffic division's investigation was officially closed. It had just been a formality, but the cops took a dim view of people skating when they'd been told to stick around. It was possible that if I was ever picked up on something minor in San Francisco, I'd be shipped back to Los Angeles and charged with some kind of obstruction. It wasn't the charge that would be problematic, but jail would actually be the easiest place for Marsellus to get at me. Anyone gang-connected could.

CJ would have stayed longer with me in San Francisco, but I hadn't let him. When we parted, we'd both acted with exaggerated casualness. He'd said, "Look, I'll come up and visit you soon. I'll be around so much you'll be sick of me," and I'd said, "Sure, I know," and we'd hugged and then he'd driven away, toward the 101 back home.

In those first weeks, I'd lived with a drab, hollow feeling not unlike how addicts describe their first day without alcohol or a cigarette: *Is this what my life's going to be, from here on out?* I'd alternated between that sense of lonely tedium and a stomach-clenching guilt. I'm not sure those feelings ever went away, but they did lessen. In time, I found an adrenaline-junkie job and threw myself into it. I made more money than I needed and stashed it carelessly in a coffee can. I made a few friends and drank with them. Drank without them, too. I met Jack Foreman.

But I still felt restless at times, particularly in early summer, when business at Aries was slowest and San Francisco was shrouded in the kind of weather coastal Californians called June gloom. That was probably why, in the end, I called Serena back and told her I'd take a girl I'd never met to the mountains of inland Mexico.

seven

Several days later, sometime after nine in the evening, I was parked in front of a house in a working-class section of Oakland. It was an inexpensively well-kept place, with a small trimmed lawn, and no weeds between the stepping-stones that led to the house. There was a geranium by the front door, blooming red. This was where Nidia Hernandez was staying with friends.

Shay had looked pretty sour when I told him I was taking nearly two weeks off, but there was nothing he could do. I was an independent contractor; I worked, or not, at both my will and his. He could have fired me just as easily.

That afternoon, packing had been quick and easy. Hot-weather clothes, one heavy jacket for the evenings. A recently purchased guidebook to Mexico. A bottle of Bacardi and several minis of Finlandia, tucked protectively between layers of clothing. The little care package Serena had sent to me—a sheaf of twenties and fifties, the promised expense money, and a handful of Benzedrines wrapped in foil, to help me stay alert on the road. The rest of my pay would wait until I was on my way back up north; Serena and I had arranged that I'd stop at her place and we'd settle up then.

Finally I'd cleaned and oiled the Airweight, which was now taped under the front seat of the car I'd rented. I didn't expect any trouble in Mexico. I was just being careful.

A young man with a peach-fuzz mustache answered the door when I knocked. "Are you Hailey?" he said.

"I'm in the right place, then."

"Yeah, hello, yeah," he said, and moved aside. I stepped into a narrow entryway of brown-checked linoleum, and the boy called to someone farther back in the house in Spanish so rapid I didn't catch much of it, except for Nidia's name.

A middle-aged woman came around the corner into the entryway. She was thin, with red-tinted hair pinned up on her head.

"Is it her?" she said in a gently accented voice. "Oh, please come in. My name is Herlinda."

"Hailey," I said.

"Come into the kitchen."

I followed her. The floorboards felt slightly warped under my feet, and the house smelled of many, many meals cooked there. We rounded a corner, and I got my first look at Nidia Hernandez.

She was sitting in a chair slightly pushed back from the kitchen table, two scuffed suitcases at her feet. I could see where she'd draw unwanted masculine attention. Her hair was cinnamon-colored, in curls weighed down into near-straightness by their length. Her eyes were green-brown, and she had a heart-shaped face. She wasn't very tall—maybe five-two—and slender except for the little potbelly a lot of girls had nowadays, the obsession for flat abs being over. She looked from Herlinda to me.

"Hey," I said. "I'm Hailey."

"Thank you for coming," she said.

"I was sorry to hear about your boyfriend. Serena told me," I said.

She nodded and said something that I thought was "Thank you" but couldn't be sure: She was that quiet. We both looked to Herlinda to take over.

Herlinda did, fixing hot chocolate and offering pan dulce, both of which I accepted, although I wasn't hungry. Then she spread a map of Mexico on the table and began the debriefing I'd been promised. "Have you ever been to Mexico?" she asked.

"To Baja California, yes," I said.

"Did you drive?"

I nodded. It had been CJ's idea, a road trip to a seaside town he'd heard about.

"Good," Herlinda said. "So you know a little about driving on Mexican roads." Even so, she went on to tell me things I'd already heard: that in isolated areas, drivers tended to go down the center of the road until they saw oncoming traffic, and that it was common for both parties to be jailed in case of a traffic accident. If I were in one, she said, I should be exceedingly polite to the police and keep my ears open for the subtle implication that a bribe would clear the whole thing up. I nodded assent. Her son leaned against the refrigerator and listened.

Then Herlinda turned her attention to the map. I saw a star, hand-drawn in ink, in the northern Sierra Madre region.

"That's where we're going?" I said.

"It's the nearest town to the village," Herlinda said.

My confusion must have shown on my face—I didn't understand the distinction she was making—so Herlinda said, "You won't take Nidia all the way; the road isn't passable by car. You'll take her to this town, and you'll see the post office there. It has a Mexican flag over it. Take Nidia inside, and the postman will take her up to the village when he goes with the mail. They do it all the time, her mother says."

"If the road's not passable by car, how does the postman go up? Horseback?"

Herlinda smiled. "He has four-wheel-drive."

I was embarrassed at my assumption. "If I'd known," I said, "I could've got something with four-wheel."

Herlinda shook her head. "It's not just that," she said. "The road's narrow and it's steep, and I guess city Mexicans don't do well with it." She left the obvious unsaid: *Not to mention gringos.*

Then she looked up at the kitchen doorway. I followed her gaze and saw a thin girl of maybe twelve or thirteen there, wearing a long pink nightshirt.

"You're supposed to be in bed," Herlinda told her.

"I wanted to say good-bye to Nidia."

I moved from the kitchen counter and told Nidia, "I'll take your bags out to the car," thinking they'd want privacy for their good-byes.

Outside, I sat behind the wheel of the car I'd rented, a powerful V6 Impala. When I'd first driven it that afternoon, I felt a small rush of elation and power. Then, just as quickly, I'd been stabbed by a memory: Wilshire Boulevard and a hard thump from the front end of my car.

He darted out of nowhere; it was an accident; there was nothing you could have done. It had become my mantra in moments like these. But I wondered, if I ever owned a vehicle again, how long it would take before I could drive without thinking of Trey Marsellus.